# WITHDRAWN

M

# Strangers Among Us

## Laurali R. Wright

Scribner

SCRIBNER
1230 Avenue of the Americas
New York, NY 10020

SCRIBNER and design are registered trademarks of
Simon & Schuster Inc.

*Designed by Brooke Zimmer*
*Text set in Stempel Garamond*
Manufactured in the United States of America

1 3 5 7 9 10 8 6 4 2

Library of Congress Cataloging-in-Publication Data
Wright, Laurali, 1939–
Strangers among us/Laurali R. Wright.
p. cm.
1. Alberg, Karl (Fictitious character)—Fiction.   2. Police—
British Columbia—Fiction.   3. British Columbia—Fiction.
I. Title.
PR9199.3.W68S76    1996
813'.54—dc20    96-20471
CIP
ISBN 0-684-81382-3

*This book is for Susan Ackland, M.D.*
*Urve Kuusk, M.D., and*
*Patricia Clugston, M.D.*
*. . . with thanks.*

# Author's Note

The author wishes to acknowledge the advice and suggestions provided by John Wright, Brian Appleby, Elaine Ferbey, Alison Maclean, and Virginia Barber; any inaccuracies are her own.

There is a Sunshine Coast, and its towns and villages are called by the names used in this book. But all the rest is fiction. The events and the characters are products of the author's imagination, and geographical and other liberties have been taken in the depiction of Greater Vancouver and the town of Sechelt.

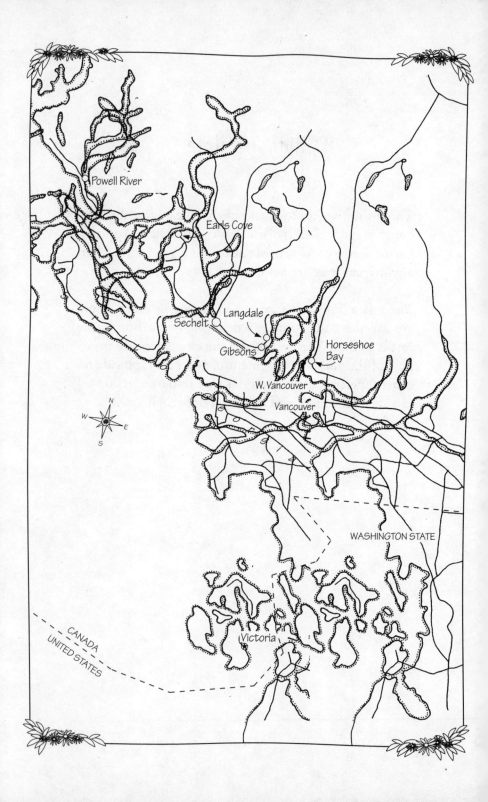

Powell River

Earls Cove

Sechelt
Langdale
Gibsons

Horseshoe
Bay

W. Vancouver

Vancouver

N
W        E
S

WASHINGTON STATE

CANADA
UNITED STATES

Victoria

# Strangers Among Us

## Friday, November 11

In the silver rain-washed morning the village of Sechelt huddled between bodies of water—a saltwater inlet rippling to the north, a wide strait lapping its southern beaches. Coastal range mountains crowded to the edge of the mainland and spilled out upon the peninsula, the dark green of coniferous forests sculpting their cragginess, softening it.

A small gray house stood in the woods close to the sea, its roof barely visible through sheltering cedars; so close to the water it stood that the Pacific Ocean must have been a continuous, restless presence within its backyard garden, around its kitchen table, inside its bedrooms.

From the house a trail led through the trees and down an incline to the beach, where a family had gathered on this mild, misty morning and were now absorbed in familiar tasks—a father, a mother, an eight-year-old girl, and a teenage boy: it was Remembrance Day, and there was no school.

The boy, Eliot, was fourteen. He was five feet ten inches tall, and thinner than he wanted to be. His shoulders were broad but carried little flesh. His hair was black and cut very short, straight across on top. This morning he was wearing long baggy shorts and a baggy T-shirt over them, and a baseball cap sat backward on his head.

His hazel eyes were the best thing about Eliot's looks. They were large eyes, almond-shaped, with long dark lashes. He already knew that girls liked his eyes.

Eliot's head was aching, a dull ache rooted in the back of his head, right in the middle, up a little bit from his neck. From here it burrowed off in several directions, causing more pain in his temples and behind his forehead. It had started sometime in the night. He had wakened, blinking, aware that he was frowning, and then had realized that his head was aching. Again. He had never gotten headaches at home.

He stopped his work, put down the tool, and leaned over, his hands gripping his knees. He thought if he let blood flow to his head the pain might ease. This was a worse headache than usual. It had hold of his entire head. He imagined his head gripped hard by a giant pair of pliers, getting squeezed, getting twisted, put totally out of shape.

He looked at his legs, the bony knees, the calves, his feet looming enormous in black military boots and white socks. The boots, he saw, were dirty, their gleaming smeared by wet sand. He shouldn't have worn them out here. He should have put on his high-tops—but then *they* would have gotten dirty, of course. And at least he could clean the boots. Polish them.

He straightened up and rubbed the back of his neck. Putting his head down had made the headache worse. It was pounding thick and hot enough to make him wince. He got a lot of headaches now. Or else it was the same one coming back again and again. It was stress that did this, he thought. He probably didn't have a real headache; that is, there probably wasn't any physical reason for it, it was just his mind's way of giving substance to his unhappiness. He was pleased with himself for figuring this out but it didn't seem to have done him much good: the headache was still there and he wasn't any happier either. He wondered if he would ever be happy again. Quite possibly he wouldn't. He glanced over his shoulder at his little sister, who was carrying the pail, helping their mom. Rosie would be happy again someday. He wasn't sure about his mom. What a waste, he thought. What a waste.

Eliot stood with his head bowed. His skin prickled, and felt clammy, and for a moment he was afraid that the headache was spreading throughout his whole body. He was truly terrified, contemplating this possibility: he didn't think it would be possible to live with that kind of pain.

He heard his father shouting at him and he stood straight again, and picked up the tool to resume his work. He was the strongest person in the family so he got the hardest job. This was logical. It made sense.

In the coolness of the November morning he started to sweat. At first the work had been satisfying. When he'd gotten into the rhythm of it he'd enjoyed the physical sensations of reaching, stretching, whacking at the brush. But now his effort was taking its toll. His shoulders ached, and his back, also. And his bare legs stung where they'd gotten scratched.

He was also very hungry. By the time he'd gotten out of bed that morning everybody else had eaten and it was time to go. He hadn't wanted to get up. It was a holiday. He shouldn't have had to get up, not at the crack of dawn for god's sake. But his dad had banged on his door, scaring the hell out of him, catapulting him into morning.

"Get your ass out of that bed," his dad had shouted.

Eliot couldn't remember the last time the beginning of a day had been a good thing. It was months and months ago and miles and miles away.

His head was aching when he awoke and he must have slept funny, too, because there was a crick in his neck, actually down in his back somewhere.

He had gotten up and gone downstairs, wearing shorts and a T-shirt. His mom wanted him to change, to put on something warmer. Eliot looked out the window and jesus christ it was one of those days when the whole fucking world was gray, and the same shade of gray, too. You couldn't tell where the sea left off and the sky started to happen. You'd never fucking know there were mountains anyplace near.

His sister was eating breakfast and reading a comic book. He could hear his dad's footsteps upstairs pounding from one room to another. "I gotta work today," he said to his mom.

"I know," she told him. "This won't take long."

"I gotta be there by noon."

"I know, Eliot," she said, being patient. But Eliot knew she didn't have much patience left, not for him, anyway. She offered him breakfast but by then his dad was coming downstairs, loudly, like he did everything, so Eliot shook his head.

Now, as he worked, he was even more hungry. It wasn't good to be missing meals. His only hope for survival in this godforsaken place, he had decided, was to turn himself into some kind of an athlete, and this required that he bulk up. He had to eat a lot, as often as possible. And start working out, too. And this made him think of Sammy, of course, Sammy back home. Eliot was pretty sure he'd never have another friend like Sammy, not ever in his whole life.

His anger was wakening again. A whole bunch of things could get it going. Being hungry could do it. Thinking about his real home could do it. So he tried not to think about home but sometimes that just made him angrier, a person ought to at least be able to take comfort from thinking about a place and people he'd never see again but oh no, there was no comfort there, just more fucking anger. Even when it wasn't threatening to boil over, he knew it was there, his anger, always there inside him, like a low-grade fever. At least the headache went away sometimes.

Suddenly he stumbled and lost his balance, clutching at a blackberry bush in a vain attempt to break his fall. He landed heavily on one knee, the palm of his hand stinging.

"Watch yourself with that thing, dumbo," his father called out, and laughed.

For a second Eliot didn't care about the laughter. For a second he welcomed it—his father was in a good mood, and Eliot was grateful for this. For a second he considered laughing, too, in acknowledgment of his clumsiness.

He lifted the tool, seeking the rhythm he'd lost, lifted and sliced downward, lifted and sliced. He opened his hands, one by one, and got a better grip, lifted it again, smashed it down. There was a burning feeling in Eliot's chest and shit there were tears in his fucking eyes; his whole body was shaking; he was trying desperately to hang on to something, he didn't even know what it was.

Suddenly his father was yelling again. "What the fuck are you doing?"

Eliot staggered backward, breathing fast. Sweat ran down his face. That was good, he thought—they wouldn't be able to tell that he was crying. The cool air sizzled on his skin. His father was striding toward him, his soiled canvas hat in his hand, waving the goddamn hat in the air, hurrying up to Eliot.

"You've cut down the fucking bamboo!" his old man cried.

Eliot didn't look at the bamboo. He looked at his father, rushing toward him. All pain lifted from him—Eliot was amazed at how light he was, all of a sudden; he felt light and giddy. His father slapped Eliot's shoulder with his hat. Eliot believed himself to be perfectly calm when he raised the machete and brought it down on his father's head.

# 2

Staff Sergeant Karl Alberg drove to the crime scene in his white Oldsmobile, down a rutted lane through a brush-clogged forest of evergreen trees. He tried not to drive as quickly as he wanted to and kept his mind on his surroundings, refusing to think about anything else, noticing big stands of ubiquitous blackberry bushes along the border of the trail, and small maple trees stationed like occasional red flares among the cedars. He saw tire tracks in the ruts ahead of him, and an A & W wrapper in the tall grass between the trail and the blackberries, and a Steller's jay, a flicker of blue calling stridently from a tree branch.

"Go to the end of the track, Staff," Sid Sokolowski had told him on the radio. "We're behind the house."

Alberg knew the track, knew the house.

The trail took a wide, slow curve. Nothing hinted of a population except the trail itself. Alberg imagined a horse-drawn cart clopping along here, taking somebody to town.

It had rained in the night, and in the early morning, and puddles had formed in the ruts. Alberg splashed through them slowly, the tires spewing mud along the fenders of the Oldsmobile.

Finally the track straightened again and he saw the small gray house. The lane formed a loop next to it. He drove around the loop and pulled off onto a grassy clearing next to several empty patrol cars and Alex Gillingham's Buick. He got out and locked the Oldsmobile, and absently tried the door of the nearest patrol car—it was locked. He crossed to the side of the house, which faced east, up the trail, and looked through the kitchen window.

A tea towel was draped over the back of a wooden chair. The linoleum on the floor was worn in places—in front of the door that led outside, and underneath the table. Alberg had sat at that table more than once over the last several months, talking to Verna.

White lace curtains hung on either side of the window. Dishes had been stacked neatly in a drainer that sat on a rubber tray on one side of the sink. There were hooks on the wall next to the door; an umbrella hung there, and several jackets. Alberg turned away—then he turned back, and tapped on the window. He waited, listening to the sea, waited for someone to appear in the living room doorway, for footsteps to pound down the stairs from the second story, for the phone to ring, and someone to rush into the kitchen to answer it. He noticed that paint was peeling from the window ledge.

Alberg went around to the back of the house. There was an overhang above the back door and a sizable porch—a small pair of red boots sat there, one upright, one fallen over. He turned around quickly and gazed westward, in the direction of the sea. He was aware of himself doing this.

He was standing in a backyard that consisted of a large vegetable garden surrounded by worn strips of grass. There were still things growing in the garden. Alberg couldn't recognize much. But he knew brussels sprouts when he saw them.

At the bottom of the yard were some deciduous trees. Alberg found a path and followed it through thirty feet of forest. The ground was springy, covered with rain-soggy fallen leaves, but there were also splotches of bright green where ferns were growing. He ducked under yellow crime scene tape and emerged onto a clearing several feet above the beach.

Below, on the sand, Alex Gillingham was crouched next to the body of a woman.

Alberg felt like weeping.

Near the doctor, Sokolowski stood stiffly, his feet apart, his hands behind his back.

Alberg wanted to pray. He thought this curious. He didn't think it had ever happened to him before. For what would he have prayed? he wondered. And to whom, or what?

Sokolowski was watching the woman intently, as if hoping she would start to move. She was wearing sneakers and socks, a gray skirt and a gray cardigan. Her skirt had gotten pushed up almost to her waist. The sergeant bent, reached out, and pulled the skirt down a little, enough to cover the inch or so of white underpants that had been showing.

Alberg saw police officers up and down the beach, searching. He wanted very much to turn his back on them, on the crime scene, and go home.

But he made his way down from the clearing. "The child," he said to Alex Gillingham. "Rosie."

The doctor pushed himself to his feet. "Hospital," he said. "She's not seriously hurt. But she's in shock."

"Will she be okay?"

"Physically? Sure." He brushed sand from the palms of his hands. "Psychologically? Who the hell knows."

Alberg turned, slightly, and saw a second body. He walked toward it, and Sokolowski followed. Together they looked down at the dead man. Alberg felt nausea clogging his throat, generated not by carnage but by failure.

"Ralph Gardener," said the sergeant. "Eliot's dad."

"I know who they are. Where's Eliot?"

"Not here," said Sokolowski.

Alberg turned away. There wasn't a single boat out on the water. That hardly ever happened. He decided that he would keep looking out to sea until something showed up out there.

Sokolowski had taken a notebook from his pocket and was tapping it against his hand. "That's the guy's wife over there," he said, gesturing.

"I said I know who they are."

Sokolowski glanced at him. Then he went on. "Looks like they were getting clams," he said, indicating an overturned pail about halfway between the two bodies.

From the south a tug had emerged from behind the biggest of the Trail Islands, its tow still blocked from view. Alberg turned back to the sergeant. "The tide's coming in."

"Body bags are on the way," said Sokolowski.

"Is there a weapon?"

Sokolowski pointed.

"Jesus." Alberg looked, and looked away, down the beach at a man and woman huddling together. "Who are those people?"

"That's the neighbors," said Sokolowski. "They're the ones made the call. Very shook up. Very."

"Somebody was using this thing on the blackberries," said Alberg. The toe of his black shoe nudged the bloody machete that lay in the sand. About four feet away the sand began giving way to grass, and somewhat farther inland grew some brush and a thicket of blackberries, about half of which had been recently hacked away: the canes littering the ground still looked fresh and alive. Next to the blackberries a stand of bamboo spread up the incline and onto the edge of the clearing. Some of this, too, had been slashed out.

They heard a muffled shout from the forest. Sokolowski lumbered toward the sound, pushing through the undergrowth, and Alberg followed. There was another shout: Alberg thought he recognized Norah Gibbons' voice. He glimpsed uniforms through the trees, heading toward the beach.

"Hold it—this way," he said, and when he and Sokolowski emerged onto the sand again they saw Norah and Henry Loewen trudging toward them, one on either side of Eliot Gardener. The boy's shoes and socks and shorts and T-shirt were splattered with blood. There was blood on his hands, and his arms, on the side of his face, and on his bare legs.

The two constables and the boy stopped in front of Alberg. All three were breathing fast. Blood was smeared on Norah Gibbons' chin, and Alberg saw a dark stain on the right shoulder of Henry Loewen's uniform jacket.

Alberg looked intently into Eliot Gardener's face. He said nothing, and neither did the boy; he just stared back at him.

Eliot looked very tired.

Nothing more.


Alberg had a place that he went to when he wanted to be on his own. He never actually decided to go there—he just sometimes found himself there, or on his way. I could go to the boat, he would think; and then he would find himself going to this place instead, because there were too many people at the marina; he'd have to be sociable there, and sometimes he didn't feel sociable.

He climbed down to a rocky beach and dropped a cushion on the ground. He tried to remember how long he'd been doing that—providing himself with padding, protecting himself against what had become inhospitable surfaces. He settled himself upon the cushion, with his hands clasped between bent knees, his back supported by an enormous boulder, and he gazed out at the water.

It was high tide now and the ocean was washing languidly

at the stones not far from his shoes. Alberg made himself concentrate on sounds: the gentle susurration of the sea, the piercing, haunting cries of seagulls, the whisper of a breeze in the underbrush that crowded through the forest and tumbled toward the ocean. He heard a cracking noise as something or someone trod among the trees, a sound that was repeated farther away, and still farther, until he finally could hear it no longer. Alberg shifted on the cushion.

Ralph Gardener had been almost decapitated. The blade of the machete had struck him in the left side of the neck. Blood had gushed across the sand, engulfing his denim hat, which had been lying several feet away.

Alberg, looking skyward, couldn't see individual clouds, just a monotone grayness brightened here and there with streaks of pewter. In the woods yellow leaves clung precariously to tree branches, trembling.

Verna had been struck in the back, probably while trying to run away. Her left hand lying curled upon the sand had looked like a child's hand.

It was a mild day, almost springlike. Before he'd left for work that morning Cassandra had taken him into the backyard and shown him a glorious russet blaze of chrysanthemums. He remembered gazing upon this sight in something approaching wonder, amazed that he hadn't noticed it before. Would the flowers have bloomed and died without his ever having seen them, if Cassandra hadn't dragged him out there? How had he ever gotten the idea that he was an observant man, discerning and perceptive? How had he ever gotten the idea that he was a good cop?

And Rosie. The child . . .

That blood-soaked beach would be gone now, devoured by the incoming tide. And in the morning the sand would reappear, and it would be clean. Unblemished.

Alberg got up and went home, taking his cushion with him.

• • •

"I don't feel like talking, Cassandra," he said later that day. "I don't feel like it and I don't think it's necessary."

He was sitting on the edge of the sofa, looking down at the rug. Cassandra Mitchell wanted to sit next to him and take him in her arms but she knew he would have pulled away.

"I don't have anything to say," he told her. Lamplight glinted on his hair, which was so fair that she couldn't easily see the gray in it. "I really don't."

They sat there for a long time. Outside, the cloud cover stirred and weakened and there was a brightening of the day; not enough sun to cast shadows, but enough to draw attention to itself. This lasted only a few minutes. Then the afternoon light began rapidly to fade, while Cassandra sat in Alberg's wingback chair, watching him, a tall, broad man, smooth-faced, with cool blue eyes he liked to hide behind. She sometimes found him every bit as enigmatic as when they first had met. When it was almost dark, he spoke.

"Have you ever been clamming?"

"Sure," said Cassandra.

"They spout, like whales. From under the sand. The mud. A couple of feet in the air. You hear this sound—'psst.' 'Psst.' And you look, and there's a jet of water, coming from a clam you can't see. 'Psst,' it goes."

He stood up and went to the window. Cassandra thought he was going to close the curtains and turn on the lights but he just stood there with his hands in his pockets, looking out.

"They had shovels," he said. "And a big pail. There were quite a few clams in the pail."

The cats were curled up on the sofa, and the light was now so dim that Cassandra couldn't distinguish them one from the other. She tried to focus on them, though, and think about them, so that not all of her would hear whatever Alberg was going to tell her.

"There was a great jeezly rock there," said Alberg. "A big flat rock. It was maybe four feet high, eight feet across. Covered with bird shit and clam shells. The seagulls drop clams on it, to break the shells."

Cassandra knew the place he was describing. She could have climbed into her car and driven directly there.

"What he used was a machete," said Alberg. Cassandra thought this must be the voice he used when he had to testify in court. "The blade is almost a foot long, and it's four inches across at the end, where it's curved, and widest. It's an old one," he said, as if in response to a question. "The handle's wrapped in electrician's tape and on the blade you can make out 'CF 8' something and then '1942.' It's a World War II weapon." He turned from the window to face her. "No. Not a weapon. A tool. Used to clear brush. That's what Eliot was using it for, too. Clearing blackberries." He reached up with one hand, and then didn't seem to know why he'd done this. "It's like a slide show. I didn't manage to get my guard up in time. Things have stuck in my head that wouldn't, usually." He wiped his forehead with the back of his hand. "Damn."

Cassandra got up and went to him, and put her arms around him. "How's the child?" she said.

"I've been afraid to call the hospital." He rested his chin on the top of her head, and linked his hands behind her back.

"Karl," she said. "Do you know why he did it?"

"I don't even know if he knows why he did it."

**3**

*Saturday, November 12*

Cassandra Mitchell was in charge of Sechelt's library. She had recently begun to find her office claustrophobic, and had decided this was yet another symptom of middle age, another of the many little things associated with growing older that nobody bothered to warn you about.

It occurred to her that she could go on calling herself middle-aged only if she intended to live to be a hundred.

She glanced uneasily at the skylight, then at her watch. She was actually looking forward to lunch with her mother, because it would get her out of there.

Cassandra got up from her desk to open the top of the Dutch door that led into the area behind the checkout counter. She could see beyond it into the stacks, where Paula was reshelving a cartful of books. She sat down again and opened a file folder marked BOARD MEETINGS. Sighed. Looked again at her watch. And began making a list of the items that would comprise her report to the board.

· · ·

"I don't understand why you haven't set the date yet," said Helen Mitchell two hours later, breaking a half-slice of toast into quarters. She looked with distaste around Earl's Café & Catering. "For some reason I never think this place is quite clean."

"For god's sake, Mother," Cassandra hissed. "Keep your voice down."

Helen ate some of her clam chowder, and then a piece of toast. "And when are we going into town to get your dress?"

Cassandra, inspecting Helen gloomily, acknowledged that her impending wedding had given her mother new reason to live. "I don't know, Mother," she said, picking at her salad. "Soon, I guess."

"There are legions of things to be done, you know. Have you at least begun to make lists?"

"Lists? Lists of what?"

"People to invite. Gifts you want."

"Oh for heaven's sake."

"Things to do. Decisions to be made. Etcetera, etcetera, etcetera." Helen's hair was just long enough to cover her ears. It cupped her face like an elegant silver frame. Her eyes were brighter and more alert than they'd been in months.

"Okay, okay," said Cassandra. "How about if I come over tomorrow."

"Bring a notebook." Helen Mitchell waved an imperious hand until she had Earl's attention, and asked for more hot water for her tea.

"Did you hear?" said Earl to Cassandra when he brought the hot water. "About my busboy?"

"I heard. It's terrible."

"It's terrible," said Earl, nodding. "Awful." He gestured over his shoulder with his thumb, toward the lunchtime crowd. "What if he'd gone nuts in here? Grabbed a butcher knife or something. People dead. People dying. Blood all over the place."

"Please," said Helen, pained. "Please."

It had been raining when Cassandra dropped her mother off at Shady Acres but now the rain had stopped and the sky was brightening. Rain clung to the world, though, in crystal drops, gleaming. The branches of the forsythia bush in Sid Sokolowski's front yard were swollen with raindrops. Cassandra, anticipating spring by several months, thought they looked like leafbuds.

She went up the steps to the front door, her big leather bag slung over her shoulder, and Sid opened it before she had a chance to knock.

"I saw you coming," he said. The aroma of coffee wafted toward them down the hall from the kitchen.

They sat at Sid's dining room table, which Cassandra remembered as being much bigger. She asked if it was new and he explained that he had taken out the leaves. "Not much need for a long table now," he said unhappily.

He brought them coffee in large white cups. "I've got some muffins, too," he said, but Cassandra declined.

"I'm here about Karl," she said, stirring cream into her coffee.

Sunlight spilled suddenly through the dining room window—and just as suddenly departed. Cassandra felt bereft.

She also felt as if she oughtn't to be there, as if confiding in Sid would grant him some kind of advantage over Karl. But then that's what a person always feels when asking for help, she told herself. Asking for help was an admission of need, sure, of course it was. You had to accept that and get on with it. People who never sought help from one another, who struggled on alone, didn't learn nearly as much in a lifetime as those who allowed others to teach them some of what they knew.

"I thought it might help if he talked about it, about these murders," she said. "But he didn't really talk about it. He just described things. It was like he was showing me pictures."

"He seems fine to me," said Sid. "Maybe a little preoccupied. That's all."

His eyes were gray, the same color as his hair, which he kept very short. He had lost weight since Elsie left, but was still an unusually large person. His size made Cassandra think of the huge men who played professional football, the ones who seemed seldom to catch or throw the ball, men whose sole job, apparently, was to try to knock down equally large men on the other team. She wondered how he kept in shape.

"He can usually separate work from the rest of his life," she said. "But he's thinking about this all the time. Literally. And it's not as if there's anything to solve, right?"

Sid nodded.

"I mean, there's no detecting to do, right?"

He nodded again.

Cassandra was aware of her growing agitation. She forced herself to pick up the coffee cup and drink, and replace the cup in its saucer. "He didn't sleep last night, either."

"He knew the kid," said Sokolowski. "Met him soon after they got here. The kid was unhappy, for some reason." He rolled his eyes. "Unhappy. Huh." He shifted position, causing his oversized captain's chair to creak. "Anyway. I think Karl thought he could help in some way."

"So—"

Sid shook his head. "Nobody could've done anything. Who's to know what's going on in somebody else's head? A thing like this—it's not predictable."

"But he feels some responsibility anyway. Is that what you're saying?"

"Oh hell, we're all responsible. Everybody's responsible. You learn to live with that." He had been looking out the window, frowning. Now he clapped his hands on his thighs and pushed himself out of his chair. "I'll be right back."

Cassandra ran her hand along the grain of wood in the tabletop, which was highly polished. She glanced into the adjoining living room and saw no clutter there. Elsie had liked a little clutter. Cassandra wondered where she was living, on her own again, for the first time in years. Did she have a tiny apartment? A duplex? A whole entire house, all to herself? Whatever Elsie had, Cassandra was pretty sure it would be cluttered.

When Sid came back he had a thick scrapbook in his hand. He put it down in front of Cassandra. "I've got a whole pile of these," he said. "Go on. Have a look." On the front cover was printed "1980–84."

The scrapbook was full of newspaper clippings that had been taped in place. CARNAGE ON THE NUMBER ONE, read the first headline.

Sid went around the table to sit down again in the captain's chair.

CYCLISTS MAKE GRISLY FIND, Cassandra read.

"Elsie didn't like me doing this," said the sergeant. "She said it was gruesome."

KNIFE-WIELDING THIEF TRAPPED IN ELEVATOR.

"But it's not gruesome," he went on. "I'm filing it away, see?" Cassandra looked up at him. "Sometimes it's hard. Sometimes the papers lose interest in a case and they don't bother to do a story that wraps it up."

MOTHER KILLS BABY, SELF.

"I don't clip anything I didn't work on. And I don't clip what they call feature stories."

RCMP ALARMED ABOUT POLICE SUICIDE RATE.

"What about that one?" said Cassandra.

Sid looked at the story, then at Cassandra. "I knew one of the guys it talks about." He rubbed one enormous hand across his face. "Had to take him home. To his folks in

Peterborough." He reached over and closed the scrapbook. "The point is, here—this is how I put things out of my mind." He tapped the cover with his fingertips. "As soon as it's in here—it's outa my head. Karl doesn't keep a scrapbook. He's got other ways. Now sometimes there's no story for me to tape in here, and then I feel yantzy for a while. But it goes away eventually."

Cassandra looked at the scrapbook. How many of them did he have? She imagined him sitting here at his dining room table, evening after evening, poring over newspapers, clipping, taping.

"He'll brood for a while," said Sokolowski. "But it'll go away eventually," he said. "It always goes away. Eventually."

Alberg was standing in his Royal Canadian Mounted Police detachment office, looking out through its only window, which was small and square. The filing cabinet stood in front of the window, whose venetian blinds were pulled all the way up to the top.

He wasn't thinking about anything in particular. He felt as if he might be waiting for something. For the phone to ring, perhaps. And whoever was on the other end of the line would be calling with stupendous news. He couldn't imagine what this news might be, or how it could make any difference in his life.

On his desk were several stacks of paperwork. Every survey Alberg had ever read about the stress of police work had named paperwork as the biggest single cause. It ought to have been relatively easy for somebody to have done something about this, but so far nobody had. So far it had, in fact, only gotten worse. If he were to retire early, as he had lately sometimes thought he might, he wouldn't have to deal with paperwork. He could set himself up as an investigator, maybe, and hire somebody else to do it. This was tremendously appealing. He tried to think where the idea had come from—Cassandra. Of course. And he had resisted it almost contemptuously, he remembered. He'd have to apologize for that. But not yet. Better wait and see if this was a real idea in his head, or just a temporary distraction.

Alberg turned from the window and looked at his office. He should move stuff around in here, he decided. Get the filing cabinet out of the way, and position his desk so that he could see out the window when he was sitting there, dealing with the goddamn paperwork.

He put the black leather chair out in the hall and yarded the filing cabinet over against the wall next to the doorway. Then he took hold of the edge of his desk, a gray metal object whose panels were badly dented, and began hauling it around so that it faced the window instead of the door. The black chair went under the window. Then he wheeled his desk chair into place and sat down.

Through the window he saw a chunk of gray sky.

There, he said to himself.

The photograph of his daughters that hung on the wall was now inconveniently behind him, of course. But he needed to get a new photo anyway. He would have it put into a frame that he could put on his desk. He'd get one of Cassandra, too. He sat back in his chair, his hands on its arms, and told himself to keep on struggling.

There was a knock on the door and Norah Gibbons looked in. "They've come for the kid," she said.

He looked out the window again. The gray sky was still there. "I want to see him first."

In the interview room, Eliot Gardener was slumped in a wooden chair that Alberg didn't remember ever having seen before. Henry Loewen had picked up some clothes for him, to replace the bloody ones he had been wearing, which were now evidence. Jeans, a long-sleeved gray sweatshirt, sneakers. That was what he had on now. And he'd had a shower. You'd never believe, looking at him, what he'd done.

Alberg straddled a chair on the opposite side of the table. Norah remained standing, next to the closed door. "What happened?" he said. There was a slight echo in the room, which contained nothing but the rectangular table, the wooden chair, and two metal ones.

"Rosie," said the kid, in a monotone. His voice had only recently changed. "Is she—" He was trying to keep his chest from heaving.

"She's in shock," said Alberg. "But she's not badly hurt." The kid's hands were shaking. He trapped them between his knees. "What happened, Eliot?"

"I don't know what happened," said Eliot. "Nothing happened. I don't have to talk to you."

"No, you don't. This isn't official, anyway."

Eliot didn't respond. Alberg couldn't get a good look at his face because Eliot was looking at the floor. Alberg heard phones ringing, and voices, and footsteps; but all that was happening in another universe.

In his peripheral vision he saw Norah shift her position slightly.

Alberg got up and walked around the table to stand behind Eliot. He saw the kid's shoulderblades beneath the sweatshirt, sharp like chicken wings, and wanted to tell him to straighten up.

"Did he do something to piss you off?" he said.

Eliot opened his mouth to speak, but changed his mind. He shook his head.

Alberg put his hands in his pockets. "Well, what happened? You were whacking away at the bush and all of a sudden you turned around and— Is that it? Is that all there is to it?" He noticed that his voice was shaking just a little.

Eliot, staring at the floor, said nothing.

Alberg went back around the table and picked up his

chair. He moved it next to Eliot and sat down. "Jesus christ, Eliot. Do you know what you've done?"

The kid's eyes flickered up to his face. Alberg didn't move. Eliot's gaze locked onto him. He stared directly at him, into him—and Alberg didn't allow himself to look away. He didn't know why this was so difficult; he didn't know if he was more afraid of what he would see, or what Eliot would see.

Jack Coutts emerged from the elevator and made his way slowly down the hall to his Kamloops apartment, carrying a large paper bag. When he arrived at the apartment he didn't go inside. He reached into his pocket and took out his keys, then raised his hand to rest it on the door frame, and leaned his forehead against the door. A few seconds later he pushed himself away and started walking back up the hall.

He stopped before he got to the elevator, and stood motionless for several moments, holding the bag, holding his keys, looking at the floor. Then he returned to his apartment. This time he unlocked the door and entered.

He emptied the paper bag onto his bed: a teddy bear with a ragged red ribbon around its neck; another stuffed animal, a donkey, patched with mismatched fabric; a tiny glass vase, painted in blues and pinks; a battered copy of *The Wizard of Oz;* a doll, wearing overalls. Jack put these items on top of his bureau, one by one.

Then he went to the recliner by the living room window and sat down.

Across the street were a couple of apartment buildings much like his own; four stories high, modest, unpretentious. Trees had been planted in the strip of earth that lay between the street and the sidewalk, and some of the apartments had window boxes.

There was snow on the ground, and more falling.

Jack rubbed his face with both hands and looked at his watch. He got out of the recliner, pulling off his overcoat, and hung the coat in the closet. In the bedroom he toed his shoes off. They were wet from the snow—his socks, too. He put on slippers and took off his tie, loosening the top buttons of his shirt. He sat on the edge of the bed and looked at the objects on the bureau.

He lay down, after a while, with his hands behind his head, and stared at the ceiling.

"There's a theory," Alberg said that evening to Cassandra, "that we've got built-in circuit breakers. So that when we're pushed to the limit, something kicks in that keeps us from committing violence."

"You mean, an antiviolence gene?" said Cassandra.

"It's a species thing. Or so the theory goes."

They were sitting at the dining room table having dinner. Alberg hadn't had much to say, but the silence, though not exactly companionable, because Alberg was too preoccupied, hadn't been uncomfortable. His voice when he did speak was so unexpected that it caused Cassandra to jump. But she didn't think he'd noticed that.

"What do you think of this theory?" she said.

He pushed his plate away. He'd eaten half of a whole wheat roll, two bites of chicken, and four green beans. "But some people don't have them," he said. "These—interceptors. Yeah. That's what they are. Interceptors." He looked at the food on his plate. "Huh. I keep this up, might lose the weight after all."

# 4

*Friday, November 18*

Enid Hargreaves turned off the vacuum cleaner, yanked its plug out of the wall, and watched with pleasure as it disappeared into the body of the appliance: this was why she'd bought that particular model. It was very satisfying not to have to deal with the damn cord.

Slightly out of breath, she looked around the small living room and was pleased. It was easy to imagine somebody living here, being happy here, in this private, self-contained suite with its own ground-level entrance. The windows were big enough so that her tenant wouldn't feel as if she was living in a basement. Enid imagined a kindergarten teacher occupying the place. Or maybe a nurse. She had provided only bare essentials in the way of furniture, because whoever rented the apartment would naturally want to put her own stamp on things. She had left the walls bare, too.

She peeked into each room one last time. The four-piece bathroom was immaculate. The stainless-steel sink in the kitchen gleamed. The double bed in the tiny bedroom was covered with a handmade quilt Enid had inherited years ago from an aunt. There was a pine bureau in there, too, and a white bedside table with a small lamp, and a high-backed chair. The living room had a love seat, a basket chair with a corduroy cover, a standing lamp, a coffee table, and a book-case. Enid had had wall-to-wall carpet laid in the bedroom and living room. The tile in the kitchen and the bathroom was patterned in large green-and-white checks.

The suite still smelled of paint. Enid decided to leave the door open, to air it out.

She expected to start getting calls any time now: her ad was to appear in today's paper. It would be nice to have somebody else living in the house, she thought, as she hauled the vacuum cleaner back upstairs. Enid didn't know why she hadn't had a suite made down there years ago.

She checked the time and decided she had half an hour to spend in her garden, so she put on a jacket over her sweats and went outside.

From a shed in the backyard she got gardening gloves and a wheelbarrow, which she trundled around to the front.

Enid was not fond of flowers, except for the artificial kind, but she enjoyed growing vegetables. She had earlier harvested enough potatoes from her front garden to fill three cardboard cartons, and her two zucchini plants had produced into October. But it was now time to get rid of them. She parked the wheelbarrow and started heaving at the first plant, grabbing hold of its huge, spiny leaves with both of her gloved hands. She suddenly got a mental glimpse of herself doing this, as if she were watching herself from over there by the fence, a fifty-nine-year-old female in a life and death struggle with a zucchini plant. Not a pretty sight, with her face squishing up and getting red from the effort. It actually gave up after only a token struggle, the zucchini did, and she thrust it at the wheelbarrow, cracking its bulbous leaf stems so as to fold it in on itself. Then she turned to the other one.

In her backyard she had grown, this year, peas and beans and tomatoes and cucumbers and carrots. She gave away a lot of her produce, but kept potatoes and carrots in her basement all winter. She also froze some vegetables, made relishes with others, and could usually pick brussels sprouts from her own garden for Christmas dinner. She particularly liked the relishes and chutneys she put up each year, though, because the jars were so bright and colorful, lined up on top of her kitchen cupboards.

She'd wrestled the second zucchini plant into the wheelbarrow, and now she dumped the two of them in the compost pile, to be broken down later. Then she parked the wheelbarrow, dropped her gloves on the counter in the shed, and closed and locked the outside door to the suite.

Half an hour later she had showered, and was selecting clothes to wear to the funeral. A dark brown suit. A silk blouse, ivory-colored. A hat with silk roses in a shade of mocha.

Enid had a large collection of hats, mostly straw hats with rolled brims and hatbands of ribbon with artificial flowers tucked in there—lily of the valley, for instance, or small roses, or violets. She used to make the flowers herself, fashioning them out of silk, but her eyesight wasn't good enough anymore.

She dressed carefully, watching in her mirror, absorbed in herself. She had only recently stopped having her hair colored and perhaps it was vanity, perhaps her eyesight again, but she believed that her face looked younger by contrast. The salt-and-pepper hair had more substance than her black hair had had, too; this was one good thing about aging. There weren't many.

Enid got herself to the funeral home by walking there. She had a car but walked a lot, to keep herself trim.

She had been a widow for seven years. She had enjoyed her husband's funeral so much that she had gone to every funeral in town since. Except when she was away, of course. Funerals, she had discovered, were an excellent way to meet new people, or to establish new relationships with people she already knew.

She and Arch had had two children. Gloria was a lawyer married to a lawyer; they lived in Vancouver. But Enid saw her son, Reggie, almost more often than she saw Gloria. This was because he lived in California. Enid loved California.

She swung along the street this Friday afternoon holding her dark brown leather purse in one hand, carrying a rolled-up umbrella in the other, and she knew she cut an attractive figure, clothed in silk and gabardine, with a charming little hat nestled in her curls.

A small crowd had gathered in front of the funeral home by the time she got there, which pleased Enid, who had been to several funerals where there had been a shockingly poor turnout. She took her place in the lineup that had formed in front of the door and before it had moved much farther she saw Bernie Peters hurrying along the street. Bernie was wearing her cherry red jacket over good black pants and a black sweater. She had on a black tam instead of her usual hairnet, and tight curls, bright brown, formed a rim around the edges of the tam. Enid waved and Bernie, spotting her, joined her in the lineup as if they'd decided all along to meet there and Enid was holding her a place as they'd agreed.

"What are you doing here?" said Enid.

Bernie's small black eyes were blinking rapidly. Her face was deeply lined, with hundreds of tiny grooves crisscrossing one another. "She was a friend of mine, Verna," she said.

Surprised, Enid said, "I didn't know that." She felt vaguely resentful.

Bernie was standing very close to her, as if taking physical comfort from her presence, and she was holding on to her big black handbag with both hands. "I always thought it was a stupid idea, you going to everybody's funeral," said

Bernie. "But today when I woke up it was the one good thing I could think of."

"I don't always stay for the food," said Enid.

"Well, you better today," said Bernie, "because I have to, and I ain't gonna do it alone."

They had shuffled their way almost to the door by now. Enid had had a good look at the people behind and in front of them and there weren't many faces she knew. "What a dreadful thing," she said in a low voice to Bernie, who shook her head and dragged a Kleenex out of her jacket pocket. Enid restrained herself from asking Bernie what she knew.

They stepped inside, where people had remained clustered around the doorway instead of spreading out across the room. Enid took Bernie by the elbow and propelled her firmly through the crowd toward the memorial chapel.

"Hold it," said Bernie, digging in her heels. "I'm not gonna be the first one in there. I want a smoke so bad," she said, looking futilely around for an ashtray. "There's no place in the world a person is allowed to smoke anymore except in her own home."

"You can smoke in Italy," said Enid, who had traveled to Europe again last year. She gazed approvingly at the vases of dried flowers flanking a long sofa that sat along the wall. Above it hung a painting of a mountain scene.

"Why is everything pink?" said Bernie irritably. "Lookit. The walls are pink. The sofa's pink. The damn mountain is pink."

"It's been scientifically proven that pink is a restful color," Enid explained. "Soothing. Come on, now. It's almost one o'clock." She led Bernie to the door of the chapel, where a tall young man in a black suit greeted them and indicated a stand on which he'd put a guest book.

"Would you be kind enough to sign, please? It's a memento for the family."

Bernie looked at him in horror. "What family?" she

snapped. "You mean that poor child in the hospital? Is that the family you mean?"

She marched into the chapel, Enid at her heels.

Alberg got there when the service was about to begin. He heard soft organ music as soon as he entered the building, and slipped into the chapel just before the young man in the black suit swung the doors closed. Alberg ignored the beckoning arm of an usher and slid into a pew near the back.

He couldn't see an organ, and decided it was probably behind and above him, but he didn't bother looking.

There were perhaps twenty rows of pews, divided by an aisle. At the front of the room a low table held photographs of Verna, and Ralph, and several vases full of flowers.

Alberg recognized Bernie, a few rows ahead of him, sitting next to a woman who was wearing a straw hat. It seemed to be the only hat in the place, and he wondered when women had stopped wearing hats to funerals, and whether they still wore them to weddings.

There were maybe fifty people in the chapel. The Gardeners were relative newcomers to Sechelt: their families lived in Nova Scotia. The bodies of Ralph and Verna Gardener were being taken home for burial by Verna's brother and his wife. But the neighbors—the Wilsons—had insisted on a memorial service. They had been walking on the beach when Rosie, screaming, bleeding, had run to them for help, and then collapsed.

"We can't let this happen and then just pretend that it didn't," Muriel Wilson had said on the phone to Alberg. She was still having nightmares, she'd told him.

A portly man with thinning hair wearing a dark suit, a modestly patterned tie, and eyeglasses with tortoiseshell frames had materialized next to the table. He clasped his hands in front of him and studied the photographs, looking somber, before turning to the assemblage and beginning to speak.

Alberg had to talk to the relatives. He wasn't looking forward to this, but it was necessary. It was one of the loose ends that had to be tied up before he could complete the paperwork, before he could put this event, and Eliot, behind him.

He noticed that the minister was wisely sticking close to the Bible, reading lengthy passages from the New Testament rather than floundering around in the here and now.

Alberg saw young people in the crowd and tried to determine from their faces whether they were friends of Eliot, or at least acquaintances. But they looked, to him, expressionless, and he couldn't even guess why they were there.

The minister was talking about Verna's gardening skills— at least he'd talked to somebody about her, then—and Ralph's concern for his family: this latter made Alberg suddenly furious.

"Let us pray," said the minister. Alberg surveyed the bowed heads surrounding him and heard the minister rejoice for souls welcomed into the kingdom of heaven and he thought about Eliot, about the blood on him, the blood of his family on him. That's all it is, then, he thought: blood on him; their blood on him.

Enid was somewhat shaken by the time the service concluded. She had never before attended the funeral of somebody who'd been murdered. And now here she was mourning the deaths of two of them.

Bernie was dabbing at her eyes with a Kleenex and muttering under her breath. She pushed the tissue into her pocket and stood up. "Let's get downstairs to the tearoom before everybody else does," she said to Enid. "I've gotta say a word to the relatives."

She rushed away, and Enid followed, but outside the

chapel Bernie stopped suddenly, then hurried up to a large man who was heading for the door. She put a hand on his arm and he turned around. He was younger than Bernie and Enid, with pale hair, light blue eyes, and a melancholy face.

"Bernie," he said. He gave her a hug.

"I'm sorry I ever told you about him," she said.

He shook his head. "No. Hey. Sometimes you can do good. Sometimes you can't. And you never know until you try."

"This is Mr. Alberg," Bernie said to Enid. "He's a policeman. I do for him. And his missus."

"Enid Hargreaves," said Enid, offering her hand. "How do you do."

He smiled, though she didn't think his heart was in it, and shook her hand. "Pretty hat," he said, and turned away and went out the door.

Jack was sitting in the recliner again. Outside, the snow continued to fall.

After a while he got up and went into the kitchen. He opened the fridge door and looked inside.

There was a knock on his door, but Jack made no response. He continued to inspect the contents of the fridge.

There was another knock, louder this time; a brisk, impatient sound. Jack opened one of the fridge drawers and took out a withered apple.

A third and final knock. Jack tossed the apple into the garbage bag under the sink.

He shut the refrigerator door and pulled open cupboards, one by one. Then he sat down again.

Five minutes later he got up quickly, stumbling, grabbing hold of the back of the chair for support, and pulled his overcoat from its hanger in the closet. He was still putting it on when he opened the door.

Sitting on the hall floor was a large basket of flowers. Jack stared at them. He looked up and down the hallway. There was a florist's envelope with his name on it, attached to the handle of the basket. He finished putting on his coat, picked up the basket, and took it inside.

Jack put the flowers on the coffee table in the living room and opened the envelope. It contained a card that had CONDOLENCES printed on the front in script and it was signed, "Maura Sullivan." And then, in brackets, so he would be sure to know who she was, she had written "(Alberg)."

He sat on the sofa and looked at the flowers, at the card in his hand, at the flowers again.

Jack tossed the card on the coffee table and sat back.

A few minutes later, he went quickly into his bedroom and started to pack a bag.

**5**

*Saturday, November 19*

Verna Gardener's brother and sister-in-law were staying in a Sechelt motel while they waited for Rosie to recover: they were going to take her back to Nova Scotia with them.

"They say it'll be another week or two," said Frances Regan. Her eyes filled with tears. "Oh the poor wee thing, it's terrible, just terrible, what this has done to her."

"She's starting to come out of it, though, Frannie," said her husband, Sandy, who was sitting next to her on the motel room sofa. He turned to Alberg. "At least now when we talk to her, she looks like she knows who we are." He fumbled for his wife's hand, and patted it. "She's going to come through it, Frannie, oh yes she is, with our help and the Lord's."

Sandy Regan was a slight man in his fifties, with coal black hair and small dark eyes, wearing a wool plaid shirt and khaki-colored denim pants. His wife was plump, with soft, creamy skin and slightly protuberant green eyes. She looked at her watch now, and said to Sandy, "It's time we got over to the hospital." She turned to Alberg. "We visit her twice a day. They let us stay as long as we want."

"I won't keep you," said Alberg, who was seated in a

straight-backed wooden chair that was crammed between the television set and one of the bedside tables. "I just want to tell you how sorry I am. I liked Verna very much."

Sandy Regan squinted at him. "Do you know what happened? Do you know why he did it?"

Alberg shook his head, his eyes on the floor, which was covered in rugged wall-to-wall carpeting, beige, that needed cleaning.

"No. I didn't think so." Regan squeezed his wife's hands and let them go.

"What can you tell me about him?" said Alberg.

"He was a perfectly ordinary lad," said Eliot's uncle. "Sullen. I admit that. But I always thought of him as a well-meaning boy."

"Very fond of the wee one, he was," said Frances. "It doesn't make any sense, you see. I mean, I can understand a boy his age having trouble with his dad. With his mom, even. But he doted on wee Rosie. Wouldn't harm her. Never. That's what I would've said." Her large green eyes gazed intently at Alberg. "He was vulnerable to Satan. And Satan embraced him. And so an evil happened. A wickedness descended."

Sandy Regan looked at his shoes, nodding gravely.

"Do you know if he ever got in trouble with the law?" said Alberg. "Back home?"

They told him no, and Sandy looked at his wristwatch. "We better be on our way," he said.

"Are you going to see Eliot while you're here?" said Alberg.

"No," said Frances firmly, picking up the raincoat she'd draped over the end of the bed.

"Maybe you'll want to talk to the psychiatrists," said Alberg, with some desperation, "once they've spent some time with him."

Sandy shrugged into his jacket and opened the door.

Frances Regan put the raincoat over her arm and stroked it. "The boy's lost," she declared with conviction. "He is lost to us forever."


"He's only a kid," Bernie had said to him months ago, on a hot, dusty day in August, while vigorously polishing Alberg's sink. "It's real important, the things that happen to him now. The people he meets."

Alberg, leaning against the kitchen wall, rolled the beer can in his hand along his forehead in an effort to cool himself. On the stove, a pot of stew was simmering. He didn't think he could handle stew today. He didn't think Cassandra could, either. But he hadn't told Bernie this. It wouldn't have made a difference anyway. Three times a week Bernie came to clean and start dinner and three times a week she prepared something hot and substantial, "something that'll stick to your ribs," she'd say, with a satisfied flourish.

"Why?" said Alberg. "What's his problem?"

"He was dragged outa house and home," said Bernie, turning to face him. "All the way across the country Verna, she was sure he was gonna run away. He didn't, though. And now he probably wishes he had. It's not like he can go back for a weekend—he's stuck here. The boy's stuck here, until he's old enough to fend for himself, and that's not gonna be for years yet. And meanwhile he gets himself into trouble, because he's miserable. And bored silly, too, because there's no school yet and he doesn't know anybody and he's got nothing to do."

The kid had been picked up the previous night, tearing up the highway in Fred Mahoney's Mazda Miata, which he'd hot-wired in Fred's driveway, watched by an interested neighbor.

"Why me, though?" said Alberg. And flinched. The phrase had a sinister resonance.

She fixed her small black eyes on him, and all of the tiny wrinkles in her face quivered. "Why not?" she snapped.

Alberg was already nodding. "Yeah. Okay. I'll talk to him."

He remembered this now, getting into the Oldsmobile, looking out through the windshield at gray sky meeting gray water.

From the beginning, there was something about Eliot that got Alberg's attention.

He had gone to the house and introduced himself to Verna—Ralph wasn't home that day. And Verna had called upstairs, where muffled music was playing. The boy either couldn't hear his mother or had decided to ignore her: with a flushed face she finally went upstairs and got him.

He was almost as tall as Alberg, but thin like a reed.

"Hi," said Alberg, holding out his hand.

Eliot took it, with obvious reluctance, and shook it, but didn't say anything.

"Are you looking for work?"

Eliot gave him a look of disbelief. "No," he said, making two syllables out of it.

"You sure? Life's a lot easier when you've got money in your pocket."

"My life's fine like it is." He dropped onto a kitchen chair, knees together, sneakers splayed apart. His voice had changed but he hadn't yet gotten used to the size of his feet.

"Let me know if you change your mind."

The boy shrugged, looking bored.

Alberg fished a card out of his shirt pocket and put it on the kitchen table. He had looked down at the top of Eliot's head, and the nape of his neck.

That's what he remembered now, driving in the rain, driving away from the motel recently vacated by Sandy and Frances Regan: the smooth, innocent, vulnerable nape of Eliot Gardener's neck.

• • •

Horace Thibideau was a small, thin man wearing a cowboy shirt with pearl buttons, jeans, a wide leather belt with a silver buckle, and western boots with two-inch heels. He was leaning on the counter, chin in hand, gazing dreamily out at the falling snow, when a brown Chevy Silverado pulled up in front of his diner.

He straightened, stretched, and poured a coffee.

"Hiya, guy," he said as Jack Coutts came inside, making the bell on the door jingle, stamping his feet to get the snow off his boots. "Long time no see," said Horace, putting the coffee down on a nearby table.

"Yeah, it's been a while," said Jack. He took off his jacket and hung it over the back of a chair. "It's quiet in here, eh?" he said, looking around. "How's business, generally speaking?"

"Hell, Jack," said Horace, "generally speaking business sucks. Ever since the Coquihalla opened."

The Coquihalla was a four-lane highway that had opened several years earlier. It cut the driving time between Kamloops and Vancouver from six hours to four. It also bypassed the town in which Horace's diner was located.

"You want something to eat?" Horace asked.

"I'll take a sandwich to go. Ham and cheese."

"It's okay, though," said Horace, going back behind the counter. "I'm scrapin' by." He got out sandwich ingredients. "My wants are few." He glanced over at Jack. "You on your way to the coast?"

"Yeah."

"Business? Nah," Horace answered himself. "You haven't been on the road in years."

"Right," said Jack.

Horace had a lot of curiosity about Jack. Horace was pretty good at sussing people out—it was the Indian blood in him, he often thought, usually while admiring himself in the mirror (he had a face like an eagle, a woman had told him once and Horace had never forgotten that). Hell, a guy'd walk through the door of the diner, Horace'd look him up and down, right away he'd have him, have the type. A boaster. A worrier. A ladies' man. Whatever. But Jack was a true challenge, he acknowledged as he fixed the sandwich. He glanced over at him sitting there looking out the window, no paper to read, just sitting there.

Butter, mayo, mustard, ham—Horace peeled off a couple of pieces of cheese and added them, and a big old lettuce leaf, slapped on the second piece of bread and cut the sandwich in two, diagonally.

Close-mouthed, that was Jack Coutts. Secretive, you might even call him. At first this had hurt Horace's feelings somewhat. Hell, Jack had been coming in here since the early seventies, right from when Horace first opened The Eatery. Horace had come to think they were friends, of a sort. And so he'd resented it that Jack never confided in him, never told him personal stuff. After all, Horace had moaned and groaned to Jack when he got broken into that time. And when he had the gall bladder attack, and surgery from hell. And when Effie walked out on him. Yeah, but that was his nature, he reminded himself. He'd just naturally complain to anybody who'd listen when things went bad in his life. It was his way of being friendly.

He slipped the sandwich into a plastic bag and filled up a take-away container with potato salad.

Jack was just not much of a talker, not when it came to his personal life. Horace knew Jack had been married, and he thought he wasn't married anymore, but he wasn't sure about that. And he knew Jack had a kid. But there was some kind of bad stuff surrounding that situation. Horace used to ask about the kid but Jack not only wouldn't answer, he'd pretend he hadn't even heard the question, so, hell, Horace didn't ask about her anymore.

He slipped the sandwich and the salad and a plastic fork into a paper bag and left it on the counter. "Mind if I join you?" he asked Jack, and when Jack shook his head, Horace got himself a coffee and sat down with him. "What're the roads like?"

"Not bad," said Jack. "They're already plowed. Sanded. Visibility's not great." He was rubbing his face with his hands, as if it were numb and he was trying to rub feeling back into it.

"Yeah," said Horace, nodding. "The wind. Blows the stuff sideways across the windshield. I hate that," he said cheerfully, polishing the toe of one of his cowboy boots with a paper napkin.

"Good coffee," said Jack. "I'll take another one with me."

Horace, studying him, said, "You're lookin' kinda zwacked, if you don't mind my sayin' it."

Jack looked at him straight on, then, for the first time, and Horace felt a shiver of concern, it was such an empty look. " 'Zwacked'?" said Jack. "What's 'zwacked'?"

"Tired," said Horace quickly. "You know. Wiped."

"Wiped. Yeah," said Jack, looking out the window. "Yeah, that's what I am." He checked his watch. "Gotta go." He stood up and reached for his jacket.

Horace went back behind the counter and poured coffee into a Styrofoam cup, put on a lid, and tucked the coffee into the bag with the sandwich and the salad.

"Stop in on your way back," he said, handing the bag over to Jack, who paid with the exact change. And then he just stood there. Horace tilted his head at him, inquiringly.

"I might not be coming back," said Jack. He was looking at the floor, and frowning a little, like he was surprised at what he'd said.

He could've meant that he might take the Coquihalla back, for once. He could've meant that he might decide to move to the coast. But Horace didn't think he'd meant either of these things.

"Hell, what's wrong, Jack?" He peered into Jack's face, looking in the eyes like he always did for clues to personality and state of mind, but not finding them in Jack's.

"But, yeah," Jack said, as if Horace hadn't spoken, "if I do, I'll stop in." He headed for the door.

"Adios, partner," Horace said, automatically, and Jack gave him a wave, without turning around.

The bell jingled again, and he was gone.

Horace watched him hurry through the snow, one hand clutching the paper bag with his lunch in it, the other pressing the remote that unlocked the pickup's doors. He kept on watching until the Silverado pulled away.

He looked around the empty diner. No traffic outside, no traffic inside. He suddenly didn't feel like being there anymore. He suddenly felt depressed. Uneasy.

Horace gazed out at the falling snow and wished he had somebody to go home to.

━ ━ ━

*The door opened and Betty could hardly believe it, but there he stood. "It's me," he called out. "I'm home."*

*She was amazed to see him, and told him so. "You said next week. I know you said next week. I made a note of it."*

*"Daddy, Daddy!" Heather was yelling, and Jack picked her up and gave her a hug. They were so thin, the two of them, compared with her.*

*Heather wasn't amazed to see him. Betty didn't understand this; how Heather always got the day right and Betty always got it wrong.*

*She took herself quickly in hand, though, and scurried around the kitchen making dinner. She found a can of stew in the cupboard, and a can of peaches, and there was a loaf of bread, of course, as well. And she* made a pot of tea. Jack cleaned his plate and seemed quite content.

After dinner Heather went outside to play, and Jack opened up the newspaper.

"Shall we talk, now?" said Betty, patting her frizzy hair. "How was your trip? How long will you be home this time?" She could see from the impatient way he turned the page of the newspaper that he didn't want to talk. But it was important that a husband and wife talk to each other. So she kept on asking questions, even though she knew he was becoming more and more annoyed; they just popped out of her mouth, like bubbles of spit.

Finally, he threw down the paper and said to her, "Have you been to the school yet, Betty? to talk to Heather's teacher?" Then he asked about her pills. "Have you been taking your pills, Betty?" And this was a personal matter. So she stood, and hurried upstairs.

But he followed her. He looked into every room up there, swearing, cursing the dirt he said he saw. Except in his own room, of course; except in his den, which he cleaned himself. Betty wasn't allowed in his den but she often looked in through the doorway, admiring its white walls.

Soon he stormed downstairs, and outside. After a while, Betty followed. She looked through the glass door in the kitchen and saw him out there watering the lawn. Heather was leaning on the fence, and the two of them were talking and laughing together in low voices.

Betty threw open the door. "Heather! Come in here at once! Come in here and help me clean this kitchen!"

Heather's smile went away. "No," she said. "I helped with dinner. I practically made the whole dinner. It's not fair." She glanced at her father and then back at Betty, and, "Do it yourself," she said.

*"Jack! Don't let her speak to me like that!"* Betty felt tears come into her eyes and blinked fast, trying to make them go away. *"I'm her mother, she must treat me with respect!"*

Jack's face turned dark red. *"You can't do anything, can you,"* he hissed at her. *"You can't—you can't wash a dish or sweep a floor or do a goddamn thing."* Betty tried to interrupt him but he kept on, getting more and more angry, shouting now. *"That house is a pigsty, every time I come home it's a pigsty. You can't even tell what color the floor in that kitchen is supposed to be; you couldn't get all the filth off those counters now if you tried. You want help? I'll give you help."* He came toward her—and pointed the hose inside the kitchen.

Betty heard Heather shriek and start to cry.

Jack went on yelling as the harsh spray struck pots and pans and dishes piled in the sink, bounced off the toaster, zinged against cupboards and stove, splatted against the walls. Betty watched, fascinated, and hardly felt the cold water that flew sideways from the nozzle of the hose, drenching her.

After a while Jack threw down the hose and turned off the water. He went quickly around the side of the house and Betty heard his car start up. Heather had disappeared.

Betty squished up to the door and peered into the kitchen. She shook her head sadly. She walked around to the front door and went upstairs. *I really must do something,* she thought, *and soon, so that eventually when he arrives I can be prepared.*

A little later she heard Heather come home.

Much later she heard Jack arrive. He was downstairs a long time, and Betty heard muffled bangings and sloshings. Then he came up and went into his den.

*A long long time later Betty tiptoed downstairs, avoiding the steps that squeaked. She went into the kitchen and turned on the light. She smiled with pleasure. The whole room was very clean. The whole room was fresh and gleaming.*

# 6

*Monday, November 21*

"I mean, what does a person do all day, when he's retired?" said Isabella Harbud, leaning against the door frame of Alberg's office. Isabella, the detachment's secretary-receptionist, was referring to her chiropractor husband, who had lately begun to muse aloud about giving up his practice.

"I don't know, Isabella. How the hell would I know?"

"Well you've been thinking about retiring yourself, haven't you? So you must have some opinions on the subject. What would *you* do, retired?"

He was astounded. "Where did you get the idea I'm thinking of retiring?"

"You mutter it under your breath every time you get fed up with something. Or somebody," she said, going to the window and peering out.

"You've been imagining things," said Alberg, flustered.

"It might be all right," said Isabella. "I guess. I'm just afraid he'll get depressed, or something." She turned to Alberg with a sigh. "I'm thinking of getting my hair cut." Her graying hair fell almost to the middle of her back. She usually wore it down, and loose, but had recently begun braiding it and pinning it in a coil on top of her head. She patted this coil now, cautiously. "It makes my head ache." Alberg liked her hair. He also liked her eyes, which were golden brown—topaz—and gave her an exotic look.

"Has he got any hobbies?" he said, leaning back in his chair. He opened the bottom desk drawer and rested his foot on it. "Has he got a boat, for instance?"

She looked at him with pity. "No, Karl. He doesn't have a boat. The world is filled with people who don't have boats. Who don't *want* boats." She looked around the room. "This is better. You were right. All you need now is a plant in here."

"No, Isabella. No plants." She was disappearing down the hall now, pretending not to have heard him. Alberg realized that he was smiling. Thank god, he thought, for Isabella.

He reached for the phone and called Eliot's Legal Aid lawyer. He had discovered that he couldn't put the whole damn thing behind him after all. At least not yet.

A few minutes later he was saying, "Just ask the kid if he'll see me, will you?"

"Why? Are you offering to help him?" said the lawyer.

Alberg sighed, drawing a parade of stick figures on the notepad in front of him. "I don't know. Maybe. It depends."

"On what?"

"On what he says." He linked their wrists with pairs of handcuffs.

"He's not saying anything, Staff Sergeant. He's not talking to anybody. What makes you think he'll talk to you?"

Isabella reappeared in his doorway.

"He probably won't," Alberg said irritably. "But it's worth a try, isn't it?" He beckoned to Isabella, tossing the notepad aside. "I did something for him. Maybe he trusts me a little."

"I'll ask him," said the lawyer wearily.

"What is it?" said Alberg to Isabella, as he hung up the phone.

"There's a person out there who wants to see you," she told him. "He says you know him. Jack Coutts?"

Alberg didn't move. Into his head came an image of Jack Coutts standing in a doorway, daylight behind him, wearing an overcoat; he held an overnight bag in one hand, and a battered briefcase in the other.

He realized that he was slightly hunched, over his desk. He straightened himself. He looked at the notepad and pen in front of him and couldn't for a moment recall whom he'd been talking to on the phone, or why. He slid the pad and pen with care into the desk's top drawer.

"Karl? Should I bring him in?"

Slowly, Alberg stood up. "Yeah. Okay." He moved from behind his desk into the middle of his small office, and there he waited.

Isabella ushered him in. Jack Coutts was about Alberg's age, tall and slightly stooped, with hair that had become mostly gray. He was paunchy, now, instead of lean. His eyes were very bright. Alberg looked at him and tasted dirt. They were both standing perfectly still, and Alberg was aware of the multitudinous sounds that constituted their silence.

"She's dead," said Coutts flatly.

It was what Alberg had known he would say. It was an event long expected—and the only thing that could have brought Jack here.

"I'm sorry, Jack."

She had been a slim pale child with yellow hair that was long and often stringy-looking.

"Sure you are." Jack's eyes flickered around the office, settling on the photograph of Alberg's daughters that hung on the wall.

"When?" Alberg asked him.

One summer evening long ago he'd been hurrying from his house to his car, late for work, and she'd called out to him. He'd looked up to see her leaning out from behind a tree, holding on to the tree and leaning far out, so that her hair hung almost low enough to touch the ground. "What is it?" he'd said, and maybe he'd sounded impatient, because she shook her head and disappeared behind the treetrunk. And he'd driven away.

"When?" he asked Jack now.

It was the only time he could remember speaking to her.

"Ten days ago," said Jack, studying the photograph. He was wearing a heavy wool jacket of red plaid, a pair of jeans, and hiking boots. He looked different, more comfortable in these clothes than in the suits and ties he'd worn as a salesman.

Alberg reached for his jacket. "Can I buy you a coffee?"

Jack turned, and looked at the mug on Alberg's desk. "There's no coffee here? In a cop shop?"

"I'm on my way out," said Alberg. "How about it?"

Jack followed him to Earl's in a brown Chevy pickup. As he drove Alberg thought about the last time he'd seen him, twelve years earlier, in Kamloops.

"I've got no reason to stay in Kamloops now," said Jack, as Earl put down two big white porcelain mugs full of coffee. "I'll probably move." He massaged his face. "I don't know. We'll see."

"You've got a lot of seniority with the company, though, haven't you?"

Jack looked him in the eyes long enough for Alberg to feel challenged. "Yeah," he said finally. "But you probably know, that means fuck-all to me now."

"Yeah," said Alberg. "I know." He watched him for a moment, fixing up his coffee. He remembered that Jack had no family—no parents, no brothers or sisters. He realized that he was trying not to feel too much sympathy for the guy. "So are you taking some time off?"

Jack nodded. "Some time off. Yeah." He added more sugar to his coffee. "I was going to go right back to work. But then—" His face creased in a baffled frown. "I decided to come here."

"Not much to do around here this time of year," said Alberg.

Jack rubbed his face again, moving it around, sculpting transitory grotesqueries with his own flesh. He didn't respond.

Alberg glanced at his watch. "I've got to go." He started to get up.

But Jack grabbed his wrist. He looked at Alberg questioningly.

Alberg forced himself to remain relaxed; not to pull free.

"I've come a long way," said Jack.

The urge to resist, to clout the sonofabitch, was exceedingly strong. But Alberg gazed steadily at Jack, into his eyes, presenting him with a fabricated calmness.

And Jack let go.

"Yeah, you have come a long way," said Alberg. "You wanted to let me know in person. Is that it?"

Jack sat back in his chair. "How're your kids, Alberg?"

Alberg stood up. "I told you I was sorry, Jack," he said quietly. "I told you then and I told you today. What more do you want from me?"

Jack looked at him with his bright eyes. "I don't know yet."

Jack remained sitting at the table after Alberg left. Several people in the restaurant threw curious glances at him. Jack looked back at them, pleasantly, one after another, and they all turned away. All except for a man in mechanic's overalls sitting at the counter, who tipped a nonexistent hat to Jack before returning to his meal.

Earl hustled over with the coffeepot. "Warm it up for you?"

"Sure," said Jack. "Warm it up."

"You want something to eat?" said Earl.

Jack looked at him, then at the clock on the wall. "Yeah. Maybe. What've you got?"

"I got a whole menu full of stuff. But the specialty of the house is spaghetti with marinara sauce."

"Is that so?"

"It comes with a green salad and garlic bread."

"Okay. Good. I'll have it."

Jack sat quietly, his hands folded on the tabletop, looking out at the street.

A while later Earl delivered a plate of spaghetti, a green salad in a glass bowl, and a basket of foil-wrapped garlic bread. "You want a beer with that?" he asked. "A glass of wine?"

"Yeah. Wine, please. Red wine." When the waiter came back with it Jack raised the glass. "To the chef."

"Chef. Owner. Bottle-washer," said Earl.

"Earl?"

"That's me. Enjoy," he said, and went back behind the counter.

Jack cleaned his plate, ate all the salad and the garlic bread, and had another glass of wine.

"What kind of work do you do?" said Earl as Jack paid the bill.

"Sales. I'm in sales."

"On the road?"

"Used to be. Now I'm part of management."

"You gonna be in Sechelt long?"

"Not sure. What time do you open?"

"Six o'clock."

"Might see you for breakfast." He gave Earl a wave and went through the café's squeaky door onto the street. He climbed into his pickup, which was parked halfway down the opposite side of the block, and sat there for a few minutes, his hands on the steering wheel.

They had lived in a succession of houses but it was the last one that Jack would remember forever, because of the things that happened there.

The last time he'd gone home to that house, the very last time . . .

. . . He had seen when he was halfway along the walk that the door was standing open, in spite of the cold, and he'd known then, instantly, that something was wrong. But he stepped inside, carrying his suitcase and his briefcase, as he always did, and called out, as he always did, "It's me. I'm home."

And then, in the archway between the hall and the living room, Alberg had appeared.

Jack stared out through the windshield at Alberg's town, hunkered down in the gray drizzle, and shuddered.

After a while he fired up the truck and drove along the street until he got to a mini-mall, where he parked and went inside to buy a copy of the local paper. He had another coffee at a little place that sold hamburgers and hotdogs, and looked through the paper, circling several ads. Then he went back to the place where he'd bought the paper and got himself a map of the town.

It was five o'clock now and almost dark. Jack drove down several streets, slowly, looking for addresses, peering at the various houses but not stopping at any of them. Until he got to the third place on the list of four he'd made. It was a well-maintained house, with a neat fence around it. Lights were on inside.

Jack parked and went through the gate and climbed the steep steps to the veranda.

Enid Hargreaves was having a light supper in front of the television set when she heard the knock on her door. She put aside the TV table, pushed herself out of her easy chair, and went down the hall and opened it. "Yes?" she said to the man on her porch.

"It just struck me now, ma'am, that I should have called you first, and not just dropped in like this." He held up the paper. "I'm here in response to your ad. Do you want me to come back another time?"

Enid hesitated. She couldn't see him well. "No, that's all right," she said finally. "You want to see the suite, then?"

"If it's no trouble, ma'am."

She glanced behind her. "That's all right," she said again. "But let me get a sweater." She pulled one from the closet, a heavy cardigan, and put it over her shoulders. "The entrance is in the back," she told him, stepping out onto the porch, pulling the door closed behind her.

Enid led him around the house and unlocked the door to the suite. "You go in and have a look around," she said, pushing the door open. "The light switch is on the left."

She stood outside on the patio as he explored the apartment. He was the first person to respond to her ad. She'd expected a flurry of calls, but had had none. Of course it was early days. And she was in no hurry.

He cast a large shadow in her basement suite.

She had never considered having a male tenant. The idea made her uneasy. But she probably couldn't refuse him because of his gender. There was probably a law against it.

"It might smell of paint," she called out to him. "It's just been newly painted." Why did I say that? she scolded herself. She ought to be telling him there were mice in the house. Or fleas.

He emerged outside. "It seems fine. I'd like to take it. On a week-to-week basis."

"Really," said Enid, slightly dazed.

"If that's okay."

He had lovely eyes, she noticed. Brown, she thought they were, with specks of gold. Kind eyes, she thought they were.

"Oh yes, of course," she said. "Good."

Jack introduced himself, arranged to move in the following day, and shook her hand warmly.

Enid, standing on the front porch, watching him drive away, was filled with a delicious curiosity.

## 7

*Tuesday, November 22*

Jack cried out, and awakened.

Quickly he sat up, his hands pressed hard on the mattress on either side of him—he was sweating; blinking—there were tears on his face. He swung his legs over the side of the bed and stumbled into the bathroom, where for a long time he scoured his body in the shower.

Half an hour later he was ordering breakfast at Earl's.

The mechanic, a youngish man with a mustache, sat at the counter looking at one of the Vancouver papers and checking his watch every couple of minutes. Over by the window was a big, burly, unpleasant-looking fellow with gray hair partly covered by a woolen cap, and a black beard that was also going gray. Under his table lay a big brown dog.

"Does that dog bite?" Jack asked Earl, when he arrived with a mug of coffee and a glass of juice.

"Fred? Nah. Wouldn't let a dog in here that bit."

The mechanic, after a final look at his watch, left money on the counter for Earl and picked up the paper. As he turned around he noticed Jack. "You want *The Province?*" he said, waving it.

"Yeah, sure," said Jack. "Thanks."

"Bye, Earl," the guy called out, heading for the door.

"Bye, Warren."

The door creaked open, slammed shut. Jack paged through the newspaper. A radio was playing from behind the counter—CBC-AM. The café was warm: Jack took off his jacket.

"Here you go," said Earl, delivering bacon and eggs and a plate of brown toast.

"Smells good," said Jack.

Earl stood back and watched him for a minute, his hands clasped, brown against the enormous white apron that was wrapped around him. Beneath it he wore a blue-and-white-checked flannel shirt, a pair of jeans, and neat black loafers, very shiny. "Are you a friend of Karl's?" he said.

Jack wiped the edges of his mouth with a paper napkin. He looked up at Earl. "We knew each other in Kamloops." Earl nodded. Jack picked up his knife and fork and went back to his breakfast. "Are *you*?" he asked. "A friend of his?"

"We're friendly, sure," said Earl.

"I'm done over here, Earl," said the man at the window table.

When Earl had taken his money and the man and his dog had left, Jack said, "He gotten himself married again?"

"Lives with his girlfriend," said Earl. "She works over at the library."

"Oh, yeah?" said Jack. He forked up a mouthful of scrambled eggs, chewed, swallowed. "They live here in Sechelt, I guess, do they?"

Earl, who was cleaning the window table, threw him a curious glance. But he said, "Uh-uh. Gibsons."

Jack drank some coffee. "He can be a hard man to get to know," he said. "I seem to remember."

"He's not gonna get close to a lot of people, though, is he?" said Earl, wiping the chair seats, one by one. "Not in his job. Can't afford to." He went back behind the counter, whistling, rinsed the cloth in the sink, and put on another pot of coffee.

Jack layered strips of bacon between pieces of toast. "Can't be much going on around here, is there?" he said. "Not in a place this small. Must be a hell of a boring place to be a cop." He took a big bite of his sandwich.

Earl shuddered. "Oh, you'd be surprised," he said. He nodded to a couple who'd just come in, and handed them menus.

Jack finished his breakfast and had more coffee, reading the paper and watching the people coming and going. When the café had gotten full, he paid the bill and left with a wave in Earl's direction.

He drove back to the little mall and steered a cart down the aisles of the supermarket, buying coffee, bread, margarine, cans of tuna and soup, salt and pepper. Then he wandered through the mall until it was time.

It was ten-fifteen when he rapped on Enid's door. "Come in," she said, smiling. "Will you have coffee? I've just made a fresh pot."

"Sure," said Jack Coutts, smiling back.

She took him into the living room and looked around, trying to see her belongings through the eyes of this male stranger. There was a small wooden chair with an oval back, the seat covered in a petit point design. A big easy chair with a matching footstool. A table made from a burl from a redwood tree. There was a brocaded love seat, and a fireplace with wood piled on the hearth and ashes in the firebox. Bookcases. In the adjoining dining room sat a table and a china cabinet with a glass front. He would like the easy chair, she thought, appraising him with a sideways glance. And the table. Maybe the bookcases. Does he like to read? she wondered. But wouldn't ask him. Not yet.

"Sit down," she said, indicating the easy chair. "I'll be

back in a minute," and she hurried down the hall to the kitchen.

He stood up as she came into the room bearing a wooden tray with two cups and saucers on it, and cream and sugar. The china was light blue with a white ring half an inch from the mouth of each piece.

She put down the tray and handed him a cup and saucer. "And here's your key," she said, taking it from the pocket of the gray cardigan she wore over sweatpants and a T-shirt. She saw him notice what she was wearing.

"Do you, uh, jog, or something?" he asked clumsily.

"I walk," she said. "And I work in my garden."

They sipped coffee in what Enid took to be a pleasantly stress-free silence. And then, "I'll need a couple of references," she said. She absolutely had to get references or she'd never hear the last of it from Bernie.

"Oh sure," said Jack. He got out his wallet and extracted a piece of paper on which he'd written three names, with phone numbers. "I figured you would. Those are out-of-town numbers, I'm afraid. Kamloops."

"Are you moving here, Mr. Coutts?"

"I don't know yet, ma'am. I'm looking the place over, you might say. The climate's better than up-country, so I'm giving it serious consideration."

The phone in the kitchen rang, and she excused herself to answer it.


. . . it had happened on a rutted, sandy road, dry yellow grass and sagebrush spreading across the landscape on either side, purple mountains rising nearby. Jack had gotten him down and he was pounding the shit out of him. Sweat was pouring from his face onto Alberg's. There was bright blood in Alberg's blond hair, upon his ashen face, drenching his uniform jacket. It was the only time in his adult life that he'd hit somebody. And it hadn't been enough. It wasn't nearly enough . . .

As Enid returned to the living room she saw that Jack Coutts' hands were trembling. He brought them together, tightly. He was a big man, slightly stooped, with thick hair that was almost completely gray, even though he was a little bit younger than Enid. What could cause his hands to tremble?

"I'm sorry about that," she said. "If I had one of those answering machines I could have just let it ring." She smiled at him. "And your family?" she said.

He looked at her uncomprehendingly. "Excuse me?"

"Your family. Will they be joining you here, if you decide to stay? Because as you saw last night, the suite really isn't big enough for more than one."

"No," said Jack, huskily. He cleared his throat. "No family."

—  —  —

*She had resolved not to be caught by surprise this time. This time she would be ready for him. This time the house would be ready for him.*

*She took an old paper grocery bag into the bathroom and dumped into it all the bottles and sponges and toothpaste tubes that cluttered the counter, and then she wiped the counter. Downstairs, she put all the newspapers into piles, and in the kitchen she washed all the dishes. Some of the food would not come off. It stayed on the plates in speckled patterns, like a bird's egg. It stayed in the cups, shadows of tea and coffee stuffed down in there. It stayed in glasses, ghosts of Heather's milk. Still, Betty thought, every plate and cup and glass and knife and fork and spoon has been in hot soapy water, and so it is clean. She washed the counters, too, and the table, and the front of the refrigerator.*

*When she had finished all this work, she was exhausted. Her head was spinning; her mind was numb. She went up to her room to lie down, to rest and collect herself.*

*Later, she got up and walked around the house. She could scarcely recognize it, it was so clean. And it had taken her only one day—just one day. It was disappointing when Heather came home, because at first she didn't notice anything. So Betty took her around the house, showing her. "Look in here, look in the kitchen," she said, and Heather followed her in there and when she saw it, she smiled.*

*"It looks good," she said.*

*But the next morning Betty realized that she had not done the floors. She knew it didn't matter that she had cleaned the bathroom and piled up newspapers and washed all the dishes. If she didn't do the floors as well it would be the floors that he would see. She was angry with him then, for a minute, as she looked around the house and saw what she still had to do.*

*With a broom she swept the floors and the rug. The dust blew up onto the furniture and into her nose and eyes. And the more she swept, the more dust and dirt there was. It came up in clouds and choked her. Finally she stopped and went outside to breathe the cold air.*

*When she returned to the house the dust had settled back onto the carpet, onto the floors. It didn't look as though she had cleaned the floors at all. He will see that the floors are still dirty, she thought. He will see that before he sees the clean bathroom, the clean kitchen, the neat piles of newspapers.*

*And then she had an idea. She would make a large sign saying,* WELCOME HOME, JACK! *He would be so surprised and pleased by the sign that he wouldn't notice the floors.*

*She jumped up from the table and started looking for a piece of paper. She looked in the kitchen and in Heather's room, but couldn't find one that was big enough. So she went into Jack's den, tiptoed in there where it was so neat and tidy and cool and clean. She tried to open his desk drawers—but they were locked.*

*A big piece of anger settled in Betty's chest. He locked them to keep Heather out of his things, but why can't he leave a key with me, she thought, in case of emergencies? She pulled and yanked at the drawers but they would not open.*

*Then a thought came into her head, bright and shining. In Heather's room she found a big fat felt pen, and she ran into Jack's den and stood up on his sofa and in big black letters, every one perfect, she wrote on the wall:* WELCOME HOME, JACK! *And then she got the chair from behind the desk and moved it closer to that wall, the one behind his desk, and she wrote the same thing on that wall, blackly on the white wall:* WELCOME HOME, JACK! *Carefully. Carefully.*

*She stood in the doorway and looked at the two signs. He might not like it, she told herself. He might not like it that I have written on his walls. I know that. I am not a child.*

*She wanted to see his face when he looked at them. She could almost see the first expression that would pop out on his face like a big pimple when he saw them. He would be astonished, bewildered . . . and something else, something she couldn't quite make out in her mind, no matter how much she peered, no matter how hard she strained to see.*

*She had never been so impatient for him to come home.*

# 8

*Wednesday, November 23*

"I think he's experienced a tragedy," said Enid. They were sitting in lawn chairs on Bernie's covered front porch, Bernie not yet having gotten around to putting away the accoutrements of summer, and they were discussing Enid's lodger. Enid sat back with a sigh, holding a glass of iced tea. "It's extremely interesting, isn't it? Getting bits and pieces of other people's lives. It's one of the—"

"That's all well and good," said Bernie severely, "as long as you don't start making up the in-between parts." She wore a hairnet over her bright brown curls and was dressed for work in a white uniform and white shoes.

"What on earth are you saying?"

"You know exactly what I'm saying. You've got too much imagination for your own good, Enid. Especially now you don't work anymore."

Enid, who had been a teacher, had retired early, when her husband died.

"What did you think of the funeral?" Bernie asked. "You being the local expert on this type of thing."

"Well goodness," said Enid. "Under the circumstances it was fine. I guess they did the best they could."

It had been a disappointing occasion, finally, although she wouldn't say this to Bernie. The funerals she attended were usually far more social in nature. People gathered around and told stories after the service, celebrating the life of the deceased. There were refreshments, there was laughter.

Of course most of these departed had died at an advanced age, and could be considered to have lived complete lives. Enid hadn't expected that the Gardeners' funeral would be a social event. She had expected to feel the shock and bewilderment and horror that was almost palpable among the gathering. But something else had been present, too, something Enid couldn't put her finger on. She had felt it as people huddling, with backs bent, averting their eyes, concealing the dead rather than acknowledging their unnaturally terminated lives.

"How's the little girl?" she asked.

"I've heard nothing," said Bernie. "So I guess that means at least she's still alive."

"And what will happen to her brother?"

"He'll go to jail," said Bernie grimly. "But not for long enough."

"How well did you know him?"

"Not as well as I thought. I got to know his ma. I knew Verna." Bernie drank the rest of her tea and stood up. "Gotta go. You gonna walk along with me?"

They put the glasses in the sink and Bernie picked up her big black handbag from the kitchen counter. On the windowsill, three African violet leaves were rooting in small jars of water. Bernie rattled the knob of the kitchen door to make sure it was locked, and they left the house through the front door.

They set off for Bernie's two o'clock housecleaning job, which was at the O'Rourkes' house, about a mile away.

Bernie trudged briskly along the side of the road and Enid glided next to her, imagining herself on rollerblades. She'd been a creditable ice skater in her time, but that was ages ago. She did those flexibility exercises almost every day, though, so who knows, she thought: maybe there was a night school class in rollerblading; they taught just about everything else there. Enid, strolling next to Bernie, pictured herself parachuting, or windsurfing, or pitching from a clifftop with one of those big kites strapped to her back.

It was warm for November but there were puddles from the recent rains, and the brush by the roadside was still wet with the fog that had crept in during the night and taken until mid-morning to recede.

"It does feel odd," Enid mused, "having somebody staying in my house."

"Huh," said Bernie. "Especially a man."

"I hear noises down there and at first I'm alarmed, then I remember it's him. And I ought to feel relieved. But I don't know if I do."

"Well but he's only just moved in. You're not used to him yet," said Bernie, squinting up at a crow that sat on a telephone pole, squawking. "I often wonder why I've never been shat upon by a bird. It's gonna happen someday. Bound to."

"Should I invite him up for dinner, do you think?"

Bernie stopped in her tracks. "What? Your lodger?"

"I thought it might be the polite thing to do." Enid glanced at her friend. "For goodness' sake, Bernie, don't look at me like that. I've never been a landlady before. I don't know the drill."

"What you've got here, Enid, is a strictly business arrangement, and don't you forget it." Bernie started walking again, almost at a trot now. "I don't like it. I don't like nothin' about this. I thought you were gonna have a young teacher in there, or a nurse or something—some young female person, anyway."

"So did I," said Enid, striding along in order to keep up. "But it doesn't matter, surely."

"I don't know if it matters or not," Bernie muttered. "I'm not one to mince my words, Enid, and you have always been a terrible flirt."

"Bernie! You can't seriously think that a woman of my age—"

"Enid, stuff it. I've known you for twenty years and you've been a flirt for every one of them. You're gonna flirt with the embalmer, you." She jabbed Enid in the shoulder. "You just better draw the line, though, at flirting with your lodger."

"He's too young for me," Enid protested, and then winced, knowing what Bernie was going to say next.

She didn't say it, though. She just stopped again and with those raisin-black eyes looked straight at Enid, her lips pursed tightly together, the wrinkles in her face exclaiming her disapproval.


That night Cassandra had a library board meeting. Alberg fixed himself a corned beef sandwich with lots of mustard and got half of it down before his appetite vanished. He put the other half on a plate, covered the plate with plastic wrap, and put it in the fridge. Then he opened a beer and sat on the sofa, watching the TV news and tossing a foil ball for the younger of his two cats while her mother, not in the mood for play, lay in his wingback chair watching them through slitted eyes.

Later, stretched out with a cushion under his head, the lamp in the corner turned on low, he tried to conduct a detached and logical examination of the past. But all he was able to do was buzz it, like a dive-bomber. He swooped down, grabbed a glimpse, and soared high, like an eagle with a piece of prey in its talons. He looked at this piece of memory for a minute, dropped it, and plunged down for another one. He wouldn't let himself collect them, retain them, fit them together so they made a whole picture. Maybe there wasn't a whole picture.

What the hell was Jack Coutts doing here? What was going on in his head?

. . . dust in his mouth, blood in his mouth, on the uniform—head wounds, they bleed like crazy. He hadn't been expecting it—who the hell would? Especially at that late date: three months had passed since the inquest.

The guy was just suddenly flying through the air toward him. His whole body hit Alberg's and the two of them crashed to the ground, and Jack had commenced to beat the crap out of him. And then Jack had collapsed. Alberg remembered the dead weight of him, crumpled across his chest, and the sound of his weeping, and the wetness of his tears, as they mingled with Alberg's blood.

Alberg had shoved him aside and gotten to his knees, then to his feet. He pulled Coutts up and leaned him against his car. Jack's eyes were closed; he was still crying. Alberg patched himself up with the first aid kit in the patrol car while the wind blew hot across the already sunburnt grass, tumbling sagebrush alongside the sandy track down which Jack had followed him, honking his horn, waving him to a stop.

Eventually Jack's sobbing had ceased. He watched dull-eyed as Alberg staunched the bleeding in his scalp and slapped a bandage on the wound. He said nothing.

Alberg decided to pretend the whole thing had never happened. He left Jack standing by his car and went to the motel he was then calling home, to change and get cleaned up, and that was the end of it.

He hadn't blamed the guy.

He still didn't.

But that was then. What was happening now? Had this final tragedy pushed him off the edge? Was Jack becoming deranged? Like his wife?

Alberg got up and turned off the lights in the living room and sat down again on the edge of the sofa, letting the darkness engulf him. The senior cat, purring, rubbed against his pants legs, turned around several times, then lay down across his stockinged feet.

**9**

*Saturday, November 26*

Alberg and Cassandra spent the afternoon looking at a house.

"Take your time," the real estate agent had said, handing them the key. He was a shy young man called Neil, a slender, ruddy-cheeked kid whose credulous smile made Cassandra want to hug him. "I think it's gonna suit you real well," he'd said. "But you gotta be careful about such a big decision. Sure."

The sun was shining again, glittering from the ocean, throbbing in the red bark of the arbutus trees that clung to a cliff face down the beach, setting aglow the bright green ferns growing thick and tall among the trees behind the house.

In front, a small, ailing lawn led halfheartedly down to a rocky beach. On the left a spit of land extended beyond the lot on which the house was built, offering shelter, creating a small cove. To the right there was another patch of weedy lawn, and then a rocky ledge that separated this lot from the next one, which was a rough piece of terrain backed up against a cliff, unlikely to be developed easily or soon.

"Look," said Cassandra, pointing into the backyard. "Wildflowers."

Alberg looked. "Weeds."

"They're only weeds if they're growing where you don't want them to grow," she told him. They had gone to seed, turned brown, been beaten by the autumn rains.

"Right. They're weeds," he said stubbornly.

Behind this patch of earth was a forest that stretched up the hill to the highway.

A gravel road wound down from the highway and turned here to run parallel to it, giving access to the several houses that had been built along the coastline to the south, squeezed between the forest and the sea.

Inside, the living room, which faced the ocean, had one wall made almost entirely of glass, and French doors led out to the front lawn.

"There ought to be a deck out there," said Cassandra. "Or a patio." The sound of the sea would put her to sleep at night, if she lived in this house.

"That's easily accomplished," said Alberg.

"I can't believe I'm getting married." She was suddenly filled with wonder, thinking about it. "I'm fifty years old for god's sake."

"I'm older," said Alberg. "Somewhat older. Not much."

"Yeah, but it's not your first wedding. It's my first damn wedding. At fifty. Some people would say it's a dumb thing to be doing, Karl."

He put an arm around her. "People like who?"

"I don't know. People."

Cassandra had once dreamed of learning Italian, and living a year in Venice; of learning German, and spending a year in Munich, or in Bonn.

"Those people don't know diddly squat," said Karl. "Come on."

He'd probably sooner be looking at houseboats, she thought, as he led her into the master bedroom.

"There should be glass doors in here, too," she said, seeking her truant enthusiasm. "Instead of just that piddly little window." She could plant lots of flowers, and they could lie in bed on weekend mornings, drinking coffee and reading the papers and gazing out at the garden.

"Glass doors are easy, too," said Alberg.

She would never have children, now. But that didn't bother her. Not much, anyway.

The kitchen faced east. "There's probably deer in the woods. We can watch them eating the wildflowers," she said, "while we're doing the dishes."

"The best thing about this kitchen," said Alberg, "is the built-in dishwasher."

The house was empty, and their footsteps echoed on hardwood floors as they walked slowly from room to room. Each time they stopped to look around they heard the sea.

There were two huge closets in the master bedroom. "Thank Christ," muttered Alberg. "We could get rid of the damn wardrobes."

"Look," said Cassandra. "A guest room. For when your kids come to visit."

"Huh," he said skeptically.

"Or your mother," said Cassandra. Whom she'd never met.

"Mmmm."

"And this third bedroom," she went on, "we could turn it into a TV room. There'd be space enough for a desk, too, if we wanted."

They wandered back into the living room, arms around each other's waists.

"Well? Do you like it?"

"Yeah," said Alberg. "Sure. I do."

"I'm not going to change my name, you know."

He grinned at her. "I never thought you would."

She looked at him and laughed, and reached up to kiss him. "Look at that fireplace," she said. "We could put candles on the mantel. Or photographs." She brushed from her mind the image of a mantelpiece crowded with pictures of Alberg's daughters, and his ex-wife.

He said, "Uh-huh," but he was looking at her, not at the fireplace. "I wish we'd brought a blanket or something. Or else I wish just one room in this damn house was carpeted."

Cassandra touched his face with her fingertips. "Are we going to be happy, Karl?"

He rubbed his nose against hers. "Are we happy now?"

Cassandra looked up at the skylight, at a patch of blue sky, dispassionate and serene.

They locked up and got into Alberg's Oldsmobile. He turned it around and headed back up the gravel road toward the highway. He kept looking into the rearview mirror, watching the house until they turned a corner and it disappeared.

Alberg lacked ebullience today. He lacked the enthusiasm that was supposed to accompany house-buying, and getting married. He felt bad about this. He glanced over at Cassandra, who was looking through the passenger window, not having much to say. "Hey," he said.

She turned her head. "What?"

"How about if we take a couple of days off and go over to Victoria?"

The road lurched into another bend and propelled them toward the intersection with the highway, fifty feet away.

Parked on the opposite side, facing north, was Jack Coutts' pickup truck.

"I think that's not a bad idea," said Cassandra.

Alberg pulled up at the intersection. Jack looked at him steadily and Alberg looked back. His mouth was suddenly dry. His hands were tight on the steering wheel.

"Next weekend? I could get Friday, too," Cassandra was saying. "How about you?"

Jack fired up the pickup and drove rapidly away.

"Karl?" said Cassandra. "What do you think?"

Alberg wrenched the wheel to the left and took off up the highway after the truck.

"Karl!"

His foot was on the floor. He felt the world whizzing past, saw only the brown pickup, getting smaller, and smaller . . .

"Karl, what are you doing!"

. . . and now gradually bigger, bigger, the sonofabitch he'd batter him into a goddamn pulp . . .

Alberg slammed on the brakes, pulling the Oldsmobile to the side of the road.

After a long moment, he looked at Cassandra. Her freckles were sprinkled upon her white face like cinnamon. He reached out to touch her cheek but she slapped his hand away.

"What was that all about?" she whispered.

"It was right in the middle of everything. Maura." He clutched the steering wheel. "Jesus. Such a bad time."


They were standing in the dining room when Maura told him. He'd just come home from work. He hadn't even taken his jacket off yet, so he was standing there in his uniform, his hat in his hand, when she said, "Karl, I want a divorce."

He put his hat down on the dining room table. "Where are the kids?"

She was across from him, clutching the back of a chair. She was dark-haired and green-eyed, like their daughter Janey, and Alberg couldn't imagine living without her.

"Out."

"Maura. Don't do this. Let's talk about it."

"I've been trying to get you to talk to me for months."

His wife was lithe and graceful, utterly confident in her physical self. When he first saw her Alberg had thought she must be a dancer.

"It's too late now," she said.

"No," said Alberg.

"Don't snap at me."

"I'm not snapping at you." He shook his head. "Jesus. I can't believe this."

"My shop is as important to me as your job is to you."

"I know that, Maura," he said wearily.

"No you don't know that, Karl. You do not understand that I do not want to give up my business, that I do not want to move, yet again, and this time to a place I've never been to, a place so goddamn small and isolated—"

"Okay, okay. Can we discuss this? Please? There are alternatives. Let's consider the alternatives. Let's think about the kids, for god's sake."

"The kids," said Maura, "are no longer children."

"They'll be devastated," he said, desperate, and had more to say, much more.

But then Betty Coutts had pounded on their door.


The sun was getting low in the sky, casting that primrose winter light that Cassandra thought was insubstantial; transparent; it lacked richness and depth. She watched it trickle through the trees on the other side of the highway from a sky the same shade of pale blue that happened on the hottest of summer days. And this seemed odd, now that she thought about it.

Alberg was still holding on to the steering wheel, staring straight out through the windshield.

"What does he want from you?" she asked.

He glanced at her. "He hasn't decided yet." He started the car, checked both ways for traffic, and made a U-turn.

"Tell me what happened, Karl. Did you put him in jail, or something?"

"This doesn't have anything to do with work," he said sharply. "It's strictly personal."

She couldn't get him to say anything else.

**10**

*Monday, November 28*

Eliot was taken to what they probably didn't know was his favorite room in this place, and told to wait there. Like all the other rooms, there were bars on its windows. But someone had tried to make this fact less obtrusive by placing a couple of tall plants in front of the windows, making it harder to see the bars. Once this person had positioned these plants just so, however, she had apparently put them from her mind: maybe she'd thought they weren't real, and therefore didn't need watering. Eliot could see that the earth they lived in was dry, shrunken from the edges of the pots, gray and powdery, and on the floor were dozens of leaves that had fallen from the potted trees, creating gaping holes among the branches. Eliot noticed these things because his mother had worked part-time in a nursery, back home. She had a lot of plants. They were probably all dead by now, he thought. Except maybe the cactus.

There was a big rectangular rug in the middle of the room, dark blue and light blue, with a yellow stripe around the edges. Eliot was looking at this rug and picking out shapes in the swirls of color. It was like looking at the sky, watching the clouds form themselves into shapes and then dissolve those shapes and form new ones. In the rug many shades of blue collided—conflicted—mixed and merged.

Eliot had now been in this place for two and a half weeks. He had been examined and discussed and talked to by a whole lot of people and there was going to be more of this before somebody finally decided what would happen to him. It seemed to be taking an awfully long time.

A big round wooden table sat on the rug. It had a very thick top which had what looked like vines carved into the side of it, vines with leaves and grapes on them. The top of the table had pale circles all over it where careless people had put down glasses or mugs.

Eliot was sitting in a chair near the fireplace, which had no grate and no screen and looked as though it hadn't been used in years. It was an upholstered chair; the fabric was severely worn on the arms and the back. Eliot had dug his thumb into a small hole on the right arm and was moving it around in a circular fashion, making the hole bigger.

He liked to sit, and even more to lie down. He didn't get to lie down very much, though, because of his roommate. He could sometimes feel comfortable, sitting or lying down. He occasionally when lying down had the sensation that he was dematerializing, becoming another kind of substance, like steam, or cloud. He thought about that now, wondering if he'd ever be able to do it on purpose. Maybe sometime, he decided, but not today. As soon as he began to examine the possibility he became acutely conscious of his feet, quivering large and sullen in huge sneakers at the ends of his legs; and of his hands on the arms of the chair, one thumb nuzzling into the fabric like it wanted sex there, a good sucking. He pulled it out and dropped his hands into his lap. They looked grimy; dirt was smeared into all their little skin crevices—he was surprised that there were so many. One of his fingernails had grown out almost to the end of his finger. He decided not to bite it but there didn't seem to be any good reason for this and so he bit it, snapped it off and nibbled at the rough edges, and the taste of his finger was as strong as a smell.

The door that was supposed to be locked suddenly opened, and Eliot looked up, mechanically, to see a kid of about ten or eleven with black hair falling all over his forehead leaning into the room, hanging on to the doorknob with one hand and yarding up a pair of dingy gray sweatpants with the other.

"Whatcha doin'?" said this kid, and although he must have been talking to Eliot, because there was nobody else in the room, he wasn't looking at him. His eyes were wandering all over the place. Eliot figured there was something wrong with him. He was blind, maybe, or maybe just crazy. He didn't bother to reply, and then he heard somebody yammering away in a scolding tone and the kid was whisked away. But the door remained open.

Eliot continued to sit, waiting, and now he could hear sounds from the hallway. He hadn't been aware until then of how much he'd been—not enjoying, because he didn't enjoy anything anymore, but—appreciating, he'd been appreciating the silence; he'd been leaning into it; burrowing his head into its bony shoulder bone; muffling his life in its flesh. The only sounds he'd heard, while waiting here, apart from those he'd made himself, were so muted as to be ignorable. But now all kinds of noises were springing through the doorway at him. He heard so many feet on the bare floor of the hallway that there might as well have been an army out there.

Except that they weren't marching footsteps; there were a lot of different kinds. There were the overlapping, careless squeaks of sneakers, running. The brisk tapping of some woman in high heels. The plodding steps of a man who was probably wearing shoes with laces.

Eliot let himself lean back in the chair. He looked up at

the ceiling, which was pretty high because where he was now was part of an old building that had once been somebody's house. They'd added pieces on to it, ineptly, so that it didn't look right anymore but from the inside, when you were in one of the old parts of the building, sometimes you could make it feel like a regular house.

Except for the bars on all the windows.

The door slammed shut, and Eliot heard it get locked.

Now he was feeling restless. He went over to one of the windows and looked out through the branches of the potted fig tree. There was a big sweep of lawn out there, and then a bunch of plants, and a fence, and beyond that a very busy street whose name he didn't know.

Some kids were huddled together at a bus stop on the corner, little kids, and one of them was wearing a jacket that Eliot—just for a second—thought he recognized. His heart jumped and he pushed the tree in its pot aside and grabbed hold of the bars and put his face close to them, to see between them. But then just as the kid turned around, enough for him to see her profile, God showed him Rosie in real life; running, in real life; screaming, in real life; running away from him, from Eliot, and screaming, while her blood flowed, red and abundant.

He had watched her as she ran. He had seen the neighbors come. He had seen Rosie fall. And then Eliot had walked from the beach into the forest.

This much he remembered.

Eliot turned away from the window.

He heard somebody unlock the door, and Staff Sergeant Alberg came in.

Eliot made himself cross the room to a chair, a wobbly chair with no arms and a round back. He sat down and concentrated on his body, which was in distress. His teeth were rattling, his hands were cold, and at the top of his chest where his throat began he felt an intense ache. If it stayed there, and grew bigger, it would not be possible for him to breathe. Eliot wanted the ache to go away but he didn't know if that meant that he wanted to live.

He opened his mouth and forced some words out—it felt like he was literally selecting and ejecting them with his tongue; the words felt like marbles in his mouth, choking him. "Rosie," he said. "Is Rosie dead?"

Alberg didn't answer for a moment, and then he said, "No," sounding surprised.

Eliot shut his eyes. The hugeness of his relief sapped him of all strength. He thought his heart might stop beating; he thought he had not even the strength for that.

"I told you before, she's not seriously hurt."

Eliot's eyes opened, and focused on the floor.

"Not physically, anyway."

Eliot stopped listening.

Alberg was silent for a while, but then began talking again. Eliot didn't hear his words, only his voice, which was gray, and reminded Eliot of the ocean. It was quite soft. But there were slivers of pain in it, and fragments of anger. Eliot listened indifferently to this voice, and the words that rippled within it were lost to him.

He noticed a figurine on the fireplace mantel, a china woman wearing a long dress with a huge skirt, the kind they wore hoops underneath, and she was carrying an umbrella. Her hair was in big curls, pinned on top of her head. Eliot thought she was very beautiful. He stood up and went to the mantel and looked at the figurine more closely. There was a chip missing from the umbrella, and another from one of the folds in her skirt.

He heard Alberg's voice change. It blackened, and got deeper and anger glittered in it, like mica. Eliot rested his forehead against the mantel. His hands hung large, empty, useless; he didn't want to make them into fists.

He felt Alberg's hand on his shoulder, Alberg's arm

around him. Eliot became very still. He tried to make himself evaporate but of course this didn't work. Alberg wasn't talking anymore but he was so close to Eliot that Eliot could hear him breathing. In his imagination he heard blood trickling through Alberg's veins and arteries. He lifted his head and eased away from the fireplace, from Alberg's sheltering arm, and returned to the window.

"I can't help you if you won't talk to me."

Eliot heard the words this time, very clear, but with a surrounding echo, as if the two of them were standing on a basketball court.

The little kids were gone from the bus stop. Now only an old woman sat there, a scarf around her head and a shopping bag at her feet. She was smoking a cigarette, jiggling it in her fingers impatiently between puffs, craning her neck to look up the street to see if the bus was coming.

Eliot shook his head.

"I'm not gonna give up on you, Eliot."

Eliot lifted his gaze from the old woman to a big tree on the opposite corner of the street. There were a lot of yellow leaves still clinging to its branches.

He heard the door open, and close.


It was mid-afternoon when Alberg got back to Sechelt. He parked in front of the detachment and sat there in his car, going over in his mind those conversations at the Gardeners' kitchen table.

"I can do something about it, if you'll let me," he'd say to Verna, but she'd just shake her head and get up from the table and find something to do—dishes to dry and put away, a countertop to clean.

"What about Rosie?" he'd say doggedly.

"Rosie is fine," Verna would say quickly. "He doesn't have a problem with Rosie."

"And you? Does he ever have a problem with you?"

"Never," she'd said, firmly, looking him in the eye. And Alberg believed this.

"Where'd you get that?" he would say to Eliot, who was wearing his white apron, clearing tables at Earl's.

"That what?" said Eliot, sullen.

"That bruise on your face."

"Fell down. Rollerblading," said Eliot.

And what if this had been true? Alberg thought.

He got out of the car and went inside, straight to his office, where he took off his jacket and hung it over the chair behind his desk. Preoccupied with thoughts of Eliot, he glanced out the window, remembering the boy looking out that other window, the one with bars.

And then he saw the brown truck parked on the side street, and Jack behind the wheel. "Sonofabitch," said Alberg under his breath.

He sat down at his desk and looked blankly at the paperwork piled up there. He was feeling claustrophobic. He stood up and took several deep breaths, trying to calm himself.

"Staff."

Sid Sokolowski was in the doorway, wearily rubbing his close-shaven head with a huge hand.

"I've gotta talk to you."

"Okay," said Alberg briskly, staring at his in basket. He sat down again and emptied it on top of the desk. "But not now. I have to do this now." He started sorting through the piles. Concentrating. Prioritizing.

"When?" said Sid plaintively.

"Tomorrow? Wednesday? Thursday? I'm at your disposal."

"Whenever," said Sokolowski, stepping back into the hall.

Alberg worked furiously all afternoon, writing memos,

completing forms, returning phone calls. He thought about nothing but the paperwork in front of him.

When he finally went home, Jack's truck didn't follow him.


That evening Cassandra wanted to talk about Christmas. "It's less than a month away, Karl."

He knew this, of course, but found that it didn't matter to him. He didn't know how to participate in this conversation. He tried to invent an expression of interest, and wondered with what body language he might contrive to convince her that although he didn't want to talk, he didn't mind listening.

"What's the matter with you?"

Alberg pretended surprise.

"Has that man shown up again?"

Alberg realized that his right shoulder ached, and had been aching for some time. He looked down. Was his gut smaller, since he'd lost his appetite? He didn't think so.

"Karl. Talk to me."

He got up from his wingback chair and went to sit next to her on the sofa. He put his left arm around her and his right hand over both of her hands, which were clasped in her lap. "I'm sorry it's sometimes hard for me to talk. But I don't take you for granted. I love you, and I will never, ever, take you for granted."

Cassandra freed her hands and put them on either side of his face, studying its planes and angles. She kissed his chin, her tongue tip delicately probing the cleft there; turned his head and kissed his ear. Then she put her lips on his, drew his tongue into her mouth, and lowered herself onto the couch, pulling him down on top of her.

— — —

*Betty was very proud of herself, later, very very proud. She gave herself no time to think about it, oh no, oh no. Just scurried right up onto the porch and knocked on the door—knock knock knock on her neighbor's door. And she opened it, the black-haired woman did, and Betty went inside. She looked down at the shiny wooden floor. "I don't know how you do it," she said. "I can see that I have certainly come to the right place." Then a man appeared in the hallway, wearing a uniform, and Betty slapped her thigh, laughing. "Oh! someone told me you were married to a policeman. And there he is!" But he brushed right past her, rudely, very rudely, and went out the door. "I have come to ask for your help," said Betty. "What is your name?"*

*"Maura," said the woman, in a hoarse voice, and she cleared her throat.*

*"And I am Betty. Yes. My goodness. It is extremely clean in here. What a clean clean house." She looked right into the woman's eyes, then, and said, "I have come to ask for your advice."*

*"Advice about what?"*

*"Cleaning. My house. I don't know how to do it."*

*The woman shook her head. "I don't understand you."*

*Betty laughed again. She liked the sound of her laughter: it rang through this tidy house like bell-noise. "I knew you would say that!" She shrugged her shoulders. "It's such a silly thing, really, yet there it is. I can't seem to clean my house, and Jack doesn't like that—Jack's my husband, you see—and of course Heather is too young to help much and—"*

*"You mean you want me to clean your house for you?" She sounded amazed.*

*"No no no no of course not, my goodness whatever must you think of me,"* said Betty, banging her feet upon the floor. *"No no no I said I wanted your* advice *your* advice *not your actual help certainly not oh my goodness."* She started toward the door, shaking, now, she was so upset.

*"Hey,"* said the woman, said Maura, and Betty turned around. *"Wait,"* said Maura. *"Sure. Why not. I can't do it now, but I'll come over after dinner."*

And they went outside together, because Maura was on her way to the bank. She was in such a hurry by now that she forgot to lock the door. She waved as Betty walked along the sidewalk to her own house, and then she got into her car, which was parked in the driveway.

Inside, Betty waited behind the curtains until Maura drove away. She thought about Jack's walls, clean and white again, because he had painted them.

She had been behind him when he first saw the signs so she couldn't see what he was thinking, she'd had to rush around in front of him and she'd grabbed hold of his face and peered straight into his eyes and she'd seen shock there, of course, and astonishment—but she was shocked herself at what else was there, at the fear that was there. She didn't know what to make of it.

Betty left her house and went back next door, through Maura's unlocked door into the hall. Her heart was pounding, so she stood still and stroked her chest until it calmed itself. Then she drank in this house, this clean house that wasn't hers. In the kitchen everything sparkled, and shone, and glittered. In the living room there were books on bookshelves, and lamps here and there, and a big leather chair. There was a huge bedroom with flowered curtains, bright flowers on a white background: Betty gasped, it was so beautiful. In two more bedrooms she saw teenage things like posters, and schoolbooks. Finally she looked in the dining room, *where a big wooden box sat on a chest. Betty opened this cautiously, and saw that it was filled with silverware, each piece in its own little sleeve except for one, a funny little fork with three tines, a pickle fork, she thought. She took this fork, looked around a little bit more, and went home.*

*Nobody had noticed, of course. She had known they wouldn't.*

*Betty hurried to her room and reached up into the closet for the shoe box in which she kept her special things, and she put the pickle fork in there, in there with her tools.*

## 11

*Tuesday, November 29*

The next morning Alberg had to drive Cassandra to work because her car was in the shop again. As they drove, she said, "Are we going to make an offer on that house?"

"I think we ought to," said Alberg. "Don't you?"

"I guess."

"Do you want to take another look first?" he said, glancing over at her.

"Maybe. Karl," she said, turning to him, "my mother wants me to go to Edmonton with her for Christmas."

"And?"

"Would you come, too?" she asked.

"To your brother's house? I've never even met the guy."

"How about if you go to Calgary, then? You could spend it with your kids."

"And the damn musician. Huh." He maneuvered the Oldsmobile into the parking space closest to the door of the library. "I don't know. They've probably got plans."

"Think about it." She kissed his cheek and got out of the car.

Alberg stayed there for a moment. He didn't want to be without Cassandra at Christmastime. He liked Christmas, had learned to like it again, because of her. He enjoyed her delight in the giving and receiving of presents. He savored the smell of the turkey, roasting. And liked to watch the cats batting away at the ornaments on the tree. He even liked having Cassandra's mother there for the day.

True, it wasn't the same as when he was married to Maura and his daughters were small. Christmas was different now. But not necessarily less splendid, he had learned. Cassandra had taught him this.

But he did miss his kids.

Maybe, if he and Cassandra bought a house, he could persuade his daughters to spend Christmas with him and Cassandra next year. And maybe, he thought, turning the ignition key, this would be easier to accomplish if he were to invite himself to Janey's house this year. The damn musician, he thought, shaking his head. He'd have to find a way to tolerate the damn musician.

As he drove off toward Sechelt he was trying to decide which Christmas had been worse, the last one in Kamloops or his first one in Sechelt.

Even though he had moved out of the house in Kamloops by Christmas, he had still been hopeful that he and Maura could patch things up. Christmas ought to be a good time to patch things up, he'd thought, and arranged to have days off. But before he could talk to Maura about it, she announced that she and the kids were going to spend Christmas in Calgary with her parents.

Alberg parked, went directly to his office and looked out the window, but Coutts and his truck weren't there.

The following year he'd been here, in Sechelt. A new arrival. Lonely. Work kept him busy during the days, but the evenings were bad. He recalled gazing unhappily from his sunporch through the rain at the Christmas lights that flickered from a forest of masts in the harbor at the bottom of the hill.

It occurred to Alberg that that second Christmas had been equally bad for Jack.

No, he thought, turning from the window, seeking out the photograph of his daughters that hung on the wall. No. Jack's had been worse. Much worse.

Shortly after noon that day, Eliot was sitting at a table in the lunchroom, next to one of two windows. There was a bowl of soup in front of him. Pea soup, a sick-making green color. And there were little chunks of ham or something in it. Little pieces of flesh floating around in the damn soup. He also had a large glass of milk, and a bun. But the bun was soft, not the crusty kind Eliot liked. It might go down if he slathered butter all over it. He didn't like the idea of being even skinnier than he already was.

Maybe if he shut his eyes he could get some of the soup down. So he did this, he closed his eyes, fumbled on the tabletop for the spoon, swiped it through the soup and up to his mouth. Shit, he thought, it even *tasted* green. He swallowed, but just barely. Opened his eyes and shoved the soup bowl aside. He tore off a piece of the bun and put some butter on it and this he managed to chew up and swallow without much effort. It didn't taste particularly good but it wasn't offensive either.

Eliot was at a table by himself. There were other kids at other tables, some of them alone, some huddled in groups. This was a cafeteria-type lunchroom so he couldn't blame anybody else for the food in front of him except that there was only one kind of soup available every day. He could have had macaroni and cheese, which used to be one of his favorite things. He'd stood there in the lineup, pushing his tray along ahead of him, and had stared at the macaroni and cheese steaming in one of those big bins. The lid was off, because the woman standing behind the food was serving a big dollop of the stuff to a kid in front of Eliot. The smell of it had made him suddenly ferociously homesick. So he'd gone right past the macaroni and cheese and asked for the soup, not knowing it was pea soup, not knowing it'd be green with lumps of flesh in it, looking like something that had rotted. He pushed the bowl farther away from him and tore off another piece of the bun.

"Can I sit here?"

It was the kid with the droopy drawers, the sagging sweat-pants. His eyes were roaming wildly again, which Eliot found exasperating.

Eliot shrugged, buttering, and shoved another piece of bun into his mouth.

The kid sat down and unloaded his tray. He had a sandwich in one of those triangular paper things with plastic wrap around it, just like the ones you can get on the ferry . . . jesus, thought Eliot, a little bit breathless because the unsummoned memory of the ferry was so strong.

The kid also had a pastry thing with icing on it and a big splotch of jam in the middle. Plus a glass of some kind of pop—Coke, maybe, or Pepsi. He slid his empty tray under Eliot's and started unwrapping the sandwich, which turned out to be peanut butter. This kid's going to have zits from hell someday, thought Eliot. He buttered the rest of the roll and slouched back in his chair.

The place was emptying now. It wasn't a huge room, and Eliot wondered what they did when they had a whole lot of kids here. Probably they'd have meals in shifts.

He reminded himself to eat the roll, and took a bite while looking out the window at the parking lot. But it felt like the damn thing had already been digested, the way it squirmed around in his mouth, greasy with butter, soft and obliging, not crusty like buns ought to be. His stomach was growling now. Jesus. Every damn part of him seemed to have its own fucking agenda. His mouth didn't want him to eat. His stomach did. Jesus. He wished they'd get together on this.

The kid was chewing like it was the last meal he was ever going to get to eat. One hand clutched the damn sandwich, made of white bread too for god's sake, while the other hung on to the glass of Coke, and the kid's eyes were rolling around the ceiling while he chewed. There was a bruise on the side of his face and one of his rolling-around eyes was swollen. His sweatshirt was light blue, frayed at the neck, and it had some stains on it.

"What's your name?" said Eliot, putting the rest of his roll on the tray, next to the bowl of soup. The kid watched this while he stuffed what was left of half his sandwich into his mouth. Then he picked up the glass and drank some pop. Eliot imagined this, white bread and peanut butter and Coke all mixed up in the kid's mouth, all headed together for his stomach. Jesus.

"Alvin," said the kid.

He darted a glance at Eliot, who was surprised to see that the kid's eyes could actually focus; and surprised, too, by the comprehension he thought he saw in them.

"Don't you want this?" said the kid, picking up the remains of Eliot's roll.

Eliot shrugged. The kid shoved it into his mouth, his other hand still clutching the glass of pop. He drank, put down the glass, and wiped his hand on the front of his sweatshirt.

He was a dumpy kid, short, and verging on squat. His forehead was perpetually furrowed. That is, his eyebrows were always way up there, as if he was surprised at something. Eliot wondered if he slept with that look on his face, with those horizontal ridges in his forehead.

"What happened to you?" Eliot said.

"Got beat up," said Alvin promptly, working on the other half of the sandwich now.

"Here?"

"Nah."

Eliot watched him eat. "I gotta go," he said a minute or two later.

He got up, pushed the chair under the table, and headed across the cafeteria toward the door, where a couple of the guards were standing. They didn't call them guards, but that's what they were. When he reached the door he realized that Alvin was beside him. Food wasn't allowed out of the eating area but the kid had wrapped his pastry in a napkin and thrust that hand under his sweatshirt.

"I got an appointment," said Eliot, walking along the hallway behind one of the guards.

"Who with?" said Alvin.

"A social worker."

"Okay," said Alvin. "Sure." He trudged after him, though.

When they got to the room with the fireplace the guard unlocked the door and Eliot stopped and said, "Seeya."

"Seeya," said the kid, a little smile trembling on his face.

Eliot watched this face, this facsimile of a grin, as he backed into the room and closed the door.

He went to the window and looked out, feeling docile; agreeable. For the moment he didn't mind that there were rules, or even what they were.

Eventually a woman came in. Her name was Ms. Tilley. Today she wore a black suit and a white blouse that had a lace frilly thing in front, foaming up between the lapels of her suit jacket. On her feet were shoes with little heels. Usually she wore pants and flat shoes. Her legs weren't bad, what Eliot could see of them. Her skirt was relatively long, hanging way past her knees. It got shorter when she sat down, of course; but not short enough to be interesting . . .

except that now of course he started to think about what he couldn't see. Shit. Fuck. He had a boner now.

"Sit down, Eliot," said Ms. Tilley.

But Eliot paid no attention. He turned back to the window and looked out again. And turned himself off, like usual. Heard her like a murmur, like a breeze in a tree, like the purring of a cat. He liked her voice. It made him feel good, warm and comforted, as long as he didn't listen to the words, as long as he didn't look at her.

He'd been here long enough now that he recognized some of the people at the bus stop. But the little kid, the girl, the one with the familiar jacket, she hadn't come back, and Eliot was glad of that.

When were you born? they'd asked him, as if they didn't already know all that stuff, and he'd said, November 11. Yesterday, he'd said. So now he was—what? Two weeks old, almost three. Good thing he could already read and write.

He could do lots of things, he reminded himself, looking out the window, gazing at the people waiting for buses. There was a Chinese girl with long black hair and glasses, who was reading a newspaper. And a kid about his own age was slouched in a corner of the bus shelter—this kid looked like he was asleep, and Eliot wondered what he'd been up to. Yeah, he could read and write, and he knew how to use a computer, and he'd done a pretty good job as a busboy, too.

She'd stopped talking, Ms. Tilley, and after a while he turned around to see what was what. She had some papers on her lap and a pen in her hand and she was looking at the papers and occasionally scrawling something. Eliot knew from the forceful way she wielded the pen that she was mad. Or maybe just frustrated. He watched her scratching away and wondered again, wearily, what was going to happen to him.

•  •  •

Alberg went home at lunchtime on Tuesday. It was one of Bernie's cleaning days. He parked the Oldsmobile in front of the house and before he got to the front door he heard Bernie whistling "When Irish Eyes Are Smiling." She had a strong, brave whistle, with a vigorous vibrato. Alberg opened the door very quietly but she was in the living room, polishing the table in the dining area, and so she saw him immediately.

She arched her eyebrows at him. "You're early. You sick?"

"Nope," said Alberg. "I wanted to talk to you."

She looked down at the jar of paste wax in her left hand and the rag in her right. "You'll have to wait till I'm done with this. I can't talk and give a proper polish at the same time."

"Okay," said Alberg. "I'll make some tea."

Fifteen minutes later they were seated at the kitchen table.

"So," said Bernie. "I hear you're getting hitched."

"It looks like it," said Alberg.

"I think it's a good idea." Bernie stirred milk into her tea. "I'm as tolerant as the next person, but it's always better to make these things legal."

"That's what we thought, too," said Alberg gravely. He drank some tea. "I went to see Eliot yesterday."

Bernie was shaking her head before he'd finished the sentence. "You're gonna have to put that boy from your mind," she said severely.

"I do," said Alberg. "Regularly. He keeps coming back into it, though."

"There ain't a thing you can do for him, you know that. I wish I'd never turned you in his direction. It happens he's nothing but bad. Bad blood, from somewhere. A bad seed, that's what that boy is."

"I don't believe in bad seeds."

She was clearly astounded, and for a few seconds, speechless. Finally she said, "A man like you, a policeman, a mature person been living in this world more than fifty years, most of the time wholly immersed in crime—"

Alberg remarked mildly, "Not *wholly* immersed, Bernie."

"—a man like you," she barreled ahead, "you can sit there and tell me you don't believe in bad seeds?"

"Yeah," said Alberg. "I can."

She peered at him across the table, inspecting him closely, as if she'd never seen him before. "And I s'pose you don't believe in evil, either?"

"Ah, Bernie. Sure I believe in evil. Neglect is evil. Abuse is evil. Look." He leaned forward, resting his arms on the table. "That's what the kid's relatives said, too. But it's too easy, Bernie. I want to know why this thing happened, and to say it's because the kid's a bad seed, or the devil made him do it, or some damn thing—that's not helpful." He sat back and watched her drink some tea.

"I think you figure you shoulda seen it coming," said Bernie.

He laughed a little. "Yeah."

She sniffed her contempt. "So you're psychic now, are you? How about reading my tea leaves here?"

"I should have seen *something* coming," said Alberg. "And I did. But I was looking in the wrong fucking place, Bernie." He had never used that word in her presence before, and it caused her lips to clinch together. "I was looking at Ralph."

━ ━ ━

*Betty was dusting her living room like Maura had shown her, flicking the duster up and down and across, and when she'd done this a certain number of times it was necessary to rush out onto the porch and shake it vigorously: that was how to make sure she actually got the dust to go away. And she was doing this, standing out on the porch, shaking the dustrag, when she saw that the policeman was standing on his porch, too. "Yoo hoo!" she called to him, waving the duster, and she hurried down the steps and along the sidewalk, calling "Yoo hoo!"*

*"Oh wait wait wait," she said when she got close to him, for he had come down the steps. "I have a question for you. Were you wearing your uniform when you met your wife? She's a very nice person, your wife, an exceedingly nice person." She flapped the dustrag energetically. "When I went to your house the other day—remember? Remember?"*

*"I remember, yes," he said, but he didn't sound friendly.*

*"I had a problem for which I needed help, and as soon as I saw the inside of your house—" She examined him closely, standing there in his uniform, so crisp and clean, just like his house. "It is extremely clean, your house, extremely clean, I have never ever seen a house so clean. And so I knew that she could help me, your wife."*

*He kept glancing at his police car, which was parked in front of the house. Betty knew that he probably wanted to get in it and drive away, so quickly she asked him again, "Were you wearing it when you met her? Your uniform?"*

*He looked left and right. "I don't know."*

*Betty was astonished. "You don't know? You don't know?" She threw back her head and clasped her hands together, laughing merrily. "I certainly know, what Jack was wearing."*

*"Look, I've got to get back to work," said the policeman, and he started to walk toward his car.*

*But Betty said, "Oh but wait! Let me tell you how I met him."*

*"Mrs. Coutts—"*

"Yes!" said Betty, and she bestowed upon him a generous smile. She shoved the duster into the pocket of her dress. "Good for you! You remembered my name!" He looked at his watch, and she tapped the face of the watch with her finger. "There there, that's good, you have a minute or two, maybe three, I can see that." She smoothed her hair with her hands. "It was at a party. Years and years ago. There were two men there when I arrived, and two women. One of the men wore a green suit and there was dandruff on his shoulders. His eyelashes were so fair that his eyes looked naked. He sold things at The Bay."

The policeman looked behind her, and Betty turned around and saw that Heather was approaching along the sidewalk. "Go home!" Betty said sharply.

The policeman consulted his watch again. "I'm sorry, but I'm going to have to—"

"Your apology is accepted," said Betty, and she ran her hands over her hips. "Then another man arrived at the party. This was Jack. He was tall, but not big. He had ordinary brown hair, short. And he wore not a suit but a sweater with a V-shaped neck, and a shirt and tie peeked out from underneath. The sweater was beige."

Again, he looked behind her. Again, Betty turned. Heather was standing in front of Betty's house, on the sidewalk, watching them. Betty gestured, furious. "Go inside! Inside!" She turned back to the policeman, who had taken a few steps toward his car. "I liked the look of him," she said, quite loudly, and he stopped. "And he liked the look of me, too. I was thin, then. Very very thin, and also quite young, and my hair was long and hung down my back." She looked back over her shoulder, but Heather was gone. Good. "Later I told him that I had to leave. And he said, 'Let me drive you home.' So politely he said this, so politely"—she clasped *her hands again, remembering, and rocked herself, ever so slightly, rocked back and forth on her tiny feet—* "*that I agreed.*"

"*That's a very interesting story,*" *said the policeman.* "*Thank you for telling me. I have to go now.*"

"*She gave me advice, your wife did. About cleaning my house.*"

*Maura's husband walked toward his car.*

*She watched him drive away, and went back inside her house. She would make some tea, she decided. She didn't feel like dusting anymore.*

12

The kid was still in the hall when Eliot emerged from the fireplace room. He was sitting on the floor with his knees up, leaning against the wall. Bits of icing and pastry crumbs were smeared all over his mouth. When he saw Eliot he scrambled to his feet, stumbling over his sweatpants.

"I'm supposed to be outside," he said. "Wanna come?"

"Those pants are too big for you," said Eliot. He sounded disapproving, as if it were the kid's fault. But the sweatpants probably didn't belong to Alvin. They'd probably been given to him when he got here. Eliot figured there was a room somewhere in the house stuffed full of kids' clothes. Used clothes, not new ones. He wondered where the kids were who'd been the original owners. He wondered how their lives had turned out.

"Yeah, they are," said Alvin, hanging on to the waistband. It was a good thing there was elastic at the ankles because in addition to being too big around, the sweatpants' legs were too long.

"Lemme see that," said Eliot, and he pulled the waistband

from the kid's hand. "Jesus. You need to cut a big piece right out of there."

Alvin sat down on the floor again and took off his right shoe, a black high-top, and peeled off the sock that was on that foot, a gray worksock. "Here," he said, handing Eliot a Swiss army knife that felt warm and damp from having been pressed against the sole of his foot.

"Shit," Eliot muttered, glancing up and down the hall. But for once there was nobody in sight. He noticed a thin strip of gleaming wood on either side of the worn-down well-trodden pathway up the middle. For a second Eliot had a vision of how this hallway might have looked when it was new, shining like a bright bronzy stream through the heart of the house, echoing with footsteps and probably laughter, too.

"Come on," he said to the kid, and they went outside into the exercise area.

A few kids were shooting baskets, a few more were lounging against the twelve-foot chain-link fence that surrounded that part of the yard. Beyond it on one side was the parking lot. Trees pressed against the fence on the other two sides. Eliot and Alvin hunkered down on the hard-packed dirt edging the concrete pad that served as a basketball court.

Eliot pulled at the threads in the waistband of the kid's sweatpants, using the scissors on the Swiss army knife, and finally freed the elastic. The kid smelled, he noticed. Not of dirt, or sweat, it was just a little kid smell. Eliot felt weary just thinking about how truly young this kid was, with his black hair, bleary and sticky, always falling into his eyes, and his forehead with the worry marks permanently impressed into it. Huddled into himself, the kid was; probably he ate so much to deliberately make himself fatter, to create more layers of himself. Eliot tugged on the elastic and tried to snip out a chunk of it, but it was too thick for the tiny pair of scissors. He finally sawed through it with the knife, and then tied the ends together.

"What kind of a knot is that?" said Alvin.

"I don't know. One end over, then the other end over. I don't know what you call it." He handed the knife to Alvin, who removed his shoe and sock and put the knife back where he'd gotten it, then put on the sock and shoe again.

They stayed there for a while, their backs against the chain-link fence, watching the halfhearted basketball game that was now going on. The day had grown suddenly cold, and Eliot realized that he was shivering in his denim jacket. The sky was cloud-swept, the sun hidden, its warmth evaporated. There'd be months of this now, he thought. Three or four months of rain and cold and gray skies. Weather had never bothered him before, not like it affected his mom, for instance. When the sun shone it was like it had lit up in her face as well as in the blue sky above. But she hated the day after day of rain that happened every winter—and it was just the same here, on the other side of the whole damn country, exactly the same kind of winter weather. . . .

*This* was what got to him. *This* was what had got to him. It was the same weather, the *same weather,* and there they were on the beach, doing the same things, *the exact same things,* so tell me, Eliot had said inside his head, tell me, *somebody please tell me why we came here.* . . .

"I gotta go," said Eliot, and he stumbled to his feet, hanging on to the chain-link fence for support.

"Sure," said Alvin, and he started to get up, too. But then his migrating gaze fixed on Eliot's face, and he sank back onto the ground. "So I'll seeya at dinner, okay?"

"Yeah, whatever," said Eliot, moving off toward the door. He pushed inside and down the hall to the fireplace room. But when he opened the door he saw a girl in there—he thought she was called Gloria something—talking to probably her social worker. So he backed out and went upstairs, heading for the room he shared with a kid named Dick, taking the steps two at a time. He burst into this room and found Dick lying on his bed, hands behind his head.

"What the fuck you want?" said Dick, who was two or three inches taller than Eliot and at least twenty pounds heavier. He had a scar on his head that crept out from under his flattop haircut and squirmed halfway down his forehead. Sometimes it looked longer than at other times. Eliot had found no explanation for this. This scar was red now, which wasn't a good sign.

"Nothin', I don't want nothin'," said Eliot, retreating, closing the door.

He stood in the hall, looking out one of the barred windows that lined the wall. He could see over the parking lot and the landscaped perimeter of the east side of the building to the four-lane street whose name he still didn't know. His predicament, his situation, was at that moment incredible to him. He shoved his hands in his pockets and looked up and down the hall, at the barred windows that faced a row of closed doors with numbers on them. The number on his door was seven. Was seven a lucky number? He couldn't remember.

He heard footsteps coming up the stairs and because he didn't want to look like he was loitering, he began walking toward them. It was one of the housekeeping staff. He saw her head first, then her neck and chest; she was wearing an apron and carrying an armload of clean towels. She ought to have had a cart, he thought, like they have in motels, with cleaning supplies on one shelf and clean towels on another. She wasn't very old, but older than Eliot, of course. Almost everybody in the world was older than Eliot—everybody except the Alvin kid. She nodded at him as they passed on the stairs, not quite smiling, too cautious for that.

Once she was out of sight he sat down on the steps, because he couldn't think of where to go or what to do. His knees were pressed together, feet splayed apart, pointing inward. Eliot scratched at the knee of his jeans with his fingernail. There was dried dirt there. He couldn't remember the last time he'd worn these jeans. He only had two pairs with him in this place. And four tops and four pairs of socks and four pairs of undershorts. Plus his denim jacket. They'd said he could bring books with him but he hadn't wanted to.

He remembered now with some surprise that he hadn't wanted to be distracted. He'd intended to spend all his life from then on thinking. His thoughts would be a great burden he would carry. This burden would cause veins to pop out on his forehead, and in his ever-larger biceps, too. He had decided never to get his hair cut again or shave the hairs that had started to grow on his face or trim his toenails or his fingernails. He was going to let his body just do it, grow, whatever, not pay it any attention, not pay attention to anything but what he'd done.

But he'd found that he couldn't do this. It wasn't that he didn't want to. He just couldn't. Somebody would be face-to-face with him, the lawyer, or a social worker, a psychiatrist, youth worker, he didn't know who the hell they were, exactly. But there was this Ms. Tilley, Eliot thought she was a social worker. And there was the lawyer—she was a woman, too, an older one, with gray hair and a face that looked tired. They had both asked him questions that he knew they already had answers to and when they asked these he looked at them, waiting, or else he looked somewhere else, waiting, until finally they asked him—both of them did, in different ways—about what he'd done.

He remembered the very first time anybody had asked him what had happened, or why, or something. It was the cop, Alberg, back in Sechelt, before they'd taken him away.

"What the hell happened?" he'd said, or something like that.

Eliot had felt like he had a mouthful of sand. He remembered that his hands were cold, too. He thought, looking back, that he'd tried to answer, or at least to get some kind of picture in his head that he could refer to. He'd figured if he could do that, then maybe he could think of some words to say about what he saw there, in his head. He had a pretty good vocabulary—at least he'd always thought he had. But it didn't do him any good on that particular occasion. And in fact it hadn't done him any good since, either, because without a picture to describe, words weren't of any use, and he couldn't get a picture to form, no matter how hard he tried. It was like his head was full of something silvery and slippery, like rain or a streamful of eels; he couldn't form shapes there, and he couldn't see colors.

Not when he tried.

. Sometimes he had sudden flashes of stuff. But he didn't even know if they were real. He didn't know if he was remembering, in flashes; or only making things up.

He sat on the stairs, looking down and along the length of the hallway to the front door at the end. There was a square of colored glass in the top of it. He heard laughter coming from the main office, which was around the corner: the hallway formed a "T" with the entrance to the house at the place where the two arms met. The main office and a reception area were off to one side and a bunch of other offices were off to the other. These other offices, which were really cubicles, were where the social workers and the lawyers usually met with kids. But sometimes they were all full, and then they took what they called their "clients" into the room with the fireplace.

Eliot liked that room. He'd have liked to spend more time in there. He'd have liked to think of stuff to say, to talk about, so that his meetings with the social worker or the lawyer would be longer.

But he couldn't.

# 13

Cassandra was watering the plants that sat next to the big front window when she saw the brown truck. It was parked across the street. There was nobody in it, but a man wearing a red plaid jacket and jeans was sitting on the bench in front of the real estate office, facing the library. Cassandra stepped behind a fig tree. She looked around the library, at the senior citizens sharing newspapers and comfortable chairs with the unemployed; at Paula, checking out books for a young mother whose infant slept in a stroller at her feet; at the shelves of books, hundreds of books—my work, my comfort and my joy, she thought, feeling slightly dizzy; Cassandra looked around the library, a place of learning, of diversion, of refuge—and looked again out the window. The truck was still there, but the man was gone from the bench.

She finished watering the plants. When she next glanced outside, she saw Sid lumbering along the street. He came in and looked around uneasily, and she called out to him.

"I was hoping I could have a word with you," he said. "If it's not a bad time."

"I want a word with you, too, as it happens."

She led him behind the counter, through the Dutch door and into her office. "Sit down, Sid," she said, indicating a large gray easy chair. "Can I get you some coffee?"

"No, thanks." He sat down gingerly, put his cap on the floor next to him, and rested his hands on his thighs.

Cassandra sat on the edge of her desk. "Have you seen—" she said. And stopped. Had he seen what, a man driving a brown truck?

"I'm hoping you can advise me," said Sid laboriously. "About me and Elsie. About how I can persuade her to come home." His brow was wrinkled in distress. "I'm not too good at talking. And the more important a thing is, the worse I get at it."

Cassandra was dismayed: she was pretty sure Elsie had no intention of going home. "Well," she said, carefully, "if she wants to come home, Sid, well, then, I guess she will. Maybe she's just not ready yet."

So he'd parked across the street, she thought, distracted. So maybe he'd sat down on the bench. So what?

"That's the thing, see," said the sergeant. "She won't say, one way or the other. But whenever she calls me up, it's because she wants to come over and collect more of her things," he said bitterly. "For her apartment. I mean, this's been going on for a long time now. I'm getting sick of it, Cassandra." He sat back, rubbing his close-cut scalp. "Keeping the place up. Eating alone. Living alone. Sick of it."

"Has she ever talked about divorce?" Cassandra asked him.

It was a small town, after all. A very small town. It was virtually impossible to avoid anybody in a town as small as this one.

Sid flinched, and shook his head.

"The problem is," said Cassandra, "that if you try to make her choose, if you give her some kind of ultimatum—"

No—she'd already discussed Karl with Sid once. And she knew Karl wouldn't appreciate that if he were to find out.

"Yeah." He was nodding, grim-faced. "I know. She might choose wrong. But I've been thinking." He shifted in the chair. "See, a lot of it was the Job. So what if I quit? Take early retirement?" He peered at her, frowning. "What do you think?"

"Why don't you ask her?"

She'd keep an eye open, make a note of how often she saw that truck, and where. And if she wanted to talk about it with anybody, she'd talk about it with Karl.

Sid was shaking his head. "She wouldn't believe me if I just said I was gonna do it. I'd have to *do* it, get the paperwork in, get it approved. And then tell her. It would have to be a done deal."

"That's a pretty tough decision, Sid," said Cassandra gently. "Don't do anything hasty, okay?"

He looked at her, anguished. "What a mess, eh?"

Cassandra wondered what kind of a new life Elsie was living. Maybe it was a relief just to be alone, after all those years looking after Sid and their five daughters.

He picked up his cap. "I better be going."

"I'm sorry I couldn't help you, Sid."

"Well, yeah, you did, though," he said, getting to his feet. "It's the first time I said it out loud, what I've been thinking. So that was good." He tried to smile at her, as she opened the door for him. "I just gotta make the decision."


Later, Cassandra met her friend Phyllis Dempter for lunch at Earl's. They had ordered sandwiches, and were drinking coffee while they waited for their food to come.

"Now," said Phyllis briskly. "Bring me up to date."

But Cassandra, studying her friend's face, said, "Why are you so skittery today?"

"I don't even know what 'skittery' means," said Phyllis. But she wouldn't meet Cassandra's eyes, and she kept adjusting and readjusting the gold wristwatch she wore.

"It's the way you acted when you quit smoking," said Cassandra. "Nervous. Jumpy." She was facing the door, and the windows, so she saw the truck pull up in front of the café. "My god. There he is again. Look at that guy," she said to Phyllis.

Phyllis craned her neck. "What guy? Where?"

"He's outside. Just got out of that brown truck. See? My god. He's coming in here." At least she'd get a good look at him, she thought, aware of her accelerated heartbeat.

He came through the door and walked straight to a table in the back of the café, a tall, middle-aged man with a stoop, fleshy, his hair mostly gray, wearing jeans and a red plaid jacket.

"What about him?" said Phyllis.

"I don't know," said Cassandra uneasily. "I keep seeing his damn truck. On the street. Here at Earl's. Out where we were house-hunting. And this morning he was sitting on that bench across from the library."

"Well who is he?"

"I have no idea. Karl won't tell me."

"Karl? This guy knows Karl?"

Cassandra watched as he gave Naomi his order. "Yes. But I don't know from where, or when."

He was sitting quietly, waiting for his meal. "It's strictly personal," Karl had said.

Naomi arrived with their sandwiches, and Cassandra looked back at her friend. "Now listen, Phyllis," she said, attempting to marshal her powers of concentration. "Seriously."

"Seriously what?" said Phyllis.

"Seriously—is there something wrong? You *are* jumpy. And you've lost weight. Are you okay?"

"Lost weight, whoopee!" Phyllis hooked her shoulder-length hair around her ears. She took off her glasses and rubbed the bridge of her nose. "This is very awkward, Cassandra, with your nuptials rapidly approaching—"

"What makes you think they're rapidly approaching? We haven't even set a date yet."

Naomi had set a hamburger and fries down in front of the man in the back of the café.

"You haven't set a date?" Phyllis was saying, incredulous.

"Valentine's Day," said Cassandra. "That's when he wants to do it. Can you believe it? Valentine's Day. I told him, no way. You haven't touched your sandwich. Eat."

"I had no idea Karl was so romantic," said Phyllis. "If you nixed February 14, I hope you offered an alternative."

"Not yet. I'm dithering between getting it over with in January, and waiting for spring. I'd like my wedding not to be rained on."

The man had finished the hamburger and was working on the fries, picking them up with his fingers, one at a time. He didn't look dangerous, thought Cassandra. Did he?

"To be reasonably certain of sunny skies," Phyllis was saying, "you'd have to put it off until August."

"What do you think I should do?" Cassandra looked down at her plate and was dismayed to see only crumbs there.

"Have it on St. Valentine's Day." She looked over at Cassandra, unsmiling. "Maybe he'll bring you luck."

"Phyllis. What's wrong?"

Phyllis sat back, her hands in her lap. "We're getting a divorce."

"Oh no." Cassandra put down her coffee cup.

"It's been coming for a long time. First he fooled around. You knew that. Then I did." She winced a little. "I don't think you knew that. Anyway. The point is. We don't even like each other anymore."

"I'm so sorry."

"Don't be. We were happy for quite a while. That's more than a lot of people get."

"What will you do? Stay here? Move? Oh I hope you don't move."

Phyllis looked down at her uneaten sandwich. "I don't know, Cass. I have to figure out my financial situation first. If it's good enough, maybe I will go away. At least for a while."

Cassandra had a succession of visions, then: Phyllis riding serenely in a gondola; Phyllis taking a chairlift in the Alps; Phyllis strolling through Hyde Park; Phyllis leaning on the railing of a cruise ship, watching the sun set.

"Oh Phyllis." Maybe she should envy her.

But she didn't.

Cassandra glanced over at the stranger's table. He was gone. She looked quickly out the window, just in time to see his truck pull smoothly away from the curb.


Somebody—Eliot couldn't remember who—maybe it was Staff Sergeant Alberg, maybe the social worker—he didn't think it could have been the lawyer—anyway, somebody had tried to talk to him about his anger. Eliot could understand this, up to a point.

Until he realized that they thought it still existed, his anger. That they'd wanted to examine it as a living, continuing thing. Which was of course pointless. He'd thought it was obvious to anyone who cared to look that his anger, strewn upon the beach with his family's blood, spewed out on the sand with their blood—which had flown through the misty silver morning in tiny unred droplets, soaring in a great swath through the air; which had not turned red until all the drops had tumbled together and fallen upon the earth—that with the gushings of their blood, Eliot's anger, with their blood, had been washed clean away by the cleansing sea.

This was the only good thing about what had happened and was maybe the reason for it, too. There was no longer any danger, any reason to be afraid, because his anger was dead.

Eliot got up from the stairs and made his way down the hall and around the corner to the office. "I want to go outside," he said to the woman behind the counter, who was typing at a computer terminal. She looked at him through glasses with a thin gold frame around them. She was about his mom's age, only fatter. She wasn't as good-looking as his mom but her clothes were nicer.

He sat on the damp ground under the canopy of a big old maple tree, leaned against the trunk and pulled up his knees. He could hear traffic, faintly, and some birds, but otherwise it was quiet. He rested his chin on his knees and wrapped his arms around his legs. He thought about his room, about his acoustic guitar, and the ghetto-blaster, and his rollerblades. And the clothes in all the closets. He didn't know what was happening to all their stuff, and to the house.

And if she recovered from what he'd done to her—what would happen to Rosie? Would Eliot ever see her again? Would she ever let him see her again?

They had told him about the Arrangements (the word had been capitalized when they said it: "Arrangements") for his parents, about the Arrangements for their funeral. They had told him about his uncle and aunt coming to take the bodies back to Nova Scotia. He liked to think of his mom and dad lying in graves in an apple orchard back there, but he knew this was unrealistic.

For the first time he wondered if it would have happened anyway, even if they'd stayed home.

It was kind of funny that his parents, who'd really wanted to come here, all the way across the fucking country, that they'd ended up being taken back home, while Eliot, who hadn't wanted to come at all, whose malignant anger he was almost certain had been born the day the decision had been made to ignore what he wanted, because he was only a kid, it was pretty funny, by which he really meant ironic, that he was now stuck here, probably for the rest of his life. Or at least the part of it that counted.

He didn't know what they were going to do with him. Where they'd put him. Or for how long. Part of it depended on whether they decided he was crazy. Eliot knew that he wasn't crazy.

The seat of his jeans was getting damp now, and he was pretty cold. But he was reluctant to go inside. It was nice out here. He couldn't see the chain-link fence, only the trees that grew on both sides of it, and their yellow or reddish leaves. He could look at the trees and pretend he was home, or at least back in Sechelt, because he was sitting with his back to the detention center. That's what it was, even though he tried to think of it as a house, a big old house with lots of history.

Like youth hostels he'd read about.

He was going to do that someday, hitchhike across North America, back to Nova Scotia. Then maybe get himself over to Europe and hitchhike there, staying in youth hostels, meeting kids from all different countries. Seeing stuff. Learning stuff.

Eliot rested his forehead on his knees and scrabbled with his fingers at the sparse grass that grew beneath the trees. He couldn't imagine the man he'd be when they finally let him go, sometime in the next century.

## 14

### *Wednesday, November 30*

Cassandra found her mother in her room, sitting in her easy chair, looking out the window at the rain.

"Hi," she said from the hall, through the half-open door.

"Hi yourself," said Helen Mitchell. "Come in. This is a surprise."

Cassandra sat on the edge of the bed. "I thought you'd like to know that we've chosen a date."

"Finally," said her mother. "When?"

"February 14."

Helen Mitchell smiled. "And whose idea was that?"

"His."

Helen laughed, and Cassandra grinned at her.

"Have you brought the notebook?" said Helen, suddenly businesslike.

Cassandra, with a sigh, hauled it out of her shoulder bag.

Eliot had on his denim jacket, his second pair of jeans and his second top, a black sweatshirt with BLACKTOP scrawled in white letters across the front and the word REEBOK printed, smaller, inside a red rectangle. He had waited until the last minute before going in for breakfast, in order to avoid Alvin, who always ate at the earliest possible moment. Every morning Alvin was hanging around in the hall, waiting, when the cafeteria door opened. He probably woke up in the middle of the night hungry, thought Eliot. Maybe the kid had a tapeworm, a big fat immensely long tapeworm curled up inside his stomach or wherever such things lived, and whenever Alvin ate anything, the worm got it, and then snoozed for a while, and then woke up and started poking at the inside of his belly, biting him, maybe, making him starving hungry so he'd eat again. Or maybe Eliot's first idea had been the right one, and Alvin was trying to get fat so that nobody would pay attention to him.

Eliot sat alone at a breakfast table, looking at a huge bowl of porridge that sat there in front of him, wondering how the hell he'd managed to get himself a bowl of porridge, which was gloop that he hated. Nobody was sitting with him because Eliot wasn't looking to make friends in this fucking place and nobody was looking to make friends with him either. The other kids were sitting around talking and laughing. Jesus. And hollering at the women who were serving the food. And sometimes somebody threw something, a bun or a piece of fruit. Eliot was disgusted. So he stood up and got out of there.

He wanted to go back to his room and lie down on his bed, maybe look out the window, but Dick was there. Dick had said he wasn't getting up yet, wasn't hungry for breakfast.

"Get the fuck out," he'd said to Eliot. He was buried in blankets with only the top part of his head sticking out, his dark eyes and the scar that crept down from his hairline like a worm of glistening blood.

So Eliot stood in the upstairs hall wishing he'd picked something else for breakfast. The glooped porridge had reminded him of mornings in his family's kitchen. The linoleum was always cold under his bare feet. Eliot, slouched at the table, would see himself in his mind as a large black-haired troll who had a humped back with lots of hair growing on it. The hump in his back was like a hiccup on the way to becoming a mountain, and grass grew on it, black and bristly grass, black bristly grass in which lived small black quick-burrowing insects that hid in the hair and tunneled into his skin but they were so small that he barely felt their gouging.

Every time Eliot looked into a mirror he was surprised to see only himself in there, the Eliot that other people saw.

He stood now in the hall outside Room Seven, looking out the window again, shivering with restlessness. It was like he'd been anesthetized all this time. Now there were prickled scratchings at his arms and sides. But it wasn't his body that was waking up—it was someplace in his mind. It was like his thinking apparatus had suddenly been pitched into a ton of nettles. He was trying to use it again, that was the problem. He'd been going around like a goddamn zombie and now his brain was trying to wake up.

Eliot felt an urgent need to phone somebody, and his mom came to mind. "Oh jesus." Eliot slumped against the window, pressed his cheek against the bars, trying to look through the space between them, trying to get close enough to see through that space and have *no bars there*.

She was—he knew, he *knew* this—she was accessible to him, somewhere, somehow. Someplace along a straight line from here to someplace else he would find her. It was only a question of walking long enough. It'd be like in a story, thought Eliot. He would strike out equipped only with an ax and a shovel. Plus other necessary stuff in a backpack: a bottle of water and a bag of crusty buns and maybe an apple or two. And he'd wear his denim jacket and take along some gloves and some earmuffs too because the weather would change. Whatever direction he picked, eventually he'd come to some real winter. And when he needed more food he'd stop and get a job or steal something and then he'd move on. And someday he would find her, walking on the road in front of him, maybe, or waiting tables in a café in some little town or big city, or maybe teaching school like she'd done before she'd had kids, before she'd had Eliot.

He pressed his forehead against the bars and closed his eyes, and was aware of the width of his shoulders and the length of his legs. They were strong legs, and would take him miles and miles.

Eliot turned and walked down the hall. He fumbled at the door of Room Seven. He didn't have to answer Dick. He didn't need to say a thing, he'd just gather his stuff together. He pushed the door open. He would ignore him. Who the hell did Dick think he was anyway?

Eliot's face turned white and his mouth sagged open. He looked and he looked. He could not move. The seasons changed and years went by and still he could not move.

He backed out of the room and closed the door.

In the main office he stood at the counter listening to phones ringing and the muted clattering of computer keyboards.

He felt somebody standing next to him and looked down and there was Alvin, one eye hidden behind his hair. Eliot saw that his face was still swollen.

"Hiya," said Alvin.

Eliot looked up, and saw the woman with the wire-rimmed glasses gazing at him, and wondered how he could ever have seen any similarity between this person and his mother.

"Yes?"

"Dick," said Eliot loudly, thickly. "The other guy in my room. He's dead."

He wondered if there was a procedure for this. If it was written down someplace, what they were supposed to do.

But now he saw with a dreadful shock, just like he'd stuck his finger in an electrical outlet, that this woman thought he'd done something to Dick. His face flushed. He opened his mouth to speak again, then changed his mind. His eyes got slitty—jesus—he'd thought that was never going to happen again—and he looked cautiously around for his anger and there it was, there it fucking was, oh jesus. . . .

"He hung himself," said Eliot flatly. He felt Alvin's hand slip into his. Eliot stepped back, pulling Alvin with him, to watch the furore.

## 15

A chill on her arms awakened Enid. For a moment she thought she had left the window open, and looked over there. But no. The curtains were open, but not the window.

Melancholy had attacked her in the night. She burrowed into the pillow and pulled the duvet up over her shoulders. Then turned over onto her back and looked up at the ceiling, which was high, because her house was an old-timer.

Like me, she thought. Like me.

Oh dear, she thought.

Mostly Enid managed to avoid acknowledgment of death. Usually when it presented itself she was able to push it firmly aside and get on with things. She would point to a corner—there, sit there, she would say to death—and turn her back on him. Never looked him straight in the face. She had a fanciful, almost flirtatious relationship with him, confident that until the last instant of her life he would continue to do as he was told, sit there in a shadowy corner, docile, humble, knowing his place. Obedient.

Sometimes, though, this image was unattainable, and

what she encountered was a cold wind from someplace unknowable. She was helpless, then, until it had passed. This dread must descend upon other people, she thought, and decided to ask Bernie what she did about it.

Enid, trying to imagine Bernie in confrontation with her own mortality, acknowledged that theirs was an unlikely friendship. Enid had a strong sense of hierarchy—of class. People in her world could and did move from one class to another, up and down the social scale: she didn't see anyone as imprisoned by birth at one level or another. But different classes did exist. And it wasn't talent or ability or character that in Enid's eyes distinguished one from another. It was the small things, like grammar, and dress, and whether one spoke with one's mouth full.

Bernie's grasp of grammar was inexact, her dress was peculiar, and she frequently talked with her mouth full.

Enid recognized her prejudices, some of them, and used her friendship with Bernie as evidence that she was capable of rising above them.

They had met on an October morning twenty years ago. Enid left her house that day wearing a suit and carrying a handbag in one hand and a Moorcroft vase in the other, a wedding present, which had just that morning been chipped. It was one of Enid's favorite possessions and she was very upset when it happened—her ten-year-old daughter Gloria who ended up becoming a lawyer was responsible. Her wildly gesticulating arm had knocked it off the mantelpiece and although she'd caught it before it could fall to the floor the base had struck the edge of the mantel and a piece had broken from it. Enid had the piece in her handbag. She was going to take the vase in to be repaired, as soon as she was finished at the doctor's office, where she had an appointment for her biennial checkup.

Thirty-five minutes later, her clothes back on, she was in her doctor's office and he was talking to her. She sat there with her handbag in her lap, slightly tilted toward him, with her head at an angle as if she couldn't hear him, as if he wasn't coming in properly, like a badly tuned radio station. Enid felt herself to be frowning in exasperation.

"It could be nothing at all," she heard him saying.

She was suddenly drenched in terror. It enveloped her like a shroud. "I beg your pardon?" she said.

"But it requires immediate attention," he said, as if she hadn't spoken.

Enid watched him write something on a piece of paper. She heard a couple more words, then watched his mouth as he uttered still more, but didn't comprehend them.

He handed her the paper. "Tomorrow at eleven," he said.

Enid looked at what he'd written, and coldness seeped through her, from something positioned in the exact center of her body. He was talking again. "What?" she said, incredulous. "What?"

Eventually she stood up, holding her purse, and left his office. She went along the corridor into the reception area and heard a chirruping sound from behind the counter, and realized that this was more speech.

"Do you need another appointment, Mrs. Hargreaves?"

Enid didn't know what this person was: receptionist, or secretary, or nurse. She looked at her for a moment, thinking about this with a small part of her brain, wondering how the woman described her job to friends and family. "I work for a doctor." That was probably what she told people, Enid decided.

She opened the door and went outside into the warm autumn sun, the piece of paper still clutched in her hand. She found her car parked half a block away, unlocked it, and got inside. Opened the window. Just sat there.

But she kept seeing people she knew, in cars that passed, on the opposite sidewalk, and soon she started the car and drove away, not far, just to where the village ended, and she parked by the side of the road.

She realized after a while that she was trying to assimilate information, to understand, to make decisions, and that these things were impossible because of the fear. Enid had never felt such fear. She recognized it—but had experienced it only for periods so brief that it was gone before her heart had settled down again: fear that she'd heard a prowler, gone when a breeze from an open window fluttered the curtains; fear of a car wreck, gone when the truck coming toward her in her lane swerved back into its own; fear for a missing child, transformed into anger when the child came home, late, unharmed. She had never known fear that clasped and clung, intent on its own presence—and it was the fear that was malevolent, not whatever might be growing in her breast.

Enid found herself staring at the dashboard with both hands over her mouth. This time tomorrow she would be giddy with relief, drunk and euphoric with it, or she would be an amputee. And that would be just the beginning.

"No," she said. "No."

She was crying now, and realized that this was going to help. She sat back and let herself do it. She wept and sobbed and blotted her face with tissues pulled from her handbag.

After a while she told herself to stop, and did.

Enid took a deep, shaky breath. She started the car. Did a U-turn and headed back into the village. She couldn't go directly to the bank in search of Arch, couldn't walk through the bank, couldn't greet people. I look different now, I know it, she thought. She fumbled in her handbag for her sunglasses and put them on.

She wanted only to be home, where the ticking of the clock on the kitchen wall would soothe her, and the purring of the cat.

I must make out my will, she thought. And then— Oh

god, she thought, how will he manage? How will Arch manage on his own, with the children?

She saw brake lights come on, saw this and understood that the car ahead was coming to a stop. She understood also that she should therefore bring her car to a stop, too. But didn't.

They weren't traveling very fast—in fact, very slowly—but all crashes are significant.

When it was over Enid was amazed to see that the vase, though it had bounced onto the floor, had not suffered further damage.

She thought her legs were too shaky to hold her upright so she remained behind the wheel of her car. She could see that the other driver wasn't hurt. He was looking into his rearview mirror and yelling, so he had to be all right.

There were a lot of people on the sidewalk, having come out of the café and the hardware store and the real estate office, but for once Enid didn't recognize anyone. A small woman of about Enid's age—Bernie—had pushed through the crowd right up to the edge of the curb and was frowning intently into Enid's car. Enid gave her a gracious smile.

Suddenly the door of the other vehicle flew open. A large man struggled out and strode back to inspect the damage, then lifted both fists and shook them in the air. He rushed to Enid's window, which she obligingly opened.

"You stupid bitch!" He waved toward the mess created by the collision. "What the fuck is your problem!"

Enid studied his face, which was flushed with anger. She reached down, then opened her door, pushed it wide open—so briskly that the large man was forced to move hastily aside—and climbed out.

She looked at the man for a moment. "This," she said to him, "has been a very bad day." And she conked him on the head with the Moorcroft vase.

She had hardly any strength, though, so the vase didn't

break, and neither—Enid was disappointed to see, as she crumpled against her car door—did his head. He did clutch himself, however, moaning theatrically.

Then Bernie bustled up and took Enid firmly by the arm. "Sit. Sit," she said, and pushed Enid down so that she was sitting on the driver's seat with her feet on the pavement. "Put your head between your knees," she said, and Enid did. "You," said Bernie to the man. "Get up. Drive away."

The man started to complain.

"Your bumper's scratched," said Bernie, interrupting him, "and your brake light's broken. Otherwise there's nothing wrong with your car. And," she went on, raising her voice over his protests, "there's certainly nothing wrong with you. I work at the hospital and I can tell you that for absolute certain."

Her job at the hospital, Enid learned later that day, was as a cleaner.

Enid had had the lump removed the following morning, and it was benign. She came to believe that the objective of the whole exercise had been to throw her and Bernie together. It was just possible sometimes to see patterns and purposes in life.

"I thought he was your man there for a minute," Bernie had said, "the way he was hollering at you."

Now Enid stretched, beneath the covers, and was aware of irritating aches in her joints.

Her melancholy persisted, and she wondered if she'd been dreaming, tried to think . . . yes, there it was, a dream about a letter. She saw her hands turning it over before her wakened self could look at the handwriting, saw herself open the envelope and take out a folded sheet of paper, typed. Enid knew at once that it was a letter from her son Reggie in California. But this was all she could remember. Distressed, her heart aching, she tried to find more dream fragments, snuffling around like a pig after truffles, but it was gone.

It bothered her that her gloom had been created, apparently, by a dream about Reggie, who had always been a sunny spot in her life.

I should get up, she thought. But of course there was no reason to do so, except that she always did. What if I were to stay in bed all morning? All day, even?

If she had a cat, she thought, it would be curled up on her bed now, and when she got up it would stretch and yawn and blink and follow her downstairs, silent on its silent cat feet, and wait for its breakfast patiently or impatiently, depending upon the kind of cat it was.

Even better would be a new person in her life. The Jaworski funeral was coming up, and Madeline Jaworski had had a wide circle of friends and acquaintances. Enid's mood brightened somewhat as she thought about this. She rolled onto her side; curled herself up, and constructed a fantasy about a tall silver-haired man of her own age or slightly younger who would arrive at the funeral in a red sports car. She would watch him for a while, discreetly, then slide within his field of vision and his eyes would widen when he noticed her. Enid would be wearing something mauve—mauve was an excellent color for her—and she would look at him gravely when their eyes met; an expression befitting the circumstances. . . .

Enid flopped over onto her back. He'd probably be married. If he wasn't married, he'd be gay.

She knew what the morning would look like; could tell from the murmur of the rain that it was a gray, monotonous day. She did not for the moment possess the courage to gaze upon it. Enid closed her eyes in something dangerously close to despair.

Far away there was the muffled sound of a door, closing. Enid's eyes opened. She had forgotten all about her lodger. She lay very still, concentrating, and heard his truck start up. It idled for a while; he was waiting for it to warm up, a sure sign that he'd come to Sechelt from a colder place, and then he drove away. The silence ticked around her again. A wave of it had rushed in to fill the space left by the departure of her lodger and his truck.

Enid, feeling considerably more cheerful, threw off the duvet and got out of bed, and before setting off down the hall to the bathroom she did a few stretching exercises to limber herself.

The day might turn out better than expected, she thought as she dressed. She resolved not to spend any time lying there thinking in the mornings. She'd hop out of bed immediately she awakened, and continue to do her exercises every morning, first thing. She stripped the bed and made it up with clean sheets, and dumped the used ones on the floor by the door to the basement.

Next she had breakfast, sitting at the dining room table, a placemat under her coffee cup and a plate holding two pieces of raisin bread, toasted and buttered. She allowed herself this treat every morning: it was the only butter she ever ate.

As she sat there Enid was suddenly keenly aware of the possessions that surrounded her, and filled the house. Furniture. Knickknacks. Sets of china. Silverware. Vases, and platters, and serving dishes. Books, umbrellas, pictures, clocks. Things she and Arch had accumulated. Things she had bought for herself since he died. Things that used to be his parents'. Things that had once belonged to hers. Enid began feeling unwell and put a questioning hand on her stomach, which was soft and jiggly. I have to do more exercises, she thought. And then heard a clear firm voice in her head remind her that no matter how many exercises she did she would never have a decent waist again, never have a flat belly again.

Enid was losing patience with herself. She was out of control today.

She cleared away her breakfast dishes and sat down in the

living room with a pad of paper and a pencil to plan her day. She would phone Reggie, in the evening. And maybe Gloria. This morning she would do some grocery shopping. She would go for a long, brisk walk.

She looked out into the silvery rain that shrouded the world, and her garden. She would do her finances, too. With the rent money from the basement suite newly added to her budget, maybe she could afford to buy a greenhouse.

# 16

Alberg, driving to work through the cold gray slant of the rain, was remembering the summer morning when he had picked up his ringing phone, pronounced his name, and at first heard only silence. Then:

"This is Eliot."

Alberg had removed his reading glasses and leaned back in his desk chair, blinking in the hot sunshine that poured in through the small window in his office wall. "Yeah. Hi. How're you doing?"

"You said something about a job."

"Yeah. What're you interested in?"

"What've you got?" said the kid.

"Well this is what I know about offhand." He began doodling on a pad of paper. "The vet needs somebody to help in the clinic. That appeal to you?"

There was more silence. "Maybe. I like animals, but—"

"Yeah?" said Alberg.

"But I don't know about sick ones. Hurt ones."

"Okay. Well, over at the paper, they always need delivery boys. And girls."

"Uh-huh."

"And, uh." Alberg wished he'd known the kid was going to call. "I think they need guys to deliver over at the super-market, too."

"But you probably need a driver's license for that."

"Oh." Shit, thought Alberg. "Right. You probably do." He drew a little car on the pad of paper.

"Not for the papers, probably," said Eliot. "Just a bike. I had one at home. But we couldn't bring it. There wasn't enough room in the trailer, you know?"

"Uh-huh." Alberg drew a bicycle, and then added a stick man, riding it.

"This U-Haul thing."

"Right. That's tough."

"Yeah."

"It's possible that Earl might need somebody. I don't know—a busboy, is that what they call them?"

"You mean the restaurant?"

"Yeah." He penciled in a bunch of trees behind the stick man on the bike. Earl really did work too hard. He could do with more help. "You know, clearing tables, doing dishes. Stuff like that."

Another silence. "That'd be good," said Eliot.

"Yeah?" said Alberg. "You'd like that?"

"Yeah," said Eliot.

And so it had been arranged.

He was trying to comfort himself, he thought, as he pulled up in front of the detachment. Struggling to convince himself that in this particular case he had done everything possible to help the boy, to help avert disaster.

But as he locked the car and hurried through the rain he was not comforted, because even though this time, yes, he had tried, he still had not helped the boy, still had not been able to avert disaster.

∙ ∙ ∙

She could get books on greenhouse gardening, thought Enid. She could make a full-time project of it. She would be able to grow so many tomatoes and peppers and cucumbers that she'd be able to give some away.

Enid hadn't considered, when preparing the suite for occupancy, that the extra money might add something special to her life. She had known, of course, that she would be paid rent: but that was as far as she'd taken it. Mostly she had just wanted that bottom part of the house inhabited: she had begun getting nervous lately, just slightly nervous.

"You ought to get yourself a dog," Bernie had told her.

But Enid had never liked dogs.

"Or one of them alarm systems." And at this Bernie had sniggered, her face dissolving into hundreds of tiny creases. "Or better yet," she went on, "save yourself the money and just put a sticker up. You know, it says 'PROTECTED BY' and then some company or other. What burglar you know's gonna take a chance when he sees that?"

But Enid didn't like alarm systems either, and she certainly wasn't going to lie about whether she had one or not.

And then one day, driving back from the ferry after a trip to Vancouver, she'd glanced across the street at the Wheatons' front yard and seen in a corner of their big picture window a sign that said ROOM TO LET. Their son Philip had been living with the Wheatons for the past year, ever since the pulp mill laid him off, and he'd gotten more and more discouraged, Enid had heard, and more and more depressed, until on a sunny day in October just a few days before Halloween he'd walked into the ocean and drowned himself in the frigid waters of the Strait of Georgia.

"My goodness," said Enid aloud, lifting her eyebrows disapprovingly at the sign. Insufficient time had passed, in her opinion, for them to be renting out the dead boy's room.

Yet it started her thinking. As soon as she got home she took a close look around, down in her basement. Then she asked Homer O'Connel to recommend someone. Of course

Homer had volunteered to do the job himself, for nothing. But Enid had refused, gently but firmly: what was over was over, and she was not one to take advantage of the past. Reluctantly, he'd given her a name. And before she knew it, there was a perfectly good suite down there. Small, but private and clean. Just right for a single person. A single woman, of course, was what she'd had in mind.

Enid was idly turning the pages of her account book, but had lost interest in her finances. She didn't know enough about greenhouse gardening to be able to decide what kind of a structure to buy. And where, exactly, ought she to put it? Some research was obviously necessary.

Enid put away her account book. Then she picked up her soiled sheets and tiptoed down the basement stairs to put them in the washing machine. She knew that her lodger had gone out. But tiptoed anyway.

All morning, as she went about her chores, the suite and the man who lived there encroached upon her thinking. She pushed them aside but they always came back, gently nudging her, like a bathtub toy—that was the image in her head: Enid lounging in a bubblebath, daydreaming, and a red rubber octopus recalled from Reggie's babyhood bobbing nearer and nearer, bouncing from the end of the tub along the length of her leg until finally she felt it, cold and curious, against her lolling breast, and pushed it away, again and again, and finally had to pick the damn thing up and chuck it right out of the tub.

Enid stared out her kitchen window, astonished. What a bizarre thing. She was holding the coffeepot in one hand and her favorite mug in the other, a white one with painted pansies all over it. Come to your senses, she admonished herself, and poured coffee into the mug.

He spent very little time down there. She didn't think he'd cooked himself a single meal. Off in his truck early every morning, usually not coming home until late evening.

Looking long and hard for employment? Just driving around?

She had left the basement door open so as to hear the washing machine complete its final cycle. When she had moved the sheets from the washer to the dryer, and turned the dryer on, she stood in the laundry room for a minute, smoothing her apron. In a plastic basket several pillowcases and some damask napkins waited to be ironed.

Would she hear his truck from down here, pulling up in front of the house? But it wasn't even noon yet.

Enid set up the ironing board and plugged in the iron. From where she stood she could see the door to her lodger's suite. She had a key, of course, in case of an emergency—or maybe simply because it was her house, after all, and she was entitled to have a key to each of its several locks. Obviously she'd never use it, except in an emergency.

The iron, she knew, took a few seconds to warm up.

Enid wandered out of the laundry room, feeling unaccountably light on her feet, as if laughter were burbling somewhere in her chest, filling her up like a balloon. She rested her fingertips on the doorknob and pushed it slightly to the right—and the door slid open. He didn't keep it locked, then. Enid was touched.

She tapped on the door. "Hello?" she called. "Hello?" She could be inviting him up for coffee. She would, in fact, invite him upstairs for coffee, if he was home. But she knew he wasn't.

She slipped through the doorway into his bedroom, leaving the door open behind her. The bed was made, an alarm clock ticked from the bedside table, and not one personal object could she see, not a single piece of clothing, not a book or a magazine—not even a used Kleenex, balled up and left on the top of the dresser.

Enid realized that her hands were clasped, as if to keep herself from touching things, like a small child in a museum;

like Enid herself, as a child, visiting her paternal grandparents. She shuddered at this flicker of memory and stepped into her lodger's small living room.

Because it was the only thing in the room that she hadn't put there herself, she noticed the photograph immediately. It was on the middle shelf of the otherwise empty bookcase, and it would be at the lodger's eye level, she thought, as he sat in the basket chair. And, yes, the cushion she had thrown onto that chair, a nice splash of red against the brown corduroy cover, that pillow was crushed, as if someone had been leaning against it.

Enid glanced into the kitchen, which looked unused except for an empty glass on the counter; she saw that the sink was water-spattered.

In the small bathroom his electric razor sat on the counter, plugged in, getting itself charged. Aligned on the counter were toothbrush and toothpaste and some spray deodorant. And on the floor, in a corner, a small pile of dirty clothes. Enid gazed upon these with some tenderness. She saw shirts, underpants, socks. And decided that her lodger slept in his underwear. She imagined him, for an instant, asleep in his bed, beneath the quilt she'd provided, lying on his back, head to one side, one arm uncovered, his hand resting palm up, fingers open.

Enid turned the light off and returned to the living room.

Here she listened for a moment for his truck, but heard nothing. Then she lowered herself into the basket chair and studied the photograph.

It was a picture of a child with long blond hair, wearing a blue sweater. She was very young—about ten, Enid estimated. The photo was in a sturdy brass frame and there was a retractable wing in the back which, when extended, as it was now, permitted the frame to stand upright. Enid leaned closer. There was something about the child's hair, and the sweater, which had a shawl collar, that spoke of an earlier decade. She looked straight into the camera, not smiling, creating in Enid a terrible sadness. There was in her contemplation of this child more genuine grief than she ever experienced at the funerals she attended. Did that mean, she wondered, that this child was dead?

Late that afternoon Alberg became aware that Jack's truck was back on the side street, and that Jack was behind the wheel. Alberg watched him for a while. Jack had a coffee mug, and a thermos, and every so often he turned on the motor to get warm.

Alberg put on his jacket and walked out of his office and down the hall. "I'll be right back," he said to Isabella, and he went outside, walked to the corner, and around, and up to Jack's truck. He approached the driver's side window and gestured to Jack to roll it down.

But Jack didn't roll it down. He started the truck and drove away, slowly.

Alberg stood in the rain feeling like a fool. And felt his anger growing.

He walked back inside, where he phoned Cassandra and learned that her car was ready, so she wouldn't need a ride home.

"I'm going to stay here for a while, then," he said, riffling through the diminished stack of his paperwork. Maybe he could actually finish it off. He hung up, put on his reading glasses, and set to work.

Half an hour later there was a tap on his door and he looked up to see Sid Sokolowski.

"Five minutes, Staff. That's all I need."

"Come on in." Alberg took off his glasses and rubbed his eyes, then tossed the glasses onto the desk.

The sergeant settled heavily into the black leather chair across from Alberg and rested his huge hands on his thighs.

"I think you oughta know," he said, "I'm considering early retirement." He shifted his weight, causing the leather to creak.

Alberg sighed. But he wasn't entirely surprised. "How early?"

Sid hesitated. "End of March."

"Jesus, Sid."

"Yeah. Well it's not definite. But I'm considering it."

"This got something to do with Elsie?"

Sokolowski turned upon him a look of pure misery. "Yeah."

"I almost quit myself once," said Alberg, surprising himself. "For the same reason." It was probably the most personal remark he'd ever made to Sid.

"I haven't totally decided yet," said Sokolowski.

But Alberg figured that he had.

He didn't look forward to acquiring a new sergeant. The dynamics in the detachment would change. This could be good, or it could be bad, depending on what kind of a new guy he got.

His phone rang. "Alberg," he said, and listened. "Gone?" he said into the phone. "What do you mean, gone? When?" He listened some more. "What the hell do you mean, you're not sure?"

Sokolowski lifted his eyebrows questioningly.

Alberg hung up, shaking his head. "Christ," he said. "It's Eliot. He's run off. With another kid."

Sokolowski stirred in his chair. "How the hell did that happen?"

"There was a commotion," said Alberg. "His roommate hung himself. Eliot found the body. And some idiotic laundry truck driver had left the gate open."

Slowly, Sokolowski shook his head. "That kid's a goner," he said flatly. "There's nothing you can do for him now."

"What makes you think I want to do anything for him?" Alberg snapped.

The sergeant just looked at him. After a while he got up, heavily, and went to the window to peer outside. "We better keep an eye on the house," he said. "In case he tries to come home."

# 17

Eliot didn't even remember deciding to escape. As soon as he'd told them about Dick everybody in the front office rushed away, all except one woman who immediately got on the phone to someone. Alvin's eyes were having no trouble at all staying focused. They were riveted on Eliot's face like they'd been glued there, and he was hanging on to Eliot's hand like—well for dear life, that was how. Eliot had never examined that phrase before: "dear life." He liked it. Dear life. Precious life.

"Come on," said Eliot, and he turned, opened the front door—and off they went. It felt like the sun ought to be shining, but it wasn't.

They hurried down the steps and along the driveway, then angled across the grass until they got to the fence. On the other side was the busy four-lane street Eliot had watched from the barred window in the fireplace room, but he knew that farther along, the fence disappeared into a wooded area, and here they might be able to climb over it without being seen. He was trying to work out in his head which of them should climb it first when they came upon the gated entrance to the driveway. Incredulous, Eliot saw that the gate was standing open. They walked through it and onto the sidewalk.

"What now?" said Alvin. He was breathing laboriously, and Eliot reminded himself that they'd have to walk slowly.

"I don't know."

"We gotta get some money," said Alvin. "We're gonna need food and stuff. You got any money?"

Eliot shook his head.

He imagined tiptoeing into the hospital room in Sechelt where Rosie lay, bandaged and sleeping. He imagined Rosie opening her eyes and seeing him standing there. And starting to scream.

"Clothes, too," said Alvin. "Shit. I feel real good." He was standing on one foot, the other lifted in the air. Eliot thought he looked like a duck: a short, squat, black-haired duck.

"Yeah, well, I don't know how the hell we're gonna get any money," he said, "unless we steal it."

"Nah. We don't gotta steal." Alvin looked up and down the street. "I know where we are. Come on." He struck off along the sidewalk, heading south, and Eliot followed, reluctant. "See, this is what we do," said Alvin, trudging. "We gotta get off this main drag first, up there at that stoplight, see?" He pointed, and Eliot nodded. "We cross the street there and we go along that big parkway for a while and then we cross it and go through a bunch of neighborhoods and we end up at a big shopping mall."

Eliot was skeptical, uneasy about putting his fate in the hands of a kid who probably wasn't right in the head. "What's the point of all that?" he said irritably.

Alvin said, "First we're looking for cans, right? And bottles. Not beer bottles, pop bottles. And cans. And when we've got all we can carry, we go to a store and cash them in and we buy something—so the guy has to give us a bag, see? And then we go get more, until the whole bag's filled up." They had reached the stoplight, and Alvin pushed the button for the WALK light. While they waited, Eliot heard him panting.

"Are you sure you're up to all this walking?" he said.

Alvin looked up at him. His face was pale and damp, and his hair was all over the place like usual, but his eyes were still focused.

"How old are you, anyhow?" said Eliot.

"Ten."

"Shit," said Eliot. Alvin was shivering a bit in his gray sweatpants and sweatshirt. "We gotta get you a jacket. We're not gonna be able to do that with pop can money."

"Yeah, but, see, after we get us enough to buy stuff to eat, then we go to the mall I told you about, there's a Skytrain station there, and we beg."

"Beg?" Eliot was horrified.

"Panhandle. Yeah." Alvin looked him over. "Not you, I guess. You look kinda, you know, unfriendly."

"Do you do this a lot? Begging?"

"Not a lot. Sometimes. Come on." They started across the street.

"We have to get us a plan," said Eliot. "A long-range one. Like, where are we gonna go, and stuff."

"Yeah," said Alvin. From the opposite sidewalk he continued west, along the edge of another four-lane street, his eyes searching the ground. "I'm not gonna go home, that's for sure." He spotted a can, then another, picked them up and pushed them into the pockets of his sweatpants.

"I think I'm gonna go to Nova Scotia," said Eliot. But could he really leave, with Rosie still here?

"Wow," said Alvin, scanning the ground. "Can I come?"

Eliot reached down and picked up a dented ginger ale can. "Hitchhiking. That's how I'll do it." And how could he ever be sure, now, that she was really going to be okay?

"You could maybe wait for spring," said Alvin generously. "You don't wanna get stranded in the middle of the mountains someplace, not in the wintertime."

"Yeah, and what the hell am I gonna do from now till spring?" said Eliot.

"We can live on the street."

Eliot stopped.

The traffic was whizzing past on his right, and on the left a bank of blackberry bushes grew out of a thicket of brown grass. The space between those bushes and the road was about ten feet wide and all kinds of stuff had been tossed there from passing cars. He and Alvin had all along been stepping over beer bottles, some smashed to pieces against rocks or other bottles, and cigarette ends, and various pieces of garbage and litter. And, occasionally, pop bottles or cans. Alvin had stuffed several into the waistband of his sweatpants and was now having difficulty leaning over. Eliot wasn't able to get them into his jeans pockets but there were two in each of his jacket pockets and he had wrapped his arms around another four.

"What street?" Eliot said numbly. But he knew what Alvin had meant.

Alvin turned around. "It's not too bad. The hard part's staying away from the do-gooders. They'd have us back inside quick as a wink."

" 'Quick as a wink'?" said Eliot, and he had to smile.

"Seriously," said Alvin. "We can do it."

"We better find a place that'll take these now," said Eliot, juggling the cans in his arms.

They walked along next to the road, looking for a crosswalk.

Eliot said, "Do you think you can get enough money panhandling to pay for a jacket?"

"Yeah," said Alvin, panting, and Eliot slowed his pace. "A secondhand one. I know a thrift store we can go to."

Eliot plodded slowly along, glancing from time to time at Alvin. "Is there something wrong with you?" he said finally. "Like, do you have asthma or something?"

Alvin, trying to keep the cans in his waistband from falling into his pants, looked at him in alarm. "What's that?"

"Never mind. It's not serious," said Eliot quickly. "But you shouldn't, you know, you should take it easy."

"Yeah," said Alvin cheerfully. "Okay."

Eliot, looking across the road at houses lining streets that rose up a steep hillside, said, "Are we in Vancouver?"

"Nope. Burnaby." Alvin looked at him curiously. "Where do you live, anyway?"

"Sechelt."

"Where's that?"

"You take a ferry," said Eliot vaguely. They came to a cross street, and waited for the light to change. "Where do you live?"

"Vancouver. East Van." Alvin suddenly took hold of Eliot's arm, and Eliot was amazed, it was as if somebody had turned on lights in Alvin's eyes, which weren't black at all, as he had thought, but a warm dark brown. "I got a better idea," Alvin whispered. "We'll cash in these cans and we'll spend the money on bus fare to my house. And then we'll steal. Like you said."

Alberg found himself in his car, driving. It was dark by this time, although still only early evening, and his headlights were poking a tunnel of light through the blackness, illuminating the rutted track that led through the trees to the Gardener house. It was still raining, and the Oldsmobile splashed through puddles as it lurched along.

Alberg pulled up where the lane looped, and let the headlights fall upon the darkened house. He didn't think Eliot would come back to this house, which had never been home to him. But the boy's escape had created in Alberg an irre-sistible need to come here again.

He got out and looked at the place, a small two-story structure whose windows threw his headlights back at him, glinting dully, revealing nothing of the interior.

He knew that the owner was getting impatient with the Nova Scotia relatives, who were supposed to have made ar-rangements to have the contents removed and the place cleaned. But it was now almost December, and Alberg fig-ured that nothing was likely to be done before Christmas.

He trudged across muddy ground, around the corner and up onto the porch. The pair of rubber boots he'd noticed the day of the homicides was still there; now both boots were over-turned, the shaft of one resting across the shaft of the other. The back door was unlocked, which he hadn't expected. Alberg went inside: he would lock up when he left.

He closed the door behind him and stood quietly in the darkness. After a moment he became aware of the perfectly ordinary sounds of a house left to its own devices. He was profoundly struck by this; it was as if nobody had told the house, yet, that its owners wouldn't be returning. The refrigerator gurgled to life. The furnace came on with a click, followed by a rattling noise Alberg figured was made by one or more of the vents, insecurely fastened. A gust of wind came up and sprayed the window with a sheaf of rain, and the window shook in its casements, then subsided. Alberg heard an occasional creak, a sporadic moan, sounds created not by man or beast but by the house itself.

He flicked on the overhead light and looked around the kitchen. Everything was just as he remembered it, looking in through the window two and a half weeks ago: the dishes were still stacked in the drainer; the tea towel was still draped over the back of a chair; the hooks on the wall by the back door still held an umbrella, a denim jacket, an orange waterproof boating jacket, and a woman's shawl.

In the living room he saw a newspaper spread in disarray upon a sofa; a beer can sitting on an end table; an ashtray full of butts on the coffee table. On a TV tray next to an easy chair sat a coloring book and a handful of crayons, and the crayon box. There was also a vase, sitting on a sideboard. Alberg went closer and saw that it contained the same kind of chrysanthemums that grew in the corner of his own backyard. Although many of the leaves were brown, and the edges of the flowers had begun to curl and discolor, they weren't yet quite dead. He thought about Verna picking them, maybe the day she died, maybe the day before. Maybe they were the last thing she saw before she left the house that morning.

He climbed the steps, clutching the banister. He was immensely weary, and suddenly bewildered to find himself here in this empty house.

And so he created a task for himself.

Alberg opened doors until he had located Rosie's room, and went inside. The bed was rumpled and unmade. Toys were scattered on the floor around a cardboard box containing more. Alberg looked around despairingly. He had thought to take something familiar to Rosie in the hospital. But he didn't know what would comfort an eight-year-old girl. He tried to remember his own daughters at that age, but couldn't. Then he spotted something partially covered by the bedclothes. He reached for it, and pulled out a large stuffed teddy bear, a koala, with one eye missing. This would do, he thought.

Alberg closed the door behind him and stood in the hall for a moment. Then he went in search of Eliot's room.

When he opened Eliot's door he was immediately aware of a foul odor, and sniffed it out as coming from under the bed. He turned on the light and looked under there, and saw a cardboard box. He put the koala bear down on the desk, pulled out the box, and took off the lid. Inside lay a dead bird, lying on a bed of cotton, wrapped in toilet paper long before it had reached its present state of decomposition. Alberg replaced the lid and hesitated for a moment, then put the box on the floor in the hall, outside the bedroom door.

Over the back of a desk chair hung the white apron Eliot had worn when working in the restaurant.

Earl had been dismayed when Alberg told him about Eliot. "I don't need a busboy," he'd said, indignant.

"Yeah, you do, Earl," Alberg said persuasively. "Look how hard you work around here."

"I like to work hard. I don't need a busboy. A busboy! I already got a waitress, I don't need a busboy." He picked up Alberg's coffee mug and swiped at the tabletop with a dishrag.

"Look," said Alberg. "Do me a favor. Hire the kid on probation. Tell him you'll give him a week to make himself indispensable."

"He'd be more trouble than he's worth." Earl folded his arms. "I got no time to train anybody. Neither does Naomi."

"That's my point," Alberg told him. "So give the kid a chance. I'll pay his wages for the first week."

Earl had reluctantly agreed.

Eliot wasn't a cheerful employee. When he talked, it was in monosyllables. He averted his eyes when Earl told him what to do. At the end of his week of probation Earl was still reluctant. But he'd taken the kid on anyway. Alberg figured this was because he didn't want to go back to washing dishes himself, and sweeping the floors, and stocking the shelves in the storeroom. Alberg folded the apron and placed it on the seat of the chair.

Eliot's closet and chest of drawers were filled with clothes, but nothing hung on the walls of his room: none of the Kurt Cobain posters Alberg had half-expected to find; no sign of teenage angst. On the floor in the corner, a pair of rollerblades. On top of a bureau, an acoustic guitar. On the desk, school texts and exercise books. Alberg thumbed through the notebooks, looking carefully at each page. Eliot hadn't taken many notes; this was no surprise. What did surprise Alberg was the lack of anything else in the notebooks. There were no drawings, no sketches, no squiggles—no sign of the doodling that even the most artistically inept of students does when his mind wanders. Eliot had been careful to keep his mind blank. Or his thoughts concealed. Alberg closed the exercise book and sat down on the edge of the boy's unmade bed.

He shut his eyes and rubbed them, and his temples, and the back of his neck. When he blinked and focused again he was looking across the room at the window in the opposite wall . . . and for just a second—maybe even less than a second—he was completely disoriented. For an instant he felt himself to be in another room, sitting in the darkness in another room, enveloped as now in sudden grief and frustration—but in another room; some other room. He saw in the gloom, on the floor in the gloom, a small pale inert figure, wearing a white blouse, a flash of gold at her throat. . . .

Alberg blinked again, and Eliot's room reasserted itself. Once again he was looking at the window in Eliot's room, aware of the sound of rain, aware of the sight of it on the window, falling harder now, sheeting across the glass, disinterested but judgmental.

Several hours later, Enid was watching the eleven o'clock news. It was in her mind to go to bed as soon as it was over. But why wait? she thought. She wasn't listening to the news—why didn't she go to bed now?

But there clung to her a feeling of sadness. She couldn't seem to shake it off. It hadn't been a good day, really, waking up with that dream in her head, and ending up snooping on her lodger, for heaven's sake. And when she had called Reggie in California he wasn't home and she had had to make conversation with The Spouse. Which was always a strain. She had hoped that Reggie would call her back, but it must have been too late when he got in. Or else The Spouse hadn't even told him that his mother had called. Which was, when she thought about it, more than likely.

So Enid continued to sit there, facing the television screen, feeling blue, uncertain about life and the future, not even cheered by the prospects of greenhouse gardening. And then she heard the lodger's truck approach, pull up in front of the house and stop.

She had closed his door, of course, and left it unlocked. She hadn't touched a single thing in the suite, only just sat down in the basket chair for a moment, had looked at the photograph but not so much as brushed it with a fingertip, even though she had wanted to do that, to offer comfort or reassurance to that solemn child.

She turned down the volume on the television and strained to hear; thought she heard him making his way around the side of the house; definitely heard him unlocking the door, opening it, closing it behind him. A few muffled footsteps, then nothing.

Enid relaxed, gradually, and turned the volume up again.

And practically leapt out of her chair when she heard a soft tapping on the door to the basement. Then she froze. Another tap. Enid still couldn't move. When she heard him start to go back down, she was released.

She hurried to the door, and opened it. "Hello!" she said, with a bright smile. "Did you knock?"

She couldn't see him well. The light had been turned on in the laundry room but that was behind and below him, and she didn't want to turn on the one in the stairwell because it might feel like a spotlight falling on him.

And so he spoke from shadow, from a shadowed face,

half-turned toward her. She was aware of the breadth of him; a large, male presence on her stairway, and when he spoke she was faintly surprised that his voice wasn't deeper.

"You left the iron on," he said.

Enid's hand covered her mouth. "Oh dear. No. Surely not."

"Yeah."

"Oh dear." Her hand fluttered away from her face. "That's right. I was going to do the napkins. And—and the phone rang."

"No harm done. I unplugged it." He turned to go back down the steps.

"Thank you," said Enid.

"No problem."

"I'm very grateful."

He looked up at her and now he stood in light, his face crinkled with fatigue, or pain. "Next time, unplug it before you answer the phone."

"I will," said Enid quickly, humbly. She began closing the door. "Good night," she called, and couldn't be sure that he answered her.

— — —

*She took the chair she always took, the one by the window, and she tried to smother a gleam of fury when once again she found it too small. I'm my own size today, she thought, my own size, not my large size, and still this chair is too small.*

*He came in and sat down beside his desk and said hello, politely, as always.*

*He was her psychologist.*

*She had not wanted to come to see him ever again. But there was despair in her.*

*"I had a dream about Heather," she said. "It fright-*

ened me." She had never told him about a dream
before.

His face looked like the bark on a tree, she thought.
It was dark, and had shattered; there were tiny lines all
over it. Yet somehow it managed to stay stuck together,
and also to appear peaceful.

"Tell me," he said.

He probably had children of his own, she thought
suddenly, amazed. Perhaps he even dreamed about
them.

"We went to Vancouver," she began. "Heather and
I. We were going to meet Jack there." Heather wore a
navy-blue suit with a pleated skirt and Betty was surprised that she looked so much like Betty had looked
when she was the same age—plumper than she nor-
mally was, her blond hair curly, her blue eyes darker.

Betty's eyes rested on the doctor. "You may take
notes, if you like," she said generously.

He looked up from his pen and paper. "Thank you,
Betty."

"We had a whole suite of rooms," she went on. "One
of them had no windows and the walls were green. It
was empty except for a stool. On the stool sat my
mother, who is dead." Betty's hands were getting
sweaty.

In the dream her mother's hair was white and her
face was old, and when Betty opened the door her
mother covered her face with one hand and with the
other waved her violently away. Her dress was wrinkled and dirty and Betty closed the door quickly; she
didn't want Heather to see. But Heather had gone off
up the hall.

Betty drew a shuddering breath. "That's one of the
bad parts," she said to the doctor, who nodded.

"I put Heather to bed, and decided to go for a walk."

*There was a red glow in the evening sky and it was warm outside. Betty strolled up and down among strangers who were happy and smiling but not bothering her, not bothering her at all. There were little bands of people playing music. . . .*

She looked frantically around the office. "Oh this will frighten me again I know it will."

"You can stay here until you aren't frightened anymore, Betty," said the doctor.

"I shall hold on to this chair," she said, gripping the armrests.

"I stopped and looked into a store window, where there was a charming thing, so charming." *It was a white statute of a young boy, sitting on a rock. He had one foot propped up upon the other knee, and he was resting his elbow on the higher knee, his chin in his hand. He gazed right at her, with a soft smile that made Betty want to cry and comfort him, even though he looked quite content. And Betty heard sweet tinkling sounds coming from a music box that was set into the base of the statue.*

*She kept walking, and soon saw, black against the red sky, a small house with a peaked roof. A crowd of people stood looking at it and muttering among themselves.*

She loosened her hands and clutched them again around the armrests of the chair. "Here comes the second bad part," she said anxiously. "There are three of them, three bad parts to this bad dream of mine."

*In the dream, the door of the little house opened and a wide shaft of light spilled out, and silhouetted against the light were three women. The middle one was taller than the others, and seemed to be leaning on the other two. They were walking slowly from the house toward the crowd of people.*

"The feeling of the dream had changed," said Betty,

"*and I was nervous, very very nervous. And then the middle woman suddenly toppled forward and lay still upon her face, and there was a big knife sticking out of her back.*"

Betty took her hands from the chair and rubbed them quickly together.

"*I was terrified, terrified,*" she said, "*and ran back to the hotel.*" But when she got to the suite, Heather was gone from her bed. And then Betty heard a tinkling musical sound—the sound of the white statue, the statue of the little boy.

"*I ran down the hall toward the sound, and opened the door of a bedroom. The statue was there, sitting on the chest of drawers at the far end of the room. And two children were there, two of them.*" They were sitting on a large cloth-covered trunk at the end of the big bed. The room looked ancient and rich and was filled with a musty smell.

Betty jerked to her feet. She turned to the window and pressed her hands against the glass.

"*The two children had their backs to me,*" she went on, hurrying. "*Both were blond: one had long straight hair, stringy, it was; the other one had hair that shone and sparkled, oh! it looked like gold.*" She was filled with terror, in the dream, despite the peacefulness of the scene, despite the sweet tinkling of the music box.

She left the window and sat down again. Her hands were trembling. "*Now comes the worst part. I can't stop now.*"

"*It's all right, Betty. You're safe here.*"

Again, she clutched the armrests. "*I made a sound. I called Heather's name. The child with the long stringy hair turned around slowly. It was Heather.*" She was holding a comb, a comb with sharp metal teeth, and she was combing her bare chest with it, her pajama top was undone and she was combing her child's chest and where she combed long thin fingers of blood were running slowly down her chest, and tears were falling from her eyes. Betty ran and picked her up and took her out of the room and told her to run to the kitchen. Then she went back.

"The white statue turned to look at me. The music still played. I called out—'Heather.'"

The second child turned around. Her blue eyes were bright and excited and she was smiling, a smile so cold Betty thought there should be fangs in her mouth but there weren't, only a child's teeth, a straight white row of them—and she slowly stood up and in her hand she held a butcher knife. She raised it slowly and began to move toward Betty.

"I turned around and ran and ran," said Betty. "I knew I was running too fast for her to catch me but I knew that she would catch me. I ran into the kitchen where the other Heather stood, still combing her chest in jerks with that comb with teeth like knives. I took it away from her and threw it—I don't know where it went—and then I put my arms around her and we waited for the other Heather to come. I could feel her coming slowly down the hall and I heard the tinkling of the music box. And then I woke up."

Tears streamed down her face. The doctor brought her a handkerchief, but she didn't look at it or reach for it. Her hands were still wrapped tightly around the armrests of the chair. He dabbed the tears from her cheeks and unwound one of her hands gently and put the handkerchief in it. He sat down on a chair that was beside hers.

"What does it mean?" she asked. "What's going to happen now?" Her face was still flooded with tears.

"What do you think it means?"

*Her mouth hung open, stupidly; she could feel it. She flapped it closed, then open, trying to know what to say. She stared hard at him, at the hair brushed back from his forehead, at his eyes.*

*"What do I think it means? What do I think?" She pulled away from him. "You tell me what it means! That's your job! That's why I came!"*

*"You must have some notion in your mind, Betty, of what the dream was trying to say to you—"*

*"Why do you think I came here!" she shouted, tugging at one hand with the other. "If I already knew what it meant why would I come?"*

*"It's a complicated dream, Betty—"*

*"Of course it's complicated!" she roared. "I dreamed it!"*

*"You need to talk to a psychiatrist about it, I think," he said gently, putting his hand over her two, which were twisted together.*

*"You can't help me," she said, her voice suddenly dead.*

*"I'll set up an appointment for you," he said, moving toward his desk.*

*"No no no!" She rushed past him to put her hands over the telephone. "I will not tell it again! What kind of a doctor are you," she said bitterly, "if you have to send me to another person? What kind of a doctor is that?"*

*"Sit down, Betty. Listen to me for a minute." He waited until she had sat. "Perhaps you should go to the hospital for a few days."*

*Betty snorted. "Hospital. Ha." She stood up and shouted at him. "I've been to one of those and it doesn't do a person any good, any good at all, people won't talk to a person when they come out of there!"*

*"Betty, of course they will, of course they do—"*

"*Not to me!*" *She shook her head.* "*I went and when I came out he wouldn't talk to me anymore, he hated me then.*" *She sat down again, exhausted.*

."*Tell me, Betty. Please.*"

"*I was a child,*" *she said dully.* "*I saw him fall, you see. From the tree. He hit his head on a rock or something. My brother.*" *She blinked rapidly.* "*Then he died. I was very upset, extremely upset. So I had to go to the hospital for a while. And when I got out—when I got out—she was different and* he would not speak to me!"

"*Who, Betty—your parents?*"

*She laughed loudly and looked down at the floor, leaned over to peer at it more closely. The carpet was dark blue. She saw that there were pieces of lint on it.*

*She stood up briskly.* "*I will think about the hospital. I will discuss it with Jack when he comes home the next time.*"

"*Betty.*"

"*Yes?*"

"*I want you to be helped. I care about you, Betty.*"

*She cocked her head and smiled at him.* "*I know,*" *she said, and left his office.*

## 18

Eliot and Alvin shivered in Alvin's backyard waiting for darkness, getting a kind of shelter from a pile of rubbish lying under a big tree. Eliot made out a big old door, on its side, with a window in the top that didn't have glass in it anymore; and an upturned wheelbarrow, its bottom rusted almost through; a scuffed soccer ball; and a swing seat with the chains still attached. Everything had been dumped in a heap underneath the tree, which was so big that its lowest branches didn't start until way above Eliot's head. Not far away stood a double car garage with its paint peeling off. When they'd first arrived, Eliot and Alvin had poked around in there. The garage, which had a dirt floor, was also full of junk, the whole interior piled with automobile parts and pieces of old gardening tools and cardboard boxes stuffed so full that photo albums and scrapbooks stuck out of the tops. You couldn't see out through the one small window because of the boxes piled up in front of it.

"This here's my stuff," Alvin had said, pointing to some

boxes just inside the door to the backyard. He pulled open the flaps of a few of them. "Yeah, see?"

Eliot saw a few books, a bunch of clothes, toys, teddy bears.

"Stuff I outgrew," said Alvin, opening another box. He looked inside for a moment, not poking around in there like he had in the others. "Except I didn't outgrow this stuff yet," he said, and now he did reach into the box, and pulled out a heavy sweater that was navy blue. He looked at Eliot in amazement. "They cleared out my room," he said. "Shit. I've only been gone a couple of days."

"This is good, though," said Eliot. "Now we don't have to go into the house."

They emptied the box onto a rickety Ping-Pong table that stood against one wall. Alvin changed into a pair of jeans and put on the navy sweater. He rummaged in another box and came up with a knapsack and a down jacket, some gloves, a scarf, and a pair of earmuffs, and stuffed these things plus several pairs of underwear and socks into the knapsack. "We should take a couple of these, too," he said, indicating some rolled-up sleeping bags. "We do so still gotta go inside," he said, wrestling himself into the jacket.

"No we don't," said Eliot urgently.

"Yeah we do. We gotta get us some food, and some money and stuff."

Eliot argued with him vigorously. He realized that here in the city—and particularly here in his own backyard—Alvin was on familiar ground and Eliot wasn't. But he didn't know if that meant that he ought to trust Alvin's judgment. In fact, he was very reluctant to trust Alvin's judgment.

"It'll be okay, Eliot," said Alvin, hefting the knapsack onto his back, hair falling over his forehead. "Come on. Grab a sleeping bag."

Eliot opened the door a crack and peered at the back of the house. "You got any sisters or brothers?"

"No," Alvin grunted, working on the knapsack.

"It's a big place for just three people."

"My grandparents used to live with us. And my aunt. There." He flexed his arms and pulled at the jacket, which had gotten scrunched up under the straps of the knapsack. He joined Eliot at the door. "Look. It's almost dark."

And then they'd moved outside, under the tree, behind the pile of junk, so they could watch the house.

Eliot was shivering by now, and trying to warm his hands by sitting on them, but the ground was so cold and damp that that didn't help.

"Here," said Alvin, turning his back toward Eliot. "Dig around in my knapsack for some gloves. I got more than one pair in there."

Eliot got out some gray leather ones for Alvin and a pair of woolen ones for himself, even though woolen gloves were dorky, because he knew they'd stretch enough to fit his hands. And they continued to wait. The house remained dark; obviously unoccupied.

"Why don't we go inside now?" said Eliot.

But Alvin shook his head. "My mom'll be home from work any minute. We gotta wait till she goes out again, or goes to bed."

Eliot groaned. "That's gonna be hours. And what about your dad?"

Alvin shrugged. "Never know about my dad," he said flatly. "Never know where he is or when he'll be back."

"Oh great," said Eliot.

Rain fell for a while, only the showery kind but still wet and cold, and then it stopped and after a while the wind began to blow, not a strong wind but more than a breeze. Eliot lifted his face to it and sniffed and thought he could smell spring a long way off.

"Okay. Well I don't know what's going on here," said Alvin. "She shoulda been here by now." He stood up, staggering a little. "My legs got pins and needles in them. Wait a minute." He stomped his feet a few times. "Okay. Come on. Let's do it."

"Jesus," said Eliot under his breath.

Alvin crept to the back of the house with Eliot, crouched over, following him.

Eliot considered this a very scary house. In the weak light from a streetlamp somewhere behind him, in the lane, it looked even scarier than in daylight. It was tall and narrow, with three stories. In the gable at the very top there was a little window, and then there was a piece of roof that looked like a big eyebrow over the two tiny windows on the next level, and below that there was another piece of roof above the next level, where there was a big porch and some stairs leading down to the yard. Under the porch it was utterly dark. This is where Alvin led them.

"See, we used to have a dog once," he said to Eliot in a hoarse whisper. He got down on his hands and knees—and then he vanished.

"Alvin?" Eliot breathed. "Alvin?" A little louder. He bent down and waved his hand around in the darkness, and brushed against a doorknob. He tried it, but it was locked.

"Come on," said Alvin, his voice muffled, and he stuck his head through a flap in the door. "See?" he said, and Eliot saw the gleam of his teeth when he grinned. "A dog door."

Eliot crawled through after him, into the basement of the house, and stood there blinking in the darkness. A tap was dripping, slowly.

"There should be a flashlight here someplace," said Alvin from somewhere on Eliot's right. Eliot heard him poking around and then a weak, quivering beam of light appeared. Alvin swept it around the basement, causing things to loom into view and then disappear again: a furnace, a double sink that looked like it was made of cement, an old-fashioned washing machine, and more piles of junk.

Alvin and Eliot made their way across the basement to a set of rickety stairs and started climbing, slowly, quietly, Alvin and the flashlight leading the way. Eliot heard the rattle of the knob as he opened the door at the top of the steps.

"Turn off the light," Eliot whispered as they went through the door into the kitchen, and Alvin did.

Alvin said, "We gotta move fast." He started opening drawers, hastily. "You get us some food—here," he said, thrusting a handful of plastic grocery bags at Eliot. "You put food in here. I'm gonna go upstairs and look for money. I gotta take the flashlight," he said apologetically, and Eliot heard the wheeze in his voice.

"Yeah, go ahead. But hurry. Shit. Hurry, okay?"

"Okay," said Alvin, already heading down the hall.

Eliot heard him going up some stairs. "Shit." His heart was pounding a mile a minute. "Shit," he said, tearing off the gloves, shoving them in his pockets. He opened a cupboard and squinted, trying to see inside, and pulled out a couple of things until he knew what kind of stuff was kept there: brown sugar, flour, things like that. So he opened the next one, and here he had better luck. Crackers, cookies, cans of tuna, cans of soup, unopened boxes of fruit juices—he loaded them into one of the plastic bags and turned next to the fridge, where he took apples and oranges and a carton of cottage cheese. He spotted a covered casserole on the bottom shelf and took off the lid. Eliot was instantly ravenous. Saliva flooded his mouth. His hands were shaking as he squatted down and started shoving handfuls of macaroni and cheese into his mouth and heard himself moaning with bliss; he couldn't chew and swallow fast enough. . . .

"Hey!" It came from upstairs.

Eliot froze, his mouth full, hands poised over the casserole dish.

"You little bastard!"

"Oh jesus, oh jesus." Eliot staggered to his feet, still holding the casserole. He put it down on the counter. Heard feet running on the floor above. Grabbed the two plastic bags and the rolled-up sleeping bag and then hovered there in the kitchen, not knowing which way to run. Heard Alvin sprinting down the stairs.

"Here! Here!" Alvin hollered from the front of the house. Eliot ran down the hall. "Oh jesus, oh god." He saw Alvin tearing open the front door, heard the pounding of heavier footsteps behind him on the stairs, pelted out onto the porch, down the steps, and along the street, following Alvin, who Eliot suddenly realized was laughing, so hard that he weaved and tottered as he ran, his whoops of laughter trailing behind him, streamers of glee.

Eliot risked one glance back over his shoulder and saw Alvin's dad standing on the porch, his long underwear a lustrous white streak in the darkness.

Enid sat in the dark in a comfortable chair next to her bedroom window. The blinds were open. She had seen her lodger's truck arrive some time earlier and had intended to go to bed then, but she was in the tender grip of a daydream and had decided to let it have its way with her.

Thus she saw him when he came around the house, carrying his duffel bag.

This puzzled her.

His bag would be filled with his clothes, clean and dirty. His electric razor would be in there, and his toothbrush and toothpaste. His deodorant. And the photograph of the child.

Enid watched him climb into the truck. An ache began, in the center of her, even though she knew he probably wasn't going anywhere.

She waited for the engine to come to life. But it didn't. Eventually he emerged and went up the walk, and disappeared around the back of the house. She couldn't hear him, from up here, but she knew he was back in his apartment.

He'd forgotten about the ferries, that's what had happened. Forgotten that the last one had left hours ago, and there wouldn't be another until early morning.

Enid sighed, and felt sad, for he had wanted to leave, had intended to leave, and probably would leave, once morning came.

She closed the blind, turned on the light, and prepared for bed. What could she do, she wondered, to persuade him not to move on just yet?

**19**

*Thursday, December 1*

It was very early the next morning. The gray day stirred around them. Eliot hadn't slept—at least he was pretty sure he hadn't. But Alvin had slept and in fact he was still doing it, his snores attested to that. Eliot found this fascinating. He had thought it was only adults who snored. He had thought snoring was the result of overindulgences like too much smoking or too much drinking or too much eating. People's interior selves got slack and listless over time, and that was what made snoring happen. Or so he had believed. But here was this kid, honking away. Eliot was afraid somebody was going to come by and hear him.

They hadn't run very far—not nearly far enough to suit Eliot. They'd gone only a few blocks from where Alvin's dad had erupted out onto the porch in his white long johns.

"He's not gonna come looking for us," Alvin had said.

"Yeah, but he's gonna call the detention center," said Eliot.

"And what do you think they're gonna do?" said Alvin. "I'll tell you what they're gonna do. They'll call the cops and the cops'll come out and talk to my old man. But it'll take them a long time to get around to it. By that time we'll be outa here. Besides they're sure not gonna start searching for us, not in this neighborhood."

But Eliot knew they'd be looking for him, all right. And they'd know that he and Alvin were together. So that when Alvin's dad called the detention center . . .

Eliot couldn't deal with this tonight. He'd think about it in the morning. Worry about it in the morning.

Alvin had led them to a small park, a square block of rolling grass and clusters of trees, and they had crawled on hands and knees underneath the lowest branches, which swept the ground, hauling the knapsack and the plastic grocery bags after them. They spread the sleeping bag out on the damp ground, which was covered with brown needles. They emptied the plastic bags onto the sleeping bag and Alvin trained the weak, trembling beam of the flashlight on it.

They selected packets of cheese and crackers, and peanut butter and crackers that came with little plastic knives, and wolfed down the food and gulped a couple of cartons of juice.

Then Alvin lay down on the sleeping bag, curled up with his back to Eliot, and almost right away he was asleep.

Eliot put their supplies away in the bags and put the bags in a hollow between two trees and sat with his back against the trunk of one of them, his arms around his knees.

It was very sheltered in there. He could just barely see out through the branches that draped themselves down around them. He had to wiggle over a little bit so that one of them wouldn't poke him in the eye. He figured that if it didn't rain too hard they wouldn't get very wet: the ground was barely damp, the layers of branches too thick to let many raindrops through. And they wouldn't feel much of a wind, either. Still, he'd rather be inside somewhere, lying on a bed.

It was much better to be warm and completely dry, if you had to stay awake.

After a while he lay down on the sleeping bag, in the corner opposite to Alvin. Now and then he closed his eyes, but never for very long. Alvin had told him before he went to sleep that there were animals in the neighborhood. Not just cats and dogs but wild animals, squirrels, and raccoons, and Alvin said he'd even seen a big old waddly skunk once when he was creeping along the alley behind his house at four in the morning. Eliot had been skeptical. But now, lying awake in the shelter of a bunch of low-slung trees, listening to the occasional pit-pat of rain, a hollow twangy sound as it struck the needles and then slid right off, and the breeze hissing around them, it was easy to start imagining creatures hiding nearby, studying them in secret with eyes like shiny black buttons. Once or twice he thought he heard something rummaging around in the plastic bags and he thought they should have hung them in the tree like people did when they went camping in the woods, so bears couldn't get at their supplies. But maybe raccoons and skunks climbed trees. He didn't know a damn thing about raccoons or skunks. He made himself sit up and turn on the flashlight but didn't see anything poking at the plastic bags.

Now, lying on his back with his hands behind his head, Eliot saw that the darkness was fading away. He squinted at his watch but it still wasn't light enough to tell the time. His stomach was rumbling. Above them a bird called out, and Eliot wondered if it was having a dream.

Alvin suddenly emitted a great snort of a snore. "I gotta take a squirt," he said, in a loud whisper.

Eliot didn't hear him move, though. "Go behind a tree," said Eliot.

"It's too dark," said Alvin. "I gotta wait for daylight."

Eliot got to his feet, stretched, and sat down again, scratching his back against a treetrunk—there was a big itch there right between his shoulder blades. Then he settled back to wait out the rest of the night, sharing it with the medicinal scent of the trees and the dim shape of Alvin and an occasional scurrying sound that might have been a smidgen of wind trying to get underneath the tree branches or else maybe it was mice.

Gradually the darkness faded into the gray of early morning, like a Polaroid photograph, and Alvin scrambled up and pushed through the tree branches.

Eliot felt better now that day was definitely coming. He stood up and brushed off his jeans and decided that he wouldn't consider the future until after he'd eaten.

A few minutes later he and Alvin once more dumped the contents of the plastic bags onto the sleeping bag. "We better eat up the cottage cheese," he said.

"Yeah. We can use those little stick things from the cheese and crackers," said Alvin.

"There's an important thing missing here," said Eliot, gazing at their supplies.

"What? What?" said Alvin, digging around in the bag they'd put their garbage in the night before, looking for the little sticks.

"A can opener."

"That'll be today's project," said Alvin.

"There's no way I'm living on the street." Eliot made this announcement after they'd eaten. Alvin was taking regular peeks through the curtain of tree branches. Eliot observed him irritably. "I thought you said nobody'd be coming after us?"

"They won't," said Alvin. "But people come here, you know, with their dogs and stuff, with their kids."

"It's too early for that," said Eliot. "It's not even six o'clock yet." He was cleaning up, stuffing things back into the bags. "There's no way," he said again.

Alvin said, "What, then?" He came over to help. "We

gotta get us a can opener, you're right, that's for sure. You want to stay here?"

"We can't stay here," said Eliot, disgusted, "with your folks three blocks away."

"Six."

"Whatever."

"So we find another park," said Alvin.

He was getting excited. Eliot knew the signs now. His eyes would start moving around like they'd come unconnected, and he'd start jiggling up and down so that his hair bounced around on his forehead, which was just as well because whenever it bounced down it covered up his eyes for a minute.

"We walk all day," said Alvin, "and I do some panhandling so we can get a can opener and other stuff we need, and when it gets dark we find another park like this one."

Eliot started to protest; he found Alvin's enthusiasm tiring.

But Alvin went on. "And once we got a bit of money we change our clothes and dry these ones in a laundromat."

Eliot admitted that this was probably a good idea. "Come on," he said, starting to roll up the sleeping bag, and a few minutes later they slipped out of the shelter of the trees and started trudging across the park.

"When it gets cold," said Eliot, "I don't know what we're gonna do."

"There's buildings nobody lives in," said Alvin.

"Yeah," said Eliot, listless. "I guess."

## 20

Enid studied herself critically in the bathroom mirror. She pulled up on the skin of her upper forehead, trying to see how much improvement might be accomplished by some judiciously executed cosmetic surgery. Bernie's hoots of derision were almost as loud in her ears as if Bernie had been standing there with her. Enid sighed and turned away from the mirror. She would find some of Bernie's attitudes irritating, if she hadn't been made aware of their origin.

One night five years after she and Bernie had met, Enid and Arch were in bed asleep, when Enid became aware of a knocking at their front door. Arch continued to snore. Enid got up and went to the window and peered outside, and saw Bernie's VW bug parked in front of the house. She hurried downstairs, quietly, so as not to wake the children, and opened the door.

It was summer, and the night air was cool and fragrant. It was so quiet that Enid could hear Bernie's breathing, which was quick and shallow.

"I am truly sorry to come here in the middle of the night,"

Bernie said, "but I need some help and it's you I thought might give it to me."

Enid ushered her inside. Bernie walked slowly and carefully down the hall, somewhat bent over, carrying her purse in front of her like a shield. She slid onto a kitchen chair and Enid sat in another.

"What is it, Bernie?"

"I been wondering for years what it would take," Bernie said dully. "Turns out it's the sum total and you don't know what that is till you get there."

Enid shook her head in confusion.

"Turns out that seventeen times was one time too many." Bernie turned her birdlike eyes upon Enid. "You never had any idea, did you?" she said proudly. "That Hector walloped me?"

Enid felt herself gawk.

"Nope. Knew you didn't." Bernie looked blankly around the kitchen. "Knew you didn't."

Enid stood up. "I'll put on some coffee."

"Do you happen to have any strong drink in the house?" said Bernie.

"We do." Enid gave her a hug, which caused Bernie to cry out. "Oh Bernie. Where do you hurt?"

"I believe a rib or two may be broken."

"We have to get you to the hospital."

"First the police station," Bernie had said. "Then the hospital."

And so it was no wonder that Bernie mistrusted men, thought Enid, dropping two slices of raisin bread into the toaster. Most men, anyway.

As she reached into the cupboard for the butter she heard her lodger's truck start up. She remained frozen, her hand in mid-air. But she had resolved to be philosophical. If he goes, he goes, she told herself. In a moment, she heard him drive away.

She took out the butter and ate her breakfast. Her mind was elsewhere, though, and she barely tasted her toast.

When she'd washed her dishes and put them away she dithered for a while, then took herself in hand. It was her house, after all. She oughtn't to have to wait around wondering whether she still had a lodger or not. So pretty soon she marched down there, flung open the door, and had a look.

His toiletries still sat on the bathroom counter. The pile of laundry had grown somewhat larger. Enid, smiling to herself, tiptoed out of the suite and closed the door gently behind her.

Alberg felt furtive just looking out his office window now, and even though this time when he looked he didn't see the damn brown Silverado parked outside, he was just as angry as if he had.

He picked up his ringing phone. "Alberg," he said, snapping a bite out of the air with it.

"Uh, it's Neil, sir. Neil Hutchon?"

"I don't know you," said Alberg, looking out the window again. Maybe he should board the damn thing up, and carve himself a skylight.

"Uh, the realtor? You looked at one of my properties the other day?"

"Oh. Yes." Alberg went around his desk and sat down. "We were going to get back to you, but something came up."

"Sure," said Neil, comfortingly. "Sure."

"We want to take another look at it," Alberg told him.

"Sure," Neil said. "When would you like to do this? Because, the thing of it is, there's another party interested, as well?"

"Can't make it before the weekend," said Alberg, paging through his desk diary. "I'll give you a call on Saturday. If it's still available we'll set something up then."

He grabbed his jacket and went out into the reception area, where a stocky man of about sixty sat on the bench reading a newspaper. Alberg's heart lurched—for a moment he'd thought it was Jack Coutts. Jesus christ, he thought in self-disgust.

"I've got that Chamber of Commerce lunch," he told Isabella. "And then I'm going to see Noah Silverton."

"Thank you, thank you," said Isabella with fervor.

Silverton had called the detachment seven times about kids running through his yard on their way to school. Alberg was making this complaint his own personal responsibility because Silverton's sailboat was moored next to Alberg's, and they had struck up a casual friendship.

"Who's the civilian over there?" said Alberg, leaning across the counter, keeping his voice low.

Isabella threw a worried glance toward the bench. "That's Richard," she whispered. "My husband. He did it. He retired."

Alberg nodded, slowly, considering the implications of this. He said hello to the guy as he left the building, and got a pleasant smile in return.

It was after the lunch, during his talk with Noah Silverton, that Alberg saw Jack Coutts for the first time that day.

"Yeah, you're right," Noah was saying crossly. They were standing outside, examining the patch of rain-sodden grass that had been torn up by the feet of running children. "But I don't like the idea."

The Silverado pulled up at the curb across the street. Alberg couldn't see Jack clearly, but well enough to recognize that he was wearing a bright yellow winter cap. It put Alberg in mind of a parrot he'd once known, a sullen, spiteful bird, but colorful. For some reason the comparison lightened his spirits and he raised his arm and offered Jack a stylized salute.

This went unnoticed by Noah Silverton, who was still

staring at his lawn. "Don't like it one bit," he was saying. "I'm ideologically opposed to fences."

"Still and all," said Alberg. "I think Mr. Frost's got the right idea. Don't you?"

Silverton nodded gloomily. "Yeah. I know. I'll do it."

Alberg returned to the detachment—where Richard Harbud was still sitting on the bench in the reception area—and picked up his messages. For the rest of the afternoon, working at his desk, he was painfully aware of the window, of not looking out the window.

After work he drove to Warren Kettleman's garage, left the Oldsmobile there to be serviced, and walked over to the library to get a ride home with Cassandra.

And from the library he saw Jack, now hatless, leaning against a telephone pole.

"Okay," said Alberg. "That's it." And he walked out of the library and down the street toward him.

As Alberg approached, Jack's expression didn't change. Alberg felt as if he were walking in deep water. He had a sense of inevitability. He was aware of every detail of the muted pattern of Jack Coutts' jacket, saw that the white lines separating the squares of different shades of red were blurred, that one pocket sagged open—maybe his keys were in it. Jack's arms were folded across his chest. He was wearing a denim shirt under the jacket and the cuffs were slightly frayed. His jeans were worn but clean; his workboots, old but polished. Alberg was concentrating intently on these things, on these details, because he was worried about the extent of his anger, which was deeper than he had realized; and because he knew that Cassandra was watching through the library's floor-to-ceiling window.

"It's not me you're pissed off with," he said to Jack, and stopped far enough away from him not to be in his face. "You know damn fucking well who you're really mad at, Jack."

Jack pushed away from the telephone pole and dropped his hands to his sides. "Yeah, right, let's have a bunch of psychological bullshit from the world's most incompetent cop," he said, his face reddening.

A couple of kids dawdling along the street stopped their chatter, stopped in their tracks.

Alberg was shaking slightly with the effort to keep himself under control. "You're the one who watched it year after year," he said. "You're the one who didn't get your wife goddamn locked up where she goddamn belonged."

"Who the fuck are you?" Jack shouted. "Who the *fuck* are *you?*"

The kids hastily crossed the street. A passing motorist slowed down.

"So you end up watching her die for twelve years, twelve fucking years, you poor sonofabitch." Alberg turned away, then turned back, lifted his hand, and pointed his index finger at Jack, wanting badly to jab him in the chest with it. "Carry your fucking cross, Jack. And stay away from me. I'm warning you." He turned around and walked back toward the library, keeping a steady pace, focusing on the library door, on breathing, on not listening, on not remembering.

"Warning me! Warning me! That's all you're good for!" Jack shouted after him. "And you didn't even do that, you didn't even do that, you useless fucking cop!" He was weeping now, and didn't seem to know it. He leaned against the telephone pole for a minute. Then wiped his face with his hands and staggered around the corner.


Enid sat in her living room that rainy, windy evening, leafing through a catalog. The TV was on, but the volume was low and Enid couldn't have said what program was showing; she had it on for company—in the evening she needed more than sound for company, she needed the muted muffled moving around of other people in her life. She looked up, occasionally, when a gust of wind flung rain against the window: it sounded like pebbles striking the glass.

Enid was Christmas shopping in the catalog. Reggie and The Spouse were going to Hawaii for the holidays and Enid's daughter the lawyer had to go to her in-laws in Montreal. Enid resented her children for avoiding her at Christmas but she would of course send them gifts nonetheless. She turned another page of the catalog—and then heard noises downstairs.

She got up and went to the window and sure enough, her lodger's truck was parked in front of the house. The wind and the rain had covered the sounds of his arrival.

Enid stood in a bubble, feeling suspended, as if the floor had drifted away from her feet without her knowing it; she felt like one of those cartoon creatures who run off the edge of a cliff and cover a considerable distance in mid-air until realization strikes, and only then do they fall.

She glided to the basement door and listened, intently. He has nothing down there to entertain him, she thought, no radio, no television, not even any books to keep him company.

It is darn near Christmas, she told herself. We're in the month of Christmas. She would offer him a glass of wine.

She ran lightly upstairs to comb her hair and she dabbed a little perfume at the base of her neck, too, then went down into the basement and knocked firmly upon his door.

It took him a long time to answer. Enid didn't knock again, but waited, patiently. Finally she heard him stirring in there. Perhaps her knock had wakened him—but no, he hadn't had time to fall asleep.

He opened the door. She lifted her head to smile at him. But when she saw his face, she didn't smile. "What's wrong?" she said. "Mr. Coutts, what's the matter?"

He tried to reply, but couldn't. She reached out to touch

his arm. He shook his head, took a step back, then stumbled, and sank onto the edge of the bed.

Enid remained in the doorway. "Can I help you? Is there something I can do for you?"

Jack shook his head again, slumped over, sitting on his bed.

"Did something happen?" said Enid.

He looked up at her now and tried to laugh.

Enid glided into the room and sat down on the high-backed chair that used to live in her upstairs hall. "Tell me," she said.

His head was bowed. His hair, she noticed again, was thick and rough. His hands, clasped between his knees, had long strong fingers: he wore no wedding ring.

The room was mostly dark. Some light drifted in from the living room where he must have turned on the lamp.

"Tell me," said Enid again, velvet-voiced, and she folded her hands in her lap, waiting. After a long time he began to speak and a softness occurred in Enid's chest, something warm began to grow there, and she tended it, encouraged it, as he talked to her.

"I was married, once—it turned out she was crazy."

He sat up straighter and looked across the room at her. Enid realized that she was sitting in the soft light floating in from the living room. He was in mostly darkness. She could make out his clothing, a denim shirt and bluejeans, and she could occasionally see the whites of his eyes. If he were to smile, or laugh, his teeth would gleam: she had observed how straight and white they were.

"That's not my fault," said Jack. "I know that. It's not my fault that she was crazy. That she didn't keep herself clean. But—"

He got up and went to the window, pulled back the curtain and looked outside. Enid was aware of the wind and the rain. It was cozy in Jack Coutts' rented bedroom; cozy like a cave, or a den.

"But what?" she said, softly.

"We had a daughter. Heather," he said, his voice thicker. "I taught her how to look after herself, do laundry, make meals but—"

He left the window and circled the bed. She heard his leg brush the bedskirt. She wouldn't have put that thing on the bed if she'd known that a man would be sleeping there. For a moment he stood close to Enid's chair and she started to rise but he sat down again, on the edge of the bed.

"But she was only a kid. A little kid. And—"

Enid waited, not knowing how to finish the sentence for him.

He rubbed his face with both hands, energetically, as if trying to erase himself. "I should have left her. I should have taken Heather and left her. Oh god." He began to weep.

Before she knew it, Enid was sitting next to him, her arm around his shoulders. "Oh dear, oh dear," she said. "There's no room for should haves, no room at all."

She admired the way he moved, quietly, almost stealthily, guarding his secrets.

Enid patted his shoulder, squeezed it, as he wept, and he turned so that she could embrace him with both arms. "Oh yes," she whispered, hugging him close. She put her hand under his chin to lift his face, gently. Softly she kissed his tears—his eyes, his cheeks. When her mouth touched his lips it was like a butterfly landing upon a rose. She felt his lips open—oh yes thought Enid. . . .

Jack stiffened in her arms. He remained for a second very still, like a deer caught in headlights, and then like the deer he leapt away.

"I'm sorry," he stammered.

"No no," said Enid calmly, standing, smoothing her dress. "There's no need to be sorry. I misread you. It's for me to apologize." She went to the door, then glanced over her shoulder at him. "You must get rid of them. All those memories. All those should haves."

He was standing awkwardly in the middle of the bedroom, his hair in disarray. He was no longer weeping.

"Thank you for confiding in me," said Enid.

## 21

*Saturday, December 3*

"I'm sick of this," said Eliot, rolling up the sleeping bag. "I gotta get outa this city. I gotta get home. I gotta get back to Nova Scotia." Rosie was going to end up back there, with relatives, he had realized. There was absolutely no reason, then, for Eliot to stay in this place.

"Huh," said Alvin, scooping the last spoonful of pork and beans out of a can. He was using a serving spoon he'd stolen from a Zellers store.

"I'm freezing cold, for one thing," said Eliot.

They had spent the last two nights in a wooded area of Stanley Park; through the trees they could get a glimpse of the Lion's Gate Bridge. Eliot didn't know much about this park but he did know that it was very big, that besides all the acres of forest there was an aquarium somewhere, and a zoo, and he thought some totem poles, as well. But he and Alvin hadn't seen any of that. They'd kept to the woods.

"How're you gonna get to Nova Scotia?" Alvin was holding the empty can and looking around like he expected to see a garbage can suddenly appear, out there in the middle of the woods.

"I've been thinking," said Eliot. "It probably doesn't cost much to take a bus."

"Geez. That's a long way to go in a bus. How far is it anyway?"

"It's six thousand one hundred and nineteen kilometers."

Alvin was struggling into his knapsack. "Wow. So how're you gonna get the money?"

"Your face is dirty," said Eliot. "You've got bean juice all over your face."

Alvin rubbed his face clean with the sleeve of his jacket.

"I'm gonna sell some stuff," said Eliot. "If it's still there."

"What stuff? Where?"

"I've got some rollerblades. And a guitar."

"Where?"

"And there'll be other stuff. My dad's got a camera." He finished tying the strings of the sleeping bag and picked it up, holding it out to Alvin. "Here. You might as well take this. I'm not gonna need it anymore."

Alvin's eyes got big and focused. "Whaddya mean? Where're you going?"

"What've I just been telling you?" said Eliot impatiently. "I'm gonna go back to Sechelt and collect some stuff and sell it and take the bus to Nova Scotia." And while he was in Sechelt, he'd call the hospital, and find out how Rosie was. He was afraid to do this—afraid that the cop was wrong, and Rosie was hurt bad, or maybe even dead—but he had to do it, had to know.

"I'm coming with you." Alvin grabbed hold of Eliot's sleeve. "Come on, we're a team," he said earnestly.

Eliot jerked away and walked off through the trees toward the path they'd found the night before. What would he do, if they told him she was dead? Eliot's heart pounded, just thinking about it.

Plus he was wet and cold and irritable, and he was tired of Alvin. He didn't see how he could just dump the kid, but he sure didn't want him tagging along all the way to Nova Scotia. And what would he do with him when they got there? Eliot knew he'd have to hide out when he got home—he was counting on Sammy to help him out with this—and that was no kind of life for a little kid.

"I know some guys," said Alvin, trotting behind him. "They can help you get rid of your stuff. Sell it."

"Yeah, sure," muttered Eliot, pushing through a bunch of waist-high underbrush, leafless, but wet with rain. He took note of this, however, because he hadn't thought out exactly how he was going to exchange his merchandise for cash.

They emerged on the path and Alvin danced ahead of Eliot, hanging on to the straps of his knapsack, jogging backward.

"Quit that," said Eliot. "You're gonna trip yourself." So Alvin took his place beside him. "Okay okay," said Eliot impatiently. "You can come to Sechelt with me." The kid needed a bath. So did Eliot, of course. He'd get him all cleaned up before he sent him on his way.

"Yea," Alvin caroled. "I've never been on a ferry."

"We'll have to find a bunch more cans first," said Eliot, "to get money for the fare."

"And they got those little cubicles, didja see that? didja see it?" said Alvin, all excited. "You can write a private letter in there if you want."

"Or plug in your laptop," said the lady, smiling as she drove. "Your portable computer."

"What? Noooo," said Alvin, drawing out the word.

"It's true," she said.

"Geez," said Alvin, and he was quiet for a moment. Which was a big relief to Eliot. He kept thinking Alvin was going to give them away.

They'd met the lady on the ferry, and she'd offered them

a ride when she heard where they were going. "I live in Garden Bay," she'd said. "I drive right through Sechelt." She was an older lady, with gray hair, and she was wearing a raincoat that was gray and a bright red rainhat with a brim on it. She looked like a nice person, somebody who had no what Eliot's mom had called ulterior motives.

So here they were in her car, going along the highway, and Alvin had been talking nonstop about the ferry, about how big it was, how big its windows were, how big the cafeteria was, and the car deck. The snack bar knocked him out. The arcade knocked him out. The bank of telephones knocked him out. Eliot had been embarrassed at first, then he felt a weird kind of pride, as if it was his damn ferry. But now he was just sick of hearing Alvin talk.

"What were you kids doing in Vancouver?" the lady asked.

It was a casual question, and an obvious one—a question she would've asked earlier if Alvin had shut up any sooner.

Before Eliot could open his mouth, Alvin said, "He's my cousin, see, and my dad's in the hospital, and my mom works, so I'm gonna stay with him for a while, until my dad gets home."

"Oh, dear," said the lady.

Eliot, riding in the backseat, knew he had a horrified look on his face and tried to wipe it off.

"I'm sorry about your dad," said the lady.

"He's not dyin' or anything," said Alvin. "It's just kinda inconvenient. Are we nearly there?" he said, peering out the window.

"We are indeed," said the lady. They were passing Trail Bay, which was a pretty enough sight when the sun shone but on a gray and gloomy day like this it was just as gray and gloomy as everything else. "We go up that hill, and there we are," she said. "Where do you want to be let off?"

"On the other side of town. Just past the shopping center," said Eliot, "if that's okay."

As they drove up the hill he bent over, pretending to be looking for something in Alvin's knapsack, which was stowed on the floor, so as not to be seen. Now that he was actually back in Sechelt he was terrified, and couldn't believe that he'd done such a stupid thing, shit, everybody in town knew what he looked like, everybody in town knew what he'd done, shit, thought Eliot, I'm an idiot, a total idiot. The lady's Toyota crawled along the town's main street and Eliot was practically lying down in the backseat by now.

Meanwhile Alvin was chattering away about this father who was supposed to be in the hospital. Apparently he'd broken his leg when he fell out of an apple tree he was pruning. Eliot listened, incredulous, as Alvin made up the tree, the yard, the house, the school he went to—and finally, finally, the lady pulled over and let them out.

They waved at her as she drove off.

"Okay, what now?" said Alvin.

Eliot trotted along the edge of the road, heading north, away from town, and Alvin trotted after him. Soon they reached the track that led from the highway to Eliot's house.

And to the beach.

It was mid-afternoon, and some rain was falling. Eliot, heading along the track, sure hoped the power was still on in that house, keeping the furnace going, and the fridge. "We can't turn on any lights," he said, though.

"Right," said Alvin. "We can use the flashlight."

Eliot, watching the ground so as to avoid the puddles, knew that they were getting closer and closer to the house. And he did not want to get there. He still thought he had a good plan. He still thought it was the only possible plan. But he did not want to get to that house. He was glad, now, that he'd let Alvin tag along. He admitted to himself that he might not have been able to do this alone. He glanced over at Alvin, walking quietly beside him.

"I was in there because I keep running away," Alvin had said last night, lying on his half of the sleeping bag.

They'd taken out all the clothes in his knapsack and Alvin was wearing half of them and Eliot had tried to wrap himself in the rest. But they were still cold. They had found a spot deep in the woods where they were pretty much protected from the rain, but there was no way Eliot could sleep. There'd be all kinds of animals in that huge park. And they had seen occasional clusters of homeless people there, too. Who knew what, or who, might stumble onto them as they lay there? But nothing and nobody did, as it turned out.

"How come you run away?" said Eliot. He sensed, more than saw, Alvin's shrug.

"You know. You saw."

"Well do you tell them?" said Eliot. "The social workers? Whoever?"

"They'd just send me to a foster home. I been there. Foster homes are no better. At least at home I know the place. I got my stuff."

Eliot lay on his back, looking up toward the sky. It was all clouded over, though, so he couldn't see stars or the moon. Only blackness.

"How come you were there?" said Alvin.

Eliot was silent for a long time. He didn't know if he could say the words. Which ones would he pick to say, if he decided he could speak of it? Alvin shifted a little, trying to get more comfortable. The ground was bumpy and lumpy even with the sleeping bag on top of it.

"I killed my parents." Eliot's voice sounded perfectly ordinary. He was disappointed. He had hoped to learn something from the sound of his voice when he said it.

Alvin lay still. Then he gave a long, low, respectful whistle. "Geez." He thought about it for a while. "Was this a planned type thing?"

"No."

"You did both of your parents?"

"Yeah. And I hurt my little sister." Eliot's stomach rose

into his throat. He threw off Alvin's extra clothes and got up and leaned against a nearby tree. "Rosie, her name is." His voice was husky, now, and there was a shake in it.

"Why?" said Alvin after a while.

Yeah, right, thought Eliot, walking next to Alvin up the track toward his house. Why. Why.

"Hey," said Alvin, coming to a halt.

"What?"

"Did it happen in this house we're going to?"

"No," said Eliot in disgust. "Of course not. You think I'd go back in there if . . . ?"

They arrived a few minutes later. Eliot first heard the ocean, and then they were there. He stood in the turn-around, staring across at the small gray house, and in the background, washing over the house and the woods and the garden and him and Alvin, was the ceaseless sound of the sea.

"Okay," he said finally. "Let's go in."


Enid was again looking into the mirror, being careful not to get too close to it. She didn't want to see herself too clearly. She wanted her outline slightly blurred, as if she were moving while being photographed. Her fingertips moved curiously across her lips. She had a lovely mouth, if she did say so herself.

She had spent the morning cleaning her house, vigorously, and would spend the afternoon shopping for groceries. Perhaps she would stop in to see Bernie. But maybe not. Bernie was eagle-eyed, and might see the kiss on Enid's lips.

She smiled in the mirror.

She had paid no attention to him this morning. She hadn't heard a sound from down there. But then she'd had the vacuum cleaner on, and had been singing as she worked. Now she went to the bedroom window and peeked out—his truck was gone.

She smoothed the duvet on her king-size bed, and had a flashing remembrance of Harry Mason, his long white legs and his cavernous armpits and his obsessive enthusiasm for open-mouthed kissing. She'd met him at Grace Markworthy's funeral. Harry himself was dead, now, of complications following some kind of surgery, Enid didn't know what kind, they hadn't been seeing each other anymore when he had it.

She went down the hall to the bathroom and turned on the shower, filling the room with steam. She peeled off her clothes and dropped them on the floor, stepped into the tub and pulled the shower curtain closed. She hummed to herself while she stroked her soapy body, long strokes of arm and thigh, circular strokes of breasts and stomach, humming "I Could Have Danced All Night," singing aloud the phrases she remembered.

Later, she dressed, in gray slacks, a blue short-sleeved tucked-in sweater that reflected her eyes, and flat shoes.

She would make some vegetable soup, she decided, for the freezer. She consulted the recipe and listed the ingredients, sitting at the kitchen table. Then added to the shopping list paper towels, aspirin, sugar-free ginger ale, cocoa powder. . . .

Enid tucked the list in her purse and went to the closet for her jacket.

But then she stopped.

She looked to make sure his truck hadn't returned, and went quietly down the stairs.

If he's locked his door, she thought, I will take that as a sign, and I won't use my key.

But he hadn't locked the door.

She left it open when she slipped inside.

His bed was slightly rumpled, as if he'd lain down again after making it. Enid resisted an urge to smooth the spread and make it wrinkle free.

She moved fitfully through her lodger's apartment, feeling like an explorer, or a scientist; a person on the lookout for data, for information that would explain the inexplicable. She bent over to look again at the photograph of the child. Heather. My goodness, thought Enid. My goodness. She had meant what she said to him, that there was no room for should haves in a livable life. But she had to ask herself, what kind of a man would stay with a woman he considered crazy? What kind of a man would leave his daughter with such a woman?

Enid straightened, uneasily. The kitchen tap was dripping. She turned the faucet tightly closed, and it stopped. He had left dishes in the sink, a mug, a cereal bowl, a spoon, and the coffeepot.

Dissatisfied, Enid moved restlessly back into the bedroom. She tried to open the drawer in the bedside table but it stuck, she couldn't get it all the way open—but far enough to see that it was empty. And no wonder. She should have remembered to have that drawer repaired.

The bottom two drawers in the bureau were also empty. The top one held piles of underwear, shorts and T-shirts, and several pairs of socks. Under the T-shirts, a rectangular box. Enid lifted the shirts, discreetly, and saw that the box contained something that was wrapped in a piece of white fabric.

She put the pile of shirts on top of the bureau and poked at this object, which was very hard, and she reached in to pick it up, to take it out of the box. Her hand closed around it. And although Enid had never in her life held a gun, she knew she was holding one now.

22

The back door was locked, but his mom always left a spare key handy. Eliot got it out from under a big plant pot that sat on a tree stump: it had had flowers in it in the summertime.

They went in that door because it was the only door the family had ever used. The front door, in the living room, was never even opened, except when Eliot's mom wanted to air the house out, by which she meant get rid of the smoke from his dad's cigarettes.

Before they actually entered, Eliot bent down to pick up a pair of boots that had been knocked over, maybe by the wind. Alvin watched him do this but didn't say anything, didn't ask whose boots they were, probably this was because they were small and red and therefore he could tell they were Rosie's.

Alvin waited out there on the porch, sheltered from the rain by the overhang, and let Eliot go in first, by himself.

Eliot, standing in the kitchen, worked out in his head how many days had passed since that morning. A lot of dust must have collected, he thought.

A tea towel was draped over the back of a chair. The table had been wiped clean. His mom had done the breakfast dishes and left them in the drainer to dry. It was all so terribly familiar and ordinary that Eliot fully expected his family to be there, concealed somewhere in the rooms of this house: Rosie asleep in her bed, his mother maybe having a bath, his father around the corner drinking beer and watching TV in the living room.

He told Alvin to come inside and Alvin did, closing the door very quietly behind him, as if he, too, believed that they were not alone there.

"I've gotta check," Eliot mumbled, and he moved silently across the kitchen. He pressed against the wall beside the doorway and looked cautiously around it. He saw a beer can and an ashtray full of butts and some other stuff lying around, but of course the living room was empty.

He took the stairs two at a time. In Rosie's room there were clothes lying on the floor and the bed wasn't made. Eliot could hear his mom—he didn't know if he'd heard this that morning or not, he might have, could have—could hear her saying, "Rosie, Rosie, sweet as a posy, Rosie make your bed," and she'd give a gentle little swat to Rosie's behind when she said the word "bed." The curtains were still closed, too. Eliot's throat had that big ache in it again. He shut the door to his sister's room and went down the hall. His parents' room was empty. The bathroom, empty. He wasn't ready yet to look inside his own room, to encounter the Eliot who would definitely be haunting that room, the Eliot who had gotten up that November morning, and put on his clothes, just like it was going to be a normal day. All the while he was in there, waking up, getting dressed, there was still hope for him and he didn't even know it, didn't even know that when he left his room that morning he was abandoning himself.

Downstairs, Alvin was still standing by the door.

"It's okay," said Eliot. "There's nobody here." He went into the living room and got rid of the beer can and emptied the ashtray and folded up the newspaper. He just wouldn't look over there where the crayons and the coloring book were. He'd ignore them. "I gotta water the plants," he said.

Alvin took off the knapsack and dumped the contents onto a countertop. Then he wandered around the house. Eliot heard him upstairs, padding along the hall. He knew the kid would stand in every doorway, looking in, but he was pretty sure Alvin wouldn't actually enter any of the rooms and start poking around.

Eliot was surprised at how many of the plants were still alive. In some pots the soil wasn't even totally dry yet and this was so scary, to be touching soil that had been carefully dampened by his mom who was dead.

Alvin skipped downstairs and went into the living room to watch him.

"I'm gonna get rid of these ones that died," said Eliot.

"Phew," said Alvin, gazing into a vase of flowers. "These died, that's for sure. They stink."

Eliot stopped watering. "Jesus. You just reminded me."

He bounded up to his room and flung open the door, bracing himself. But he smelled nothing. Nothing except maybe a dusty smell, a musty smell, because the room had been shut up for all those days. He got down on the floor and looked under the bed.

And it was gone. The shoe box with the bird in it was gone. Eliot hunkered back on his heels, thinking. This was weird. This was very weird. It was making the skin on the back of his neck shrivel up. He looked carefully around his room. There was his school stuff on the desk. His restaurant apron folded up on the chair. His rollerblades in the corner, and his guitar up on the chest of drawers where Rosie couldn't get to it. Maybe he'd buried the bird and forgotten about it.

Alvin leaned into the room, hanging on to the edges of the doorway. "I'm gonna do some exploring around here. Okay?"

"Are you crazy?" Eliot got up and took a last look around his bedroom. "No it's not okay. What if somebody saw you?"

"I'm real good at sneakin' around. But anyway, so what if they did?" said Alvin, following him back downstairs.

"This is a small town," Eliot said. "Somebody would say, 'Hey, who's that kid, never seen that kid around here before.' And they'd start poking around and pretty soon we'd look up and see somebody staring in the window at us."

"I'm bored," Alvin complained, throwing himself on the sofa.

"So watch TV," said Eliot, and he picked up the watering can.

Alvin turned on the set and Eliot finished watering the plants. Then he threw out the dead ones, and the dead flowers, into a black plastic garbage bag.

"We're going to leave here tomorrow," he told Alvin, digging around in the closet, looking for his dad's camera.

"And we'll sell the stuff," said Alvin, "and get that bus to wherever. Yea."

Eliot turned to say something to him and saw that he was coloring, with Rosie's crayons, in Rosie's coloring book, his black hair flopped over his eyes while he concentrated. Eliot felt sick, as if he was going to throw up. He struggled to his feet and leaned against the wall. *Oh God please God dear God please let her be alive please let my sister be alive. . . .* Eliot didn't care if he never got to see Rosie again, ever in his entire life. *Oh God please let her be alive just please let her be alive. . . .*

Eliot went into the kitchen, to the telephone that sat on the countertop, a plain black one, and in his mind he saw Rosie sitting cross-legged on the floor, talking on the phone to her friend Ginny, and for a minute he couldn't do it, couldn't pick up the receiver. And when he finally did, there was no dial tone.

"I can't deal with this," he said. He put the receiver down. "I gotta go out for a minute." Alvin looked up quickly, his eyes big, those lines raking across his forehead. "You stay here," said Eliot. "I'll be right back."

He hurried out of the house and across the back lawn and through the trees to the clearing, where he stood for several moments with his gaze fixed on the horizon. Finally he looked down at the beach. It was clean. He had known it would be clean. He blinked tears from his eyes. He'd make the call tomorrow. From a pay phone. On the way to the ferry. Or maybe he'd get Alvin to do it.

Eliot turned and walked back to the house. Halfway there he realized that it was raining again.

Alvin hadn't budged. He was sitting in the easy chair with the TV tray in front of him, still holding the same orange crayon in his fist.

"You've gotta have a bath," said Eliot.

"Now?" said Alvin, dismayed.

"Not now. Later. After we eat." Eliot went over to the cupboards, to see what there was to eat . . . and from the kitchen window he saw a police car bouncing slowly along the track, splashing through the puddles. "Holy shit," said Eliot.

He didn't panic, though. The cops knew the house was empty, so they were keeping an eye on it, that made sense.

But he turned swiftly around, and told Alvin to hide. Eliot rushed into the living room and quickly turned off the TV and Alvin ran upstairs.

From his hiding place behind his dad's big chair, Eliot heard the police car come to a stop in the turnaround. He heard the door open and shut. He heard somebody walking, slow, and figured after a minute that the guy must be walking clear around the house. This was good. He was right, then, Eliot told himself, they were checking the place out, probably did this on some kind of regular basis.

But then he heard the guy at the back door. He knocked a couple of times, and then tried the door—which of course wasn't locked anymore—and opened it. Oh god oh jesus, thought Eliot, crouched behind the chair, his eyes shut tight. He didn't move. He heard the policeman come inside, into the kitchen.

"Eliot?"

Eliot's heart lunged and stopped beating for a while, and he wasn't doing any breathing either.

"Eliot Gardener."

It was like the voice of doom, right there in his own living room. Eliot opened his eyes and looked at the back of the easy chair, which he saw was less worn and faded than the front. Then, slowly, he stood up.

Oh jesus jesus, thought Eliot, looking across the room at the policeman, who was huge, and very stern-looking. Oh jesus what now? The cop was wearing the hat and the uniform and he had a radio and a pair of handcuffs and a gun and the whole nine yards.

The cop stood there for a minute and then he moved slowly into the living room and sat down on the sofa. Trying to be casual. "Hi," he said. "Where's your friend?"

Eliot couldn't speak. He willed himself not to look behind the cop at Alvin, who was slipping out of the stairwell into the kitchen.

"You guys are in big trouble," the policeman was saying. But to Eliot he sounded pleased with himself.

As Alvin advanced across the kitchen Eliot felt his eyes bugging out of their sockets. He was frozen. He could make no decision, could make no move, could only watch as Alvin raised Eliot's guitar and brought it crashing down on the policeman's skull.

Sid Sokolowski staggered to his feet, and one hand went protectively to his holstered weapon while the other went to his head. Then he reached out and grabbed his assailant by the front of his sweatshirt.

"Yes!" shouted Alvin. "Go!"

Sid looked quickly across the room. The front door stood open, and Eliot Gardener was gone.

— — —

*In the school gymnasium, big black cut-outs of human figures doing exercises and throwing balls were stuck to the walls. The big room was filled with people. Betty heard shreds of their conversation, comments about her good coat and the blue woolen hat she wore, about her gloves and her handbag, and about her size. She began shaking her head gently from side to side, distorting the voices before they reached her ears.*

*A man appeared on the stage and said he was the principal. He introduced the teachers. From throughout the audience they popped to their feet and bobbed their heads and sat quickly back down again. Betty tried to get a good look at them, but couldn't; they popped up and down too fast, like jackrabbits.*

*Finally the principal stopped talking, and the people got up and began moving toward the doors in a buzz of talking that became a roar, and again the undercurrent was there, the thorny undercurrent that spoke of Betty in rasping whispers. She moved, helpless, with the throng out into the hall. Sweat was pouring down her scalp, and she wished she could take off her coat, only the dress underneath it was dirty, somewhat dirty. Her feet hurt in her rubber boots, which were too small for her.*

*She found the classroom of Heather's teacher. There were two people already waiting. Betty peered inside.*

*And instantly, with a tremendous shock, she knew that this was not a room in which Heather spent much time. If Heather had spent a lot of time there, Betty would have been able to smell her. And she couldn't smell her.*

*The teacher was sitting at a long table, talking earnestly to a man and woman sitting opposite her. A sign on the table said* MISS JORGENSON.

*Why had she not called Betty to tell her that Heather was not coming to school? Probably she had craftily waited, not saying anything about Heather's absences, until Betty showed up for this, the parent-teacher conference, so that she could confront her with it face-to-face.*

*Betty played with the clasp on her handbag. Could they blame her for it? For Heather not going to school? Could they?*

*Time sped past, then, as it sometimes did, so fast that Betty had to hang on to the edge of the doorway so as not to be swept away by it—and it was suddenly her turn.*

*"Hello," smiled Miss Jorgenson.*

*"Hello!" said Betty jovially.*

*"I teach one of your children, do I?"*

*Betty laughed. "Heather! Her name is Heather."*

*"Oh yes, Heather. She's a lovely child, Mrs. Coutts." The teacher shuffled through some papers on the table. "She is doing just fine. She's a bright little girl, a hard worker. About the only comment I have to make other than that is that she's very quiet."*

*"That's good!" Betty was enormously relieved. The teacher hadn't even noticed that Heather wasn't often here! Because she was so quiet!*

*"But perhaps she's too quiet," said Miss Jorgenson seriously. "She doesn't spend much time talking to the*

*other children. She keeps to herself. Is she like that at home? Does she have many friends in the neighborhood?"*

*"Oh yes, yes, she has many friends, many."*

*Betty was very tense. She hadn't known what it would be like to meet a teacher. She didn't like it, she decided.*

*"And why should it matter," she said to the teacher, "if she's quiet? There are a lot of quiet people in the world. They are quiet so that other people can be heard."*

*She was sweating profusely. She could feel drops on her forehead and knew that in a minute they would begin to fall down the front of her head and be seen. There were murmurings in the line of waiting parents; she could feel their breath. She reached behind her and made swatting motions.*

*"I see," said Miss Jorgenson, her smile gone. "Mrs. Coutts—"*

*But Betty had gotten up from the chair. She pushed through the people who were waiting in the doorway and in the hall she leaned against the wall and stood on one foot and then the other, easing the pain in one and then the other. Occasionally a parent or two parents together scuttled out of a classroom and headed for the front door of the school. As people came out of the classroom Betty had been in they looked at her strangely, and she knew they were talking about her. A man in a pair of overalls, carrying a big mop and a pail with a wringer thing on it, sauntered down the hall, whistling. He was short and bent over, and he had gray hair. He nodded to Betty as he passed, which startled her.*

*She decided to go home.*

*On the way, as she hurried along in her too-tight rubbers, huddled into her coat, clutching her handbag, she thought about that classroom, a room where*

*Heather hardly ever went, and Betty wondered, urgently, What does she do, then, when she's supposed to be going to school? Where does she go every morning, if not to school?*

# 23

"What happened to your head?" said Alberg to Sokolowski, who was standing in his doorway.

"I got one of them."

"One of what?"

"One of those damn kids. Out at the Gardener house. I told you he was gonna come home. Didn't I tell you?"

"Which one did you get?" Alberg asked, taking off his reading glasses.

"The other one," said the sergeant reluctantly. "Name of Alvin Hobbes."

"And what about Eliot?"

Sokolowski's expression grew sullen. "He got away. While I was grabbing hold of the other kid. By the time I got this one to the car, he was long gone."

"Shit," Alberg muttered. "Okay. Let's move on. Get the word out to the ferries."

"Yeah. Right away."

"And what do we know about Alvin?"

"He's ten. A chronic runaway."

201 — STRANGERS AMONG US

"Anything else?"

"Nah. All he does is run away from home. I've called Social Services. They're sending someone over to take him back to the detention center."

"What the hell is he doing in a detention center, anyway?" said Alberg irritably.

"Waiting to be assigned to a foster home, probably."

Alberg studied the bandage that adorned the right side of Sokolowski's head. "Now tell me what happened."

The sergeant lifted his hand to touch it, delicately. "It's nothing. A cut. Isabella put this on it. You want to talk to this little shit, while I do the ferries?"

When Alberg and Sokolowski got to the interview room, Constable Henry Loewen was standing by the door watching Alvin Hobbes and wearing an expression of intense interest. Alvin was sitting in a metal chair, and the loudest sound in the room was the sound of his breathing, harsh and rasping.

"You been running, Alvin?" said Alberg.

The kid didn't reply, didn't even look at him. He seemed unable to sit still. His feet were jiggling, or tapping, or kicking. His hands were in almost constant motion, too. He'd shake them, as if he'd just held them under a water tap. Or he'd squeeze them together. Or move the fingers around as if he were playing a piano. And his eyes traveled continuously around the room, yet with a gaze so blank and aimless that Alberg wondered if the kid's vision was impaired.

"Hobbes," said the sergeant, turning to leave. "I think that's a Limey name," he said disapprovingly, to no one in particular.

"Are you okay, Alvin?" said Alberg. "You're having trouble breathing. You got a cold, maybe?"

"Ezma," said Alvin promptly. "I got ezma."

Alberg sat down opposite him, in another scuffed metal chair. "You've got what?"

"Ezma." Alvin's gaze rested on Alberg's face for an instant, then scurried away.

"Ah," said Alberg, nodding. "Asthma."

"Yeah." He was kicking the leg of the table now.

"I'm Staff Sergeant Alberg." He held out his hand to Alvin, who looked at it incredulously and then slowly stuck out his own, which was completely enveloped in Alberg's grasp for about a second, until he pulled it away.

The sun was going to shine on Madeline Jaworski's funeral, Enid observed, looking out from her bedroom window as she readied herself for the event. She dressed with care, as always, in a navy suit, a pale pink blouse, a navy hat with a cluster of tiny pink roses at the front, and navy pantyhose and pumps. She had made her selections automatically, however, almost absently, her mind not on the task at hand.

Madeline Jaworski had once been on a bowling team with Bernie, so Enid knew that Bernie would be attending the funeral, too.

It was a cold day, though sunny, and Enid decided as she pulled on a pair of navy kid gloves that she would take her car.

Bernie was there ahead of her, talking to a group of people Enid didn't recognize. Enid joined another group, and looked discreetly among them, fantasizing about a new romance . . . then realized that this, too, she was doing absently, because it was what she always did, not because it was at this moment something she felt like doing.

People had begun to fill up the chapel, and Bernie was trying to catch her eye. Enid pretended not to have seen her: today she preferred to sit alone. But when she slipped into a pew, Bernie caught up to her and slid in beside her, occupying the aisle seat.

"Now this is what I call a good turnout," said Bernie, scanning the assemblage with satisfaction. "The whole bowling league's here. Not to mention the church crowd, Madeline was busy as a bee with her church work. Plus those Eastern Star types." Bernie dusted her hands and gave a little shudder. "Can't stand those Eastern Star types."

"Madeline was one of them," Enid pointed out.

"Yeah." Bernie sighed. "There's just no accounting for some things." She was wearing the same outfit she'd had on at the Gardeners' funerals, Enid noticed, and experienced a familiar pang of guilt because she had more material wealth than Bernie.

The organ music swelled to a climax and came to a stop, and the minister began talking. At least he had actually known Madeline, Enid thought. Everybody here had known her. Had memories of her, and a certain amount of affection for her. Well, most people, anyway. Some had no doubt come for the free food.

Enid leaned close to Bernie and whispered in her ear. "Yesterday I found a gun."

Bernie jerked away from her, stared at her in amazement. "What?"

"Shhhh." Enid gazed attentively at the minister, her gloved hands folded in her lap, on top of her small flat navy handbag.

"What?" said Bernie again, in a whisper, this time.

"A gun," said Enid, barely mouthing it.

A ripple of appreciative laughter spread through the pews: the minister had related a story about an embarrassing moment Madeline had once created for him.

"What kind of a—what kind of a one?" Bernie hissed. She was perched tensely on the edge of the pew, clutching her black plastic purse close to her.

"Medium-sized," whispered Enid. She lifted her index fingers and from her lap, measured the air.

Bernie looked at Enid's handbag, and then, in horror, at Enid's face. "Is it—?" she said, pointing at the handbag.

Enid shook her head, frowning. "Don't be ridiculous." Then she almost giggled at the thought of it, of herself so primly properly dressed in navy and pale pink standing, suddenly, opening her bag, saying to the people whose heads would have turned to stare at her, "Excuse me," taking out the gun and shooting it. She glanced up at the hideous light fixtures that adorned the ceiling. Not a bad idea, she thought.

"Where?" said Bernie.

"I put it back exactly where I found it," said Enid.

"No, I mean, where was it, when you found it?"

The woman directly in front of Bernie tilted her head toward them and made a sound of irritation.

"Shhh," said Enid to Bernie.

They faced front. Enid put on an earnest expression, meant to signify a warm personal interest in the minister's discourse. She glanced at Bernie, whose face seemed more corrugated with wrinkles than ever, and who was chewing industriously on the inside of her mouth, a habit she'd been trying for months—maybe years—to break.

Enid, amazed by her wickedness, leaned toward Bernie again and said, her lips inches from Bernie's ear, "I found it in my lodger's underwear drawer," and then she had to grab Bernie's arm to prevent her from springing to her feet.

The second after the guitar came down on the cop's head, Eliot had been at the front door, turning the catch, tugging it open. He heard Alvin yell, "Yes! Go!" and he felt like he was doing it for both of them when he sprinted away from the house, away from the sea, up the track, and then off into the bush.

Eliot ran until he couldn't run another step. Then he sank to his knees. There was a rich, powerful scent in the air that he knew was fallen leaves, forest stuff rotting, feeding the soil. He stayed on his knees for a long time, panting, his hands leaning heavily on his thighs, until the roaring in his ears stopped and his breath was coming more slowly. He was warm, because he'd been running, but the fallen leaves beneath his knees were soggy from the rain and he knew he was going to be very cold any minute now; he only had a T-shirt on over his jeans.

Eliot decided almost in spite of himself to return to the house: he couldn't think what else to do. He wouldn't stay there—he wasn't that stupid—but he had to get stuff, clothes, and food. He knew the cop might have called another cop to come and take Alvin away while the first one stayed there in case Eliot showed up again. But he decided that even if they thought he might go back, they wouldn't expect him to do it this soon. They'd figure he'd keep on running for a while, maybe break in to some house and steal what he needed. So the quicker he returned, he told himself, the better.

He got up and made his way back along the trail he'd left through the forest—which was another reason for going back, he thought. When they came after him, they'd follow his trail and it would just end there, all of a sudden, there in the middle of the woods.

When he got to the house he skirted it, cautiously, slipping from tree to tree. The cop car was gone, which was a good sign. The front door was closed. Eliot went around to the back, where he thought there was less chance he'd be seen, and went inside.

His guitar lay smashed on the floor. The crayons and coloring book were on the floor, too—scattered there when Alvin upset the TV tray in his haste to flee upstairs. The cop had probably heard that, Eliot thought.

He couldn't believe how little time had passed since he looked out the window and saw that cop car.

Despite the bright sun that had suddenly started to shine, Eliot was afraid. He was afraid of the house but even more, he was afraid of the beach that was so near. Terrified that if he were to go back down there again and stand in the clearing and look down, this time it wouldn't be clean; this time there'd be blood there, rivers of it. . . .

He stumbled blindly upstairs, his heart hammering, and shoved his door open—couldn't let himself think about it *couldn't let himself think*—pulled off his clothes, shivering now, and put on dry socks, dry jeans, a T-shirt, and a sweatshirt over it.

Then he made himself go into his parents' room, because he'd remembered that sometimes his dad left money—change from his pockets—on the lopsided night table that was on his side of the bed. And yeah, there was—Eliot scooped it up, not bothering to count it: a handful of change and some bills, folded; the one he could see was a twenty, good.

He rushed downstairs, almost tripping in his hurry, and pulled on his denim jacket and the wool gloves that were Alvin's. Then he grabbed Alvin's knapsack and hastily filled it with cans and boxes from the kitchen cupboard and pop cans from the fridge. He remembered to take a can opener, too, and a spoon.

Eliot, standing in the doorway, ready to leave, looked around him and felt himself to be a foreigner, somebody dropped someplace where nobody knew him and he couldn't speak the language.

What am I doing? he thought. And there was no answer to that.

So Eliot picked up the rolled-up sleeping bag and grabbed the overloaded knapsack and left.

# 24

"It would be good if I could stay here," said Alvin, swinging his legs. He was hanging on to the seat of his chair, and his eyes were scrawling expansive messages all over the walls and ceiling of the interrogation room.

"Why?" said Alberg, and Alvin shrugged.

"What's gonna happen to Eliot?" the boy asked suddenly. "If you catch him. You might not catch him. But if you do."

"I don't know, Alvin. That depends on a bunch of things."

"Like what?"

"Like if he turns himself in. Things would be better for him if he did that."

Alvin's black hair flopped across his forehead as he bounced in his chair. "So what's gonna happen to me?"

"If the woman from Social Services gets here in time, she'll take you back to Vancouver. Otherwise she'll find you a foster home for the night, and take you back in the morning."

"I hate foster homes."

"How come you run away from your own home, then?"

"Oh, well," said Alvin vaguely, kicking the table leg. "I'm pretty hungry, by the way."

"We can do something about that," said Alberg, standing up. "Come on." He took Alvin by the hand. "We'll be at Earl's," he told Henry Loewen, "if anybody asks."

He noticed, as he unlocked his car and got Alvin belted into the passenger seat, that Jack Coutts' truck was nowhere to be seen, and he allowed himself a cautious surge of hope.

When Enid got home from the funeral she went straight upstairs to change into a long robe and a pair of matching slippers. It wasn't a bathrobe, it was a comfortable but elegant garment to wear in the house instead of a sweatsuit. She believed that she looked trim in her sweatsuits but today she wished to feel not trim, but elegant.

She cleaned her teeth, washed her face, and brushed her soft gray curls. It was almost dinnertime but she wasn't hungry, even though she hadn't been able to enjoy any of the refreshments after the funeral. Bernie hadn't let her. Bernie had hauled her out of there right after the service, then climbed into the car after her—well, Enid had to admit that she'd brought this behavior on herself. If she'd only kept her mouth shut about the damned gun. . . .

"What is he doing with a gun!" Bernie had said, almost shouting it, as soon as they were both in Enid's car.

Enid had immediately turned on the motor and started driving, in a hurry to get Bernie home. "I don't know what he's doing with it for heaven's sake. Maybe it's some kind of souvenir."

"Souvenir of what!"

"I told you," Enid said, "I don't know—maybe he was in a war somewhere. God knows there've been enough of them."

"I have a bad feeling about this, Enid, a very bad feeling, a very very bad feeling."

"Oh, Bernie. I just told you about it to be mischievous. I'm not the slightest bit alarmed. He probably does target practicing," she added, "as a hobby."

Bernie was staring hard at the side of her face. "You know your trouble, Enid, every bit as well as I do, and that's men, where men are concerned you've got no sense whatsoever, no good judgment whatsoever."

Enid stopped the car in front of Bernie's house. "Well what do you suggest I do?" she said, exasperated.

"Give the man his notice!" said Bernie, raising her voice again.

Enid turned to look at her. "I will consider it," she said, with dignity.

Bernie had a lot more to say, but it was really the same message repeated again and again, with only minor variations. Finally she stopped, and directed her gaze out through the windshield. "If you haven't given him notice by this time tomorrow, Enid," she said, "I'm going to take the matter up with Staff Sergeant Alberg."

"Oh for heaven's sake," Enid muttered, nearing the end of her rope.

"There are laws in this country," Bernie announced sonorously, "about the possession of weapons. And I bet he's broke them all, keeping that thing in a drawer with his underwear, in an underwear drawer in somebody else's house for pete's sake, without telling them it's there." She looked at Enid truculently. "I will telephone you tomorrow afternoon, Enid, and if you don't answer, I will assume you're dead, shot to death in your own kitchen. And if you do answer, and you tell me you haven't given your lodger notice, then I will march myself straight over to Mr. Alberg."

Enid, powdering her nose, dismissed her friend's warnings.

She descended two floors and tapped on Jack Coutts' door.

• • •

The sky had been entirely cleared of clouds, and as the sun descended into the ocean Eliot realized that with the change in the weather had come a substantial drop in temperature. He wasn't going to be able to sleep outside anymore. He almost wept, then, because if things had worked out the way he'd expected he'd have been sleeping in his own bed again this very night. Now he'd have to wait until it was real late, then prowl around the town and look for a place where he could be warm and dry and safe for a few hours, and maybe get some sleep.

Meanwhile, he was huddled against the trunk of a big old tree out in the middle of the woods somewhere, he wasn't exactly sure where, wrapped in the sleeping bag, the knapsack next to him. He'd eaten tinned spaghetti and some stale chips and drunk a can of Pepsi and was now trying to think through his situation.

His dad had left thirty-seven dollars on the bedside table. This was at least a start on the bus fare to Nova Scotia. But he had to spend some of it on a ferry ticket.

There were really two parts to his situation. The first part, getting back to Vancouver, that was the hardest part. He'd have to go around the town somehow, and get a long way toward Gibsons before trying to hitchhike. In fact it would be a whole lot safer to walk the entire way, which would take him a couple of days . . . but there'd be cops looking for him everywhere. Including on the ferry. So maybe it'd be better to hitchhike. And then on the ferry he could maybe hide on the car deck while the people who'd picked him up went to the cafeteria or whatever, and meet them back at their car when they got to Horseshoe Bay. And he could hide his face behind a newspaper or something when they drove off the ferry.

And the second part, that was getting from Vancouver to Nova Scotia. Maybe he could get another busboy job, make enough money that way. But where could he live while he did this? And how could he get some kind of disguise happening? This situation, thought Eliot, this two-part situation, it was pretty hopeless. And he shook his head, holding back tears.

But, yeah, he'd done a pretty good job as a busboy, so there was that, at least. He saw himself at Earl's, cleaning tables, and doing dishes, and sweeping up in the storage area that was in the back. The café was closed from ten o'clock at night until six in the morning, he remembered. He wondered if it might be possible to get himself in there.

Eliot yearned for the place, suddenly, because it was familiar, because it was a place he'd made partly his own. So after ten, he'd check it out. There was a small window, high in the wall. And he knew Earl didn't have an alarm. He was starting to feel a little bit more optimistic.

Meanwhile, though, his teeth were chattering with the cold, despite the sleeping bag. He'd better walk some more, get himself warmed up. The daylight was almost gone but maybe there'd be moonlight, if he could just get himself out from under these trees, onto a beach maybe. Eliot stood up and put the knapsack back on, and doubled the sleeping bag and draped it over his shoulders, and set off in the general direction of the sea.

## 25

Alberg had let his coffee grow cold while he watched Alvin devour one of Earl's jumbo hamburgers with fries and gulp down two glasses of milk and a Coke. Alvin's attention had been so wholly on his food that he hadn't been moving around much more than would a regular kid. But now he finished a second Coke and pushed the glass away, and immediately started bouncing on his chair. Alberg had an image of the kid asleep in his bed, eyes shut, bouncing.

Alvin squinted up at the clock. "What time does the ferry go?"

"Last one's at eight-thirty," said Alberg.

"That's pretty late for a ten-year-old kid to be up, you know," said Alvin, hanging on to the sides of the table. "I mean, I wouldn't get to bed till, like—when?"

"The ferry takes thirty-five minutes, another thirty to the detention center—you'd be in bed before ten."

"Wow. That's late," said Alvin, shaking his head, his unfocused gaze voyaging all over the café.

"How come your clothes are so dirty?" said Alberg.

Alvin looked at him straight on for a second, and Alberg wondered again how much of all this hyperactivity was an act.

"Well we been sleepin' outside, haven't we? Whaddya expect?"

A woman hurried into the café, looked around, and approached their table. "I'm Rebecca Webster," she said. "Social Services."

"Karl Alberg. And this is Alvin. Sit down, Ms. Webster."

She pulled out a chair and sat. "I'm going to take you to a house in Sechelt for the night, Alvin."

Alvin's hands were drumming the tabletop, quietly, and one of his restless feet suddenly hit Alberg in the knee. He said, "Argh." Alberg didn't know if that indicated assent, or dismay, or apology.

Rebecca Webster, a plump woman of about forty, had a lot of thick brown hair, a pink complexion, and a very steady gaze. She spoke slowly, directly to Alvin. "In this house lives a mother, and a father, and two kids, both of them a lot older than you."

Alvin said something that sounded to Alberg like "Goop!" and picked up his hands and waved them around in the air.

"Also in this house," said Rebecca Webster, lifting her hand, "is a cat"—she placed the palm of her hand against one of Alvin's—"and there is also a dog"—their hands, still touching, descended slowly to the tabletop—"a little dog, very friendly"—and Alvin's hand lay quiet, while Rebecca Webster stroked it with her fingertips—"who when she walks across the kitchen floor makes a click-click-click sound with her nails, and you know what?"

Alvin shook his head.

"She sounds just like a little guy wearing tap-dancing shoes."

"I know what those are," said Alvin. "My aunt had some."

"I've got the paperwork with me," said Rebecca Webster to Alberg. "It's a good place. He'll be fine there."


There was no response when Enid tapped on her lodger's door. She knew he was there, because his truck was parked outside. She arranged the folds of her robe while she waited. Finally, though, she realized that he wasn't going to answer her knock, so she turned the handle and pushed open the door.

He was lying on his bed. Again, there was a light on in the living room but the bedroom was dark. Enid had the impression that he had been lying there for a long time—not sleeping, since his hands were behind his head—thinking. She couldn't see his face.

"Mr. Coutts," she said softly, and heard the rustle of the pillowcase as he turned his head.

"What do you want?" he said flatly.

"Will you tell me about your daughter?"

Enid had clasped her hands in front of her and was standing in the doorway, not yet having received permission to enter. She waited for a long time.

Finally he got off the bed—slowly, as if it hurt to do this, and Enid felt it empathetically in her own joints, the ache of moving again after being still for a long time. He got up and came around the bed until he was close to her, facing her. She could smell his breath, which was stale, and saw that he hadn't shaved today.

He took her face in his two hands. "I killed her."

But Enid knew this couldn't be true, unless it had been an accident; there was too much pain in his eyes. "No," she said. He was still cupping her face with his hands: Enid felt like a rose about to be plucked.

"Have you ever killed anyone?" he said.

"No," she said.

He continued to look intently into her face; she had no idea what he saw there. Finally he let her go, and sat down on the edge of the bed.

"The man knows fuck-all," he said. "But he was right about one thing. For twelve years I watched her die."

Enid let herself sink quietly into the high-backed chair. He was staring at the doorway that led to the living room. A streak of light fell softly across the threshold, beckoning. But they stayed in the shadowy bedroom.

"I had this fantasy," he said. "That I'd be sitting in the chair next to her bed, with the television on, and all of a sudden something would touch my hand. I'd turn, and I'd see that she had touched me. I'd see that her eyes were open, and she was starting to smile at me. This is what kept me going." He took a deep, irregular breath, and scoured his face with his hands. "But when I dreamed about it—in the dream, when she wakes up and touches me, her eyes are empty; in the dream I see nothing in her eyes but her dead brain." He turned his head slightly in Enid's direction. "It's a funny thing, time. Sometimes it doesn't move at all. Then one day you look up, and a dozen years have passed."

He stood and moved to the doorway, looking into the living room. "When I did it, when I told them to pull the plug, I was afraid she'd breathe on her own. Like the Quinlan girl."

He turned to look at her. Enid felt the light on her face, but his was in darkness.

"She didn't, though," he said.

He went to the door, and opened it wider. "I think you should go now, Mrs. Hargreaves."

Enid, her head bowed, rose from the chair and exited.

Eliot's gloves were getting shredded and his entire body was shaking with cold. He was climbing an enormous pile of rocks that had just suddenly appeared, right in front of him. He could hardly see a damn thing—there was just a thin little strip of moon in the sky, plus a whole bunch of stars. He wished he'd thought to stick the flashlight in the knapsack. It was a struggle trying to hang on to the sleeping bag because he really needed to use both hands for climbing.

There were no houses nearby, which is why he'd headed off in this direction, but of course that meant no lights were shining anywhere and that's how he'd ended up climbing the damn rocks. Now he heaved himself to the top and saw that he was on a ridge. Below him was a shelf of rock, and below that—a house. He could just make out the shape of it. There were no lights on inside, so he figured nobody was home. He wondered hopefully if there might be a shed or something behind it, a place for him to hole up in until it was time to check out Earl's.

Eliot carefully dropped the sleeping bag onto the rock shelf, and followed it, the straps of the backpack digging into his shoulders. Then he tossed it onto the lawn of the house, and climbed down.

He stood still for a minute, listening hard; but all he could hear was the ocean—a familiar sound, and one that he found for the moment comforting.

He crept around to the backyard but there was nothing there, nothing at all, just the flat yard and then the forest again, and nothing on the other side of the house, either.

But in the front, facing the ocean, there was a little more light from the sky, enough for Eliot to see when he peered through a window that the house was vacant. And he was so cold by now that his hands and feet were getting numb.

He went back to where he'd climbed down from the shelf and found a good-sized rock. Then he circled the house again and selected the smallest window that he could get through. He took off the knapsack and his jacket, wrapped the rock in the jacket and struck at the window. But breaking it wasn't as easy as he'd expected. He had to clobber it twice. And as he wielded the second blow, suddenly furious with the glass for not shattering the first time, bringing his arm back, swinging it forward, his body remembered swinging the machete. . . .

"No!" Eliot cried. "No!"

The window broke, then, and he leaned against the house, panting, and smeared the bottom of his sweatshirt across his eyes. After a while he cleared the windowframe of broken glass, dropped the sleeping bag and the knapsack through, and climbed inside.

He found himself in a bathroom. In the hallway beyond, he closed the bathroom door to keep the cold air from coming into the rest of the house and made a slow circuit of the place, to make sure that it was truly unoccupied. And it was. There wasn't a stick of furniture in the whole house.

Eliot checked out all of the rooms and finally settled in what he decided must be the living room, because it had a fireplace. He spread the sleeping bag on the floor in a corner and sat down and looked out into the night, through a pair of big glass doors across the room. He was surprised by the amount of light that came in. It wasn't bright, and there weren't big rays of it, but the light generated by the stars and the sliver of a moon radiated, quietly, illuminating things with a gentleness that soothed him: the trees and the rocks outside, the wood floor and the white walls inside.

He opened the knapsack, intending to eat again. But either he wasn't hungry or he lacked the energy necessary to open a can—he didn't know which. Maybe he'd make himself something at Earl's, he thought, putting the knapsack aside.

Eliot let his mind turn to Alvin, now. He saw Alvin's floppy black hair, and his expression of perpetual astonishment; he heard him yell "Yes! Go!"

And Eliot had gone. Because he'd have had to abandon Alvin soon anyway.

He leaned his head back, to rest against the wall, and

blinked hard several times. Then he closed his eyes, concentrating on the sound the ocean made: it was closer, here, than it was at his own house. Eliot listened to it very hard, hoping it would wash away the hopelessness that crowded his heart.

— — —

*Betty heard the front door close and stood in the kitchen smiling and breathing and thinking about all the things there were to do and wondering which one of them she would do first.*

*And then she knew that Heather hadn't gone.*

*The whole house turned to watch her. She hurried to the front door and as she came into the hall she saw a flash of white disappearing up the stairway, saw it from the corner of her right eye, and felt the skin on the right side of her body wrinkle.*

*She heard a muffled sound from above and ran heavily up the stairs, calling, "Heather, Heather!"*

*A quiet giggle, she heard. The bathroom door was open; to the right, down the hall, Heather's door swung closed.*

*Betty went into the bathroom first. There was the little plastic bottle that kept her green headache pills; there it was lying beside the bathroom sink with its top off and it was empty, empty. The sink was all wet. She must have put them all down the drain, all my pills. Betty saw something flash in the mirror and looked quickly but there was nothing there, just the memory of a white flash. She ran down the hall to Heather's room and threw open the door.*

*The bed was not made. Betty saw the hollow in the pillow where the child's head had lain. The sheet and the blanket and the green-and-white-striped bedspread were thrown back and teddy bears lay there, sprawling,* twitching their limbs. Heather's clothes were scattered all over the floor; there was a pile of comic books on the floor beside the bed, pushed over like a deck of cards. The curtains were closed. Over everything in the room a gray light filtered, like the light inside a cave, or a big balloon.

Betty yanked open the door to the closet, where there were empty hangers and piles of clothes on the floor and boxes filled with games and handicrafts on the shelf. I have never seen her playing those games, thought Betty, never seen her making feather flowers or doing bead-work, but the boxes look worn, and they are put up there neatly, not like her clothes.

A scurrying sound came from the hall. She pushed herself out of the room. "I have a headache, Heather," she called, "and I need my pills, have you seen them, have you seen my pills?" Her voice echoed in the house, and the echo didn't sound like her at all. Could there be two Bettys in that house? Was there another Betty walking around somewhere?

She groped her way to her bedroom and lay down, and pulled the yellow spread right up over her head and looked through it. Everything was yellow and pleas-ant—that steady yellow light flowing down upon her like sunshine, like the heat of sunshine in a tropical country.

She heard a click, and the light went off . . .

. . . She stops breathing, sees a shadow over her bed-spread, over her, her poor heart is so terrified it starts beating loud and fast like a drum being struck by some-one, bang, bang, bang, and her heart becomes more and more terrified—she throws off the cover and sits up.

There is nobody there.

Heather has gone. She has stopped pounding on Betty's chest on Betty's heart and has gone.

*Betty sits soothing her heart, calming it, and as it calms, her head becomes very clear. She sits on her bed and laughs and laughs, and then calls out cheerily, "All right, Heather, I know you are here and I am coming to find you, just like in hide-and-seek."*

*She is very large.*

*She pats and strokes her chest to soothe her heart, and then she looms from the bed and strides from her room, ducking her head so as not to hit it on the top of the doorway. She walks, stooped, down the stairs, treading softly on the carpet in her red slippers. She doesn't make a single sound going down the stairs, and into the kitchen she goes, and right up to the door to the basement.*

*She stops there, just for a second. Then she reaches out her huge hand and the knob disappears into it and she opens the door, steps down onto the first basement stair, and closes the door behind her. She chuckles, and the chuckle booms down into the basement.*

*"I'm coming, Heather, I'm coming, you can't get past me I'll see you and stretch out my long arm and catch you by your white blouse."*

*Heather doesn't answer. Not even a laugh, not even a scuffle does Betty hear. Heather is nervous now, Betty knows; she will catch her, because she has no fear of the basement now, no fear at all.*

*She walks down the stairs one at a time. It is a long long flight of stairs, the basement is deep, miles deep beneath the house, beneath the earth, and there are no windows.*

*It is dark, so dark, and there are things flitting about in the darkness, bats and cobwebs slowly making their way toward her.*

*There are squeakings and rustlings and creakings, and she smells choking musty smells and sees huge boxes filled with things, the tops of the boxes slowly opening and shapes beginning to drift out. . . .* Why did I not turn on the light at the top of the stairs that was so stupid so stupid. . . .

*Her size is changing again. She is becoming small, smaller than Heather, and now she hears a tiny giggle and sees a flash of white, the collar of a blouse, the top pearl button of a blouse, the pale throat and chin above it, the gold chain winking on the throat—Heather has flitted behind one of the boxes, and one white hand is reaching up behind it to open the top of the box wider, to let the shapes drift out faster.*

*Betty turns around and starts crawling back up the stairs, each step so tall now. Little drifts of air chill the back of her neck; the things drifting through the air make small cold breezes that change her sweat to ice. She hears Heather laugh as she laughs when she is with a friend, or with Jack, only this time she laughs as she watches Betty crawling up the stairs.*

*The anger comes back in a tired spurt, but the oozing, floating things behind her are much stronger. Her knees hurt on the slivery wood of the stairs but she keeps going, eyes squeezed shut, hands clutching the edge of each stair, knees following one at a time . . . and now her hands bump something, she opens her eyes and sees a crack of light beneath a door, presses her hands against the concrete wall, pushes herself up, touches the doorknob, turns it, and falls into the kitchen.*

*She lies here on the floor; hears the laughter from below. Her face is pressed to the floor.*

*If I get up fast and slam the basement door and ram a chair under the handle she will be trapped down there.*

*She gets up and turns around, quickly—and Heather flashes around the corner from the basement into the living room*, I see you I see you, *she sees her yellow hair hanging over her white collar, sees her white skinny wrist disappear around the corner, hears the front door slam.*

Betty shuts the basement door and stands still, listening.

There is nothing in the house but her.

## Sunday, December 4

Enid sat at her bedroom window, looking out upon a cold, bright day. She watched the houses across the street, for signs of Sunday morning life. She observed the trees that lined the road, saw that they still wore a few of their bronzy leaves but that most were gone, heaped on the ground below or carted away by now to compost piles in backyard gardens. She admired the mountains in the near distance. They were sheathed in coniferous green, but the recent rains had been snowfalls at higher levels, and the mountaintops were white, now, blinding white against the blue glare of the sky. Enid sat, sipping coffee, clothed again in her elegant robe, and waited for her lodger to leave her.

And soon, he did.

He came around the house, wearing his red plaid jacket and a pair of jeans and some hiking boots—and sunglasses, which turned him into a stranger. And he carried his duffel bag, as she had known he would.

He climbed into his truck, let it warm up, and drove away. He didn't glance at the front of the house, or up at her window. He just drove away.

Enid sipped her coffee. The Jantzens, who lived directly opposite, emerged in their Sunday best and got into Hank Jantzen's four-by-four and disappeared down the street.

Enid considered calling Gloria. Perhaps they could arrange to meet, in Vancouver, and go to the art gallery, or have lunch at the Van Dusen Gardens.

A group of teenaged girls strolled down the block, smoking cigarettes and laughing. None of them looked warmly enough dressed. But they shook their long hair and spun their lithe bodies and lifted their laughing faces to the winter sun.

Enid stood up and took her coffee cup to the kitchen. From there she heard the washing machine, and went downstairs into the suite.

The bed had been stripped, the blankets and quilt neatly folded. The bureau drawers were empty, and the closet—the wire hangers looked forlorn and shivery.

No dishes had been left unwashed. The refrigerator and the food cupboards were empty. A small white plastic bag, secured with a twist-tie, sat on the table. This was his garbage, Enid surmised.

The shower curtain was wet. There were a few hairs in the tub, and a splotch of toothpaste in the sink. The towels were gone: they would be spinning around in the washing machine, with the sheets.

He had of course taken his alarm clock. And the photograph of his daughter.

He had paid two weeks' rent in advance, so he owed her no money—in fact Enid owed him some, two days' worth. But he hadn't left his address behind.

She sat down and folded her hands in her lap. It was very quiet down here. Very peaceful. Enid rested her head on the back of the love seat. The suite no longer smelled of paint, she realized.

· · ·

Alberg was on his way to the detachment, intending to make some phone calls before picking up Cassandra, who was having breakfast with her mother. He was approaching the intersection at the eastern edge of town when he saw Jack Coutts' pickup approaching opposite. There was no other traffic in any direction.

Alberg's Oldsmobile pulled up at the red light, facing west. The Silverado pulled up across the street, facing east. It wasn't a very wide street and Alberg could see Jack clearly, except for his eyes, which were hidden behind sunglasses.

Despite the surge of adrenaline, the realization that all his senses were on full alert, ludicrous parallels came to his mind. Gunfighters facing off on dusty streets, hands poised over their holsters—or in politer company, striding fifty paces from back-to-back positions before turning, calmly, to fire. Or swordsmen, touching the tips of their weapons in a bizarre salute before attempting to stab one another to death.

"Shit," he muttered, sitting in the Oldsmobile, motor running, staring across the street at Jack Coutts, who was sitting higher than Alberg in his brown Chevy Silverado.

The door of the Silverado opened, abruptly, and Jack stepped out onto the street. He looked across at Alberg and started walking toward him, picking up speed.

"Shit," said Alberg. He cut the motor, got out of his car, closed the door, and waited.

Coutts stopped about six feet away from him. The traffic light, Alberg noticed, was now green.

"You know why I came here?" said Jack. Alberg could see the tension in his shoulders, and his balled fists.

A car pulled up behind the Silverado, then cautiously drove around it and turned right, into town.

"No," said Alberg quietly. "Why did you come, Jack?"

"I came to shoot you, you sonofabitch."

Jack wrenched off his sunglasses, as if he were ripping off a bandage. Alberg saw that his hands were shaking. He wondered if he was going to have to arrest him.

"I came to shoot you dead."

He held no weapon, though, and none of his pockets sagged with the weight of a handgun.

"You had special responsibilities," said Jack, "because you're a goddamn cop." He punched the air. "Right? Right?"

A car pulled up behind the Oldsmobile. Alberg heard the driver tap lightly on the horn.

Jack turned away for a moment, and then back. "Or myself. Maybe I was going to shoot myself."

The car behind Alberg's Oldsmobile drove around it, slowly, the driver craning her neck to see what was going on.

"I don't know why I didn't do it," said Jack. "Why didn't I do it?"

Alberg watched him rub his face.

"Maybe I just don't have the guts." He sounded exhausted, now.

Jack looked Alberg directly in the eyes for a long time. Alberg felt this not as a challenge but as a legitimate, justifiable search, and he found himself trying to open his mind to Jack, trying to make available to him whatever he needed to know.

Finally, Jack said, dully, "Ah, fuck. There's been enough dying." He was silent for a while. Then he looked around him as if surprised to find himself there, in the middle of the street.

"Jack."

Jack looked at him. "I'm going home," he said. "I'm gonna pick up a coffee and drive home to Kamloops."

"Jack. I'm very sorry for your trouble."

Again, Coutts gazed intently into Alberg's eyes, then shook his head, put his sunglasses back on, and headed across the intersection.

Alberg got in his car, started the motor, and waited for the red light to become green again, and as he waited he watched Jack climb into the Silverado and drive away, turning right.

Jack parked in front of Earl's Café & Catering and climbed out. The restaurant was locked, although Earl was in there, sweeping the floor with a wide, black-bristled push-broom. The sound of his whistling could be heard out on the street. Jack knocked, and Earl came to the door.

"I don't open until noon on Sunday," he explained.

"Yeah, I just noticed the sign," said Jack. He took off his sunglasses. "You got coffee on yet? Could I get a cup to go? I'm about to hit the road."

Earl looked behind Jack, up and down the sidewalk, as if checking to make sure there wasn't a big crowd there waiting for a chance to rush in.

"Sure," he said. He held the door open for Jack, then locked it again. "The coffee's on, but it's not ready yet. Have a seat." He retrieved the broom from where he'd leaned it against the wall and resumed sweeping.

Jack dropped his sunglasses onto the counter. "Is there another broom somewhere? I'll give you a hand."

"You're kidding," said Earl. He saw, though, that the man was agitated, so maybe he needed to be active.

"No I'm not kidding. Through there?" said Jack, indicating a door next to the washrooms.

"Yeah," said Earl. He leaned on his broomhandle, watching, as Jack disappeared for a moment and returned with another one, a regular broom, a smaller one.

They swept in silence, and the job didn't take long, because Earl had already cleared the floor by putting the chairs upside down on top of the tables.

By the time they'd finished, the coffee was brewed. Earl filled two mugs while Jack put the chairs back down on the floor. "Here," said Earl, setting the mugs on one of the tables. "On the house."

"Thanks." Jack took off his jacket and arranged it on the back of a chair before he sat down.

"Where're you off to?" said Earl.

"Kamloops. Home." He sounded preoccupied.

"Oh yeah?" said Earl politely, sitting across from him. "Too bad. Just when we're getting some good weather."

"I didn't come here for the weather." Jack rubbed at his face.

"I remember you said you're in sales," said Earl. "Here on business, then?" He leaned back in his chair, enjoying the Sunday morning quiet. He took a glance at the clock and saw that he had half an hour to visit with the guy, if he felt like it.

Jack was looking at him, but not really seeing him. He kept on looking at him, until Earl started to feel nervous. Uneasy. Then Jack said, "I was gonna kill somebody."

Earl stiffened, and his skin prickled. He didn't say anything, just watched Jack, who was now looking at his coffee.

"You know," said Jack. "Revenge."

Earl thought: First the busboy, now this. . . .

"Yeah. Because of my daughter."

Earl wondered if he was going to have to call the cops. But the guy sounded tired, not mad. The floor creaked as he moved wearily in his chair.

"Yeah. My daughter . . ."

Earl snatched a hopeful glance through the windows, but saw nobody.

"Oh jesus," said Jack Coutts, rubbing his face again.

Earl watched him intently. Jack was slowly shaking his head. He looked as if he was going to cry. Which dismayed Earl. But it was better than if he shot somebody.

"I didn't know how she'd change," he said, and Earl had to lean forward, to hear him. His voice kept catching on itself. "I didn't know her arms and legs would get so thin, would get to be . . . matchsticks. Pulled up against her body."

Earl tried to imagine what the guy was seeing in his head, but then he stopped, because it was something he really didn't want to behold. "Listen," he said hesitantly. "Do you want something? Can I get you something? Something to eat?"

"I thought she'd be quiet and peaceful," said Jack, "like she'd gone to sleep. I thought that was what a coma *was.* I didn't know she'd make noises."

Earl sank back in his chair and gave a little sigh.

"They said she didn't feel any pain," said Jack. "But she sounded like she was in pain."

"She wasn't, though," Earl said earnestly. "I'm sure she wasn't. Yeah."

"One chance in a million," said Jack. "That's what they told me, at the beginning." He leaned forward urgently. "That meant—to me, that meant that it wasn't impossible."

"Yeah. That gave you hope," said Earl.

"But it *was* impossible. All along, it was impossible." Jack raised his hands, palms down, fingers spread. "Look. See that? See that shaking? Shit." He put them in his lap. "I read a bunch of books. The books said, talk to her. So I talked to her. I touched her. I brushed her hair."

Earl shivered.

"She was *there,* do you understand? There. Year after year she changed, she got less and less like herself. But she was still *there.*"

Tears had filled his eyes and spilled out. Earl tore paper napkins out of the dispenser and pushed them into his hand.

"As long as she was still there, and alive—" Jack wiped his face. He breathed in, hard, and out. "And then one day I'm sitting there, next to her bed, and the little TV's on, and I think, 'What am I doing here—going for the record?' " He looked at Earl. His face was wet, his eyes red and puffy. "There was a woman, she was in a coma from 1941 until 1978. She died then. After thirty-seven years."

Earl was leaning on the table, his chin in his hand. He made an exclamation of disbelief.

"And another one," Jack said, "she lasted from 1960 until 1977."

Earl sat back, shaking his head.

"So I looked at her lying there, and I thought jesus christ, twelve years is long enough."

He stopped talking then. He held up his hands, which were still shaking, and put them back in his lap.

Earl reached across the table and patted Jack's shoulder several times.

A while later, Jack held up his hands again. "Huh," he said. "Steady enough to drive." He stood up and put on his jacket, took gloves from the pockets and pulled them on, too.

"You didn't drink your coffee," said Earl. "I'll get you some to go," and he did this, while Jack waited at the door, putting on his sunglasses.

"Thanks," said Jack, taking the coffee from him.

Earl watched through the window as Jack climbed into his truck and drove away. Then he sat down at the table again and sipped cold coffee, staring out the window. Finally he wiped his eyes with a napkin, took the coffee mugs behind the counter, and put on his big white apron.

Who'd he want revenge from? Earl wondered.


"He's gone?" said Cassandra doubtfully.

Alberg shrugged. "Yeah. I think so."

"I hope you're right."

Cassandra looked out the passenger window as he drove: they were going back to have another look at the house, before making an offer. It was such a bright day that it made her eyes hurt.

"When you were yelling at each other," she said, "out on the street the other day, in front of the library." She turned to him, shading her eyes with her hand. "I was thinking, who will I call if they start hitting each other? See, a person usually calls the cops in a situation like that."

"Yeah, yeah," said Alberg uncomfortably. "Don't rub it in. How's your mother?"

"She got a little breathless at one point," said Cassandra, gazing past Alberg at the ocean, which was visible through gaps in the forest. "But she assured me that she'll live through Christmas and the wedding. Beyond that she's not making any promises."

Cassandra's mother had been having spells of breathlessness, due to a mysteriously faulty heart, for two decades.

"The wedding," said Alberg in disbelief. "Hmmm. What kind of an event is it going to be, the wedding?"

"It'll be whatever we want it to be."

"Hmmm."

"Karl," said Cassandra.

"Yeah?" He glanced at her. "What?"

"I think you'd better tell me what it was all about. That man in the truck."

He signaled, turned off the highway onto the gravel road, and drove slowly down the hill. He pulled up next to the house and cut the motor. They sat without speaking, listening to the ticking of the cooling engine, and the soughing of the sea.

He hadn't been completely sure that Maura wasn't having an affair. This made discussion of their situation delicate. Difficult. There had to be more to it than her goddamn boutique, he thought, pulling up in front of the house. Had to be.

He couldn't lose her. If he lost her he might lose his kids. If he lost her he'd flounder around in a purgatory of loneliness. If he lost her, he would have failed.

As he climbed out of the patrol car he was rehearsing the

speech he'd come to deliver. "Look, please listen to me one more time," that's what he'd say. And he'd promise that it would be the last time. And he'd get her to promise that she wouldn't react to what he said until she'd thought about it.

"I'll leave the Force." That was to be his offering to her. He wondered if he could say it. If the words might not stick in his throat, and gag him.

— — —

*She had gone to her bedroom window to lower the blind against the sun when she saw him. Betty liked the sun best when it was filtered; found it less frightening when it was filtered. She was reaching for the little cord that hung from the bottom edge of the blind, and looking out the window, and she saw the police car stop in front of her neighbor's house, Maura's house, Maura's clean clean house. He climbed out of the car, Maura's husband did. Betty watched as he walked up to his house but then she couldn't see him anymore, couldn't see the front of his house from her bedroom window.*

*She rushed downstairs and out the door, not stopping to think, oh no, she mustn't stop to think: sometimes it was important to do things that felt reckless.*

*"Yoo-hoo!" she called, waving, hurrying up Maura's walk. He was still standing on the front porch, and he seemed to be ringing the bell.*

*"Why are you doing that?" said Betty, breathless, one hand on her chest, where her heart was thumping. "Why are you ringing your own doorbell?"*

*He had a haughty look on his face. Betty wondered if it was possible for her to change it—because it was very important that he feel friendly toward her. She smiled at him, wanting him to think of her as shy.*

*"Have you lost your key?" she asked him. "Try the*

door, maybe she left it open; she does that sometimes,"
said Betty, nodding. She climbed up onto the porch and
tried the door, but this time it was locked. "Have you
lost your key?" she said again.

"I don't have a key," he said. "I don't live here anymore." And Betty thought he sounded sullen, quite
sullen.

It was cold outside, even though the sun was shining,
and Betty began to shiver. "I forgot my coat," she said.

The policeman started to go down the porch steps.

"Oh dear oh dear, please," said Betty, "please."

He stopped and looked at her. She was holding on to
the sleeve of his jacket.

"You have a very distant face," she said. "Your expression is extremely distant."

"What do you want, Mrs. Coutts?"

Betty felt the blistering cold, made blistering by the
glinty sun, but I won't die of it, she told herself, not of
the cold.

"I need—I need—oh dear." She brought her hands
together, clasped them together in front of her, and
thought of when the rest of her body had matched her
hands, which were small and dainty, and now her
hands were embarrassed by the rest of her, by the size of
the rest of her.

"You need what?" he said, and Betty could tell he
was impatient.

"Well I'm afraid, you see."

"What are you afraid of?" he said, and he was impatient, all right, oh yes, Betty could hear it in his voice.

Suddenly everything was in slow motion. Betty was
amazed. She was standing at an angle from the policeman. He was half-turned toward her and half-turned
toward his car. She looked down as she spoke, at her
feet, in pink slippers, at a sidewalk that had been shoveled

*clean of snow. But there was snow piled beside it and the
sun made sparks fly from the snow straight into Betty's
eyes. "It is my child, you see. My child—" With snow-
sparks blinding her, she reached out with her left hand
and let her fingertips rest on the fabric of his sleeve. "I
don't understand what is happening. And I am afraid."*

*He didn't move at all for a minute. And then she felt
him turn toward her.*

*"I don't understand what you mean," he said. "How
do you want me to help you?"*

*"Oh dear. Oh no," said Betty, and laughed, trilling
her way down the scale. She clasped her hands together
again and looked up into his face. At first it was all
darkness there, because of the blinding sun, the blinding snow, and then she could make it out . . . yes. Good.
It was a different look he was wearing now. "Of course
you don't understand," she said. "Of course. Silly silly
silly." And there were tears, made for her by the sun,
and an ache in her chest, made for her by herself.*

*She started walking back to her house, wiping her
eyes, shaking her head, chuckling to herself.*

*"Mrs. Coutts," he called after her. She could feel him
thinking, behind her.*

*Betty sailed on, more quickly now, and felt him
deciding, behind her. The ache in her chest got bigger.
She gave it a thump.*

"Mrs. Coutts," Alberg called after her. He could see her
shaking her head, and thought she was laughing.

He heard himself breathing.

He wondered what he was going to do.

He looked up and down the street, at the houses slumber-
ing in the snow. Why me? he thought. Why me? Isn't there
enough goddamn shit happening in my life? I don't need
this goddamn woman in my life.

*She heard his car start up. It drove slowly past her and she waved her hand, not looking at him, and it didn't stop, oh no, it didn't stop, he didn't get out, he didn't say, "I'll help you, Mrs. Coutts." Oh no. Oh no.*

He had intended to tell Maura, though. To pass Betty Coutts and her problems over to Maura. He intended to do it the next time they met.

But the next time they met she wouldn't let him talk, wouldn't let him say anything, and the speech he had prepared, the offering he was going to make, it all went down the toilet because Maura held up both of her hands and shut her eyes and said, "I don't love you anymore."

In the silence that followed he knew the truth of that, and he knew that his marriage was, indeed, dead.

And in that silence, Betty Coutts was sacrificed.

And Heather, too.

"Karl?"

He had been staring out at the ocean. Now he turned back to her. He did not wish to appear less, to her. Less good, than whatever she thought of him now. He was going to try to tell her this, and as he searched for the words he needed, he looked for a moment beyond her, at the house—where something caught his eye.

"For pete's sake, Karl," said Cassandra, exasperated, now.

"Wait a minute." He got out of the car. "Stay there," he said, and walked cautiously toward the house, toward the broken window. "I just have to check this out."

## 27

Eliot had fallen asleep while studying the big tree out by the rocks, and the way the dim starlight made its branches glow. And when he woke up it was dawn—too late to go to Earl's, because Earl himself would have been there by then. And so he went to sleep again . . .

. . . in his dream Eliot fell from an apple tree and when he scrambled to his feet he found that he'd been hurt, and so he headed for home, which he knew to be a house with wooden floors and a blue door. He climbed over big scary rocks to get there and opened the blue door and went inside, where his mom and Rosie waited for him. "I'm hurt," he said, and his mom got out the first aid kit, and told Rosie to get a basin of water and some clean rags. And she kneeled down next to him—he was sitting on the floor by now—and it turned out that it was his arm that was hurt, there was a big old scrape all down one arm. Rosie took a soft clean rag and dipped it in the basin of water and gently gently she cleaned the dirt away, and then his mom put some salve on it and wrapped a bandage around his arm, and she stood up and said, "What do you want to eat?" with a smile on her face . . .

When he woke, he was crying. He pulled the knapsack close to him and hugged it. What was he gonna do with himself? What was he gonna do? Through the window he saw the big tree he'd been looking at the night before and the sight of it filled him with misery. At first he couldn't figure this out, and then he knew it was because the tree had no perception of Eliot. It stood there, swaying slightly when the wind blew hard enough, and it was just there, being, it didn't care about Eliot because it didn't know about Eliot, and neither did the scary rocks and neither did the ocean.

He told himself that these were stupid thoughts to be having.

He wiped his face, shakily, with his hands, and took some deep breaths. Nobody knows anything about anybody, he thought. Nobody knows a goddamn thing about anybody.

Eliot stood up, thinking that he should go to the bathroom, or get himself something to eat. But the hopelessness he'd felt last night suddenly came again, in a big rush, like a tidal wave, and it was so strong that he couldn't do anything except lean against the wall.

He was trying to struggle, because that's what you were supposed to do. But part of him didn't want to struggle any more. This part—he could feel it getting stronger and stronger, and Eliot was desperate, unable to tell which part he should be listening to. Where's the wisdom, here? he thought. Where's the wisdom in me? Because he knew he had some. And even if it was just a little bit, he treasured it, and wanted to hear it now, would listen to it now. . . .

Calmness fell upon him, like a shaft of sunlight. He was made almost breathless by the clarity this calmness brought with it.

Eliot went into the bathroom and selected the biggest, sharpest piece of glass, then went back into the living room and sat down on the sleeping bag. He noticed some indentations in the floor, and wondered if maybe a piano had stood there; if it had, whoever had played it had been able to look out at the ocean, if they wanted, while they played.

The thing of it was, he thought, that a life was as long as it was, and that when it was over, that length became the true genuine length that it was meant to be.

Eliot sat crosslegged on the sleeping bag, with the shard of glass in his right hand. He took a deep breath, bent his left hand back, and closed his eyes.

An hour later, Alberg found him there.

Across town, Enid picked up her ringing phone.

"It's me," said Bernie. "Didja do it?"

"I didn't have to," said Enid. "He left."

"Good." Bernie sighed. "Good. Did he take his gun?"

"Of course he did." I should go for a walk, thought Enid, before the rain comes back.

"Whatcha doin'?" said Bernie.

Enid looked at her gardening books, spread across the dining room table. "I'm planning a trip," she said. And suddenly, she was.

"Where to?"

"I'm going to California," said Enid. "To see Reggie." Yes indeed, she thought. "Yes," she told Bernie, pushing her fingertips into her curls, "I'll go tomorrow, I think. I need some warm sun to shine on me."

Alberg was sitting in a chair next to Eliot's hospital bed.

"How come I'm not dead?" said Eliot.

"You bent your hand back, right?" said Alberg. "That moved stuff around in there. You didn't get a good shot at the vein."

"Shit." He looked at his bandaged wrist and turned away.

He had lost weight since November 11. And he was very pale. Otherwise, Alberg thought he looked about the same.

"My sister," said Eliot, not looking at him.

"She's just fine."

Eliot drew a long, shuddering breath, and wiped his eyes with the back of his hand. He looked slight and fragile, lying there, thought Alberg. He had lost enough blood to pass out, if not to die. It had soaked his sweatshirt, and his jeans, and the sleeping bag.

"I didn't want to hurt her. I didn't want to hurt any of them—I just—I just get so fucking *mad*—" He was holding on to the sheet with both hands, twisting it, and his head was averted from Alberg. "I miss them so much. Rosie. And my mom."

Alberg put his hand over Eliot's fists.

"I get so fucking *mad*," the boy said again, and turned his head swiftly to look at Alberg. "I thought for a while it was gone, now." He struggled to speak. "But it isn't. It isn't."

"You can get help for that."

"Yeah, right," said Eliot bitterly, and turned away again. He pulled some tissues from a box on the nightstand and wiped his face.

"Your friend Alvin—" Alberg began.

Eliot sighed. "Yeah? What about him?"

"I saw the bruises," said Alberg. "Do you know how he got them?"

Eliot looked up at him. "How do you think he got them? Somebody beat him up."

"Who?"

"I don't know who. His father."

"I called Social Services this morning," said Alberg. "They're going to talk to his aunt. Maybe he can go to her. She's in Salmon Arm."

The boy lifted his arm, wincing, and looked at the bandage. "Where is he now?"

"They took him back to the detention center."

"He's a funny little guy." Slowly, Eliot shook his head. "I'm never gonna see Rosie again. She won't ever want to see me again. I killed her mom and dad. I almost killed her."

"But you didn't kill her."

Eliot sat up in bed and clung to the sides of the mattress. "I remember—I remember my dad coming at me, smacking me with his hat. And I don't remember anything else, until— jesus. I pulled back. I'd hit her, but I pulled back. And I watched her run down the beach, and she was bleeding. And on the sand there they were, lying there, all over blood." His face glittered with sweat. "Why didn't I pull back sooner? Why didn't I stop? Why did I kill my mom?" He began to sob, and covered his face with his hands.

Alberg sat next to him, waiting. When the sobbing had stopped, and Eliot had fallen back on the pillow, exhausted, Alberg said, "I might be able to help you."

Eliot absorbed this, and his glance flickered across Alberg's face. "But why would you?"

Alberg shrugged. "Why not?"

"I killed people for god's sake." Tears fell again. "That's why not."

"You're going to have to start talking, though," said Alberg, standing up. "I can't help you if you won't talk. To your lawyer. The social worker. The psychiatrists." He looked down on Eliot. "Yeah, you killed people," he said wearily. "And you'll suffer your whole life for it. That's why you're worth helping." He gave Eliot's shoulder a squeeze and went in search of Rosie.


"She's in here." The nurse tapped on the open door before entering.

Rosie sat in a chair by the window, holding the stuffed koala bear.

"We thought she'd be better off in an adult ward," said

the nurse, who had to keep tucking stray strands of dark hair back under her cap.

There were four beds. Privacy curtains had been pulled around one, and another was obviously unoccupied. The third was rumpled, and on the nightstand next to it sat a vase of carnations and several get well cards. Rosie's bed was one by the window.

She was wearing a pink bathrobe and pink slippers, and her long light brown hair had been drawn into a ponytail and tied with a pink ribbon. Alberg could see the cut in the side of her neck, unbandaged now, a dark red healing wound three inches long.

"Hi, Rosie." The child turned, slightly, to look at the nurse, who then bent to kiss Rosie's cheek. "You know Mr. Alberg, don't you? He's the one who got your koala for you."

Rosie didn't speak. She looked at Alberg. She had blue eyes, which Alberg hadn't expected. He had remembered them as hazel, like her mother's, like Eliot's. The teddy bear was cradled in her arms.

"Hi, Rosie," said Alberg. He got down on his haunches. "I hear you're going back to Nova Scotia. With your aunt and uncle."

She looked at him sideways, not moving her head, then shifted her gaze again to look out the window.

"Is it pretty there?"

Slowly, Rosie nodded.

The nurse was tidying up, removing dead blooms from the six floral arrangements that were lined up on the wide window ledge, along with several cards.

"Tell me about their house."

The child held the koala bear a little bit tighter.

"Do they have kids of their own?" said Alberg.

She nodded again.

"Big kids? Or little ones?"

She pursed her lips and pulled the corners of her mouth down. "Big."

A large woman sailed into the room, wearing a white terrycloth robe over her hospital gown, her feet flapping in white heelless slippers. She threw a magazine down on the bed next to the carnations, swept over to Rosie, and gave her a big hug. "You been good while I been gone?" she asked sternly, and Rosie, with a faint grin, said yes.

"Good," said the woman. "Hi," she said to Alberg, and turned her back on him to climb onto her bed, where she started paging energetically through the magazine.

"Hi," said Alberg, stupidly, from the floor.

"That's Mary," said Rosie. "She had her gall bladder out. They gave it to her to keep. In a jar."

"Ah," said Alberg. "Really."

Rosie shifted in her chair. "They've got a swing. In the backyard."

"Hey. That's good. What else?"

"Apple trees."

"I'd like to have an apple tree," said Alberg.

She turned her head to look at him. "Will Eliot come there?"

Alberg felt a great sinking in his chest. "No, sweetie. Eliot has to stay here."

"Is he crazy?"

"He was, I think, when he did what he did. Don't you think so?"

She looked out the window again, and Alberg felt himself to be dismissed.

He got awkwardly to his feet.

"Just look at that sunshine," said Mary. "You want to go for a walk, later, out in that sunshine, Rosie?"

Rosie shrugged.

The nurse said, "I think that's a good idea." But Rosie, looking out the window, didn't respond. "I'll come back after lunch, and help you get dressed."

Mary winked at her, and nodded encouragingly.

"Did somebody bring clothes for her?" said Alberg, when he and the nurse were out in the hall.

"We've had so many people drop off stuff for Rosie—" She smiled at him, tucking in her hair. "It's kinda good to be reminded how nice people can be."

"What's likely to happen to him?" asked Cassandra.

They were having coffee in the living room, curtains pulled against the darkness outside. She was sitting on the sofa, and Alberg was in his wingback chair.

"He'll probably get three years in a youth facility. Unless they transfer him to adult court." He rubbed his thighs. "They've got anger management programs. I hope to Christ they work."

Cassandra pushed from her mind the bloody sight of Alberg coming out of that house with Eliot in his arms.

Alberg got to his feet. At the window, he pulled the curtain aside and looked out. Then he turned to Cassandra and folded his arms in front of him. "I'm going to try to help the kid. Because I misinterpreted that whole situation."

She started to protest, but changed her mind. He was grateful for that.

"I also screwed up with Jack Coutts' crazy wife."

She was listening gravely, her head bent, and the light glittered in her hair, which had a lot of silver in it now. "And people died," he said evenly. "People sometimes die, when cops screw up."

He could tell that she didn't want to hear this. But she wouldn't stop listening, and he loved her for that.

"I had decided not to tell you about this. But now I've changed my mind."

Alberg sat down again, on the edge of his chair, and clasped his hands between his knees. "It happened twelve years ago," he said. "I went home— No. Not home. It wasn't home anymore. I went to the house. To get the rest of my things. I'd brought some boxes, packing cartons. Flattened. A stack of them. I parked on the street. I remember it was a very cold day. But I think it was sunny. Maybe there was a lot of snow. Because it was very quiet on the street. Everything seemed—muffled. Although"—he shrugged—"maybe I'm making that up."

He concentrated hard, needing to report only the actual. "I'd gotten out of the car, carrying the boxes, and locked it, and yeah, there was a lot of snow, I remember crunching through it when I went around the front of the car. And something next door made me look over there—it was Christmas lights. Yeah. Two months or more after Christmas, and the lights were still up, and still lit. So I looked at this and at the same time I was thinking about the reason I was there, trying to decide what to pack in the boxes, what belonged to me, and not to the two of us. And then I saw that their front door was open."

He looked at Cassandra. She nodded slightly, encouraging him to go on.

"I almost didn't go in there," he said. "I didn't want to go in there." He gazed around the room, looking for an anchor, something to secure him in the here and now. "I put the cartons on the roof of the car and walked toward the house, looking at that open door, hoping like hell that somebody would suddenly slam it shut." He took a deep breath. "But nobody did.

"I went up the walk—the snow was pretty deep, and there were footprints in it—and onto the porch. And I called out. But nobody answered. So I went inside. . . ."

— — —

*Betty took out her tools. Then she fetched the plastic bottle from the bathroom, the one with her pills in it —*

*there were lots and lots of them in there. She displayed her tools in a straight line on top of her bedspread and stared at them, frowning.*

*She picked up the tweezers and went into the bathroom, so she could watch herself in the mirror there, and she plucked the hairs from her eyebrows, all of them, every single one, although it hurt badly and caused her eyes to flood with tears. She decided she liked the way she looked with no eyebrows, naked and astonished. She wet a washcloth and put it on the places where her eyebrows had been, soothing the red raw skin there.*

*Betty returned to the bedroom and threw the tweezers into the wastepaper basket, and studied the rest of her tools. With the sewing scissors she cut off all her hair, cut it again and again, ran her hand over her prickly scalp and everywhere she felt a piece of hair that had escaped she said "Aha!" and cut it off. She looked in the bathroom mirror and admired the shape of her head, which she had never seen before. Then she went back into the bedroom and threw the scissors away.*

*She hung the eyeglasses from her box of tools over her ears and on top of her nose—they had no glass in them and she saw perfectly through the holes.*

*She looked at what was left. The big kilt pin. She pinned it to her robe. That left the long hat pin with the pearl knob on the top; the jackknife with the leather handle and the leather pouch to hold it; the pickle fork she'd taken from Maura's house; the screwdriver with the bright orange handle; the pliers.*

*Betty sat on her bed and undid her yellow bathrobe. She picked up the hat pin. Delicately, she traced a line on her left thigh. When she took away the hat pin, though, the line disappeared, so she pressed harder. She felt a sharp squeal from her skin but she went on, one letter after another. Blood raced to the faint fragile tears in her skin and the skin squealed more loudly. Impatiently she shook the pain out of her head and plodded on. After a while she took away the pin and looked at her thighs. "B E" was on the left one and "T T Y" was on the right one. Her thighs were hurting a lot, so she went into the bathroom again and wet the washcloth and pressed it onto the letters in her thighs. Betty patiently waited and pressed it down again and again. Finally the weak, thin trickles of blood stopped coming.*

*She went back to the bedroom, dropped the hat pin into the trash basket, and took hold of the pickle fork. She pushed up the left sleeve of her robe and dragged the fork up her arm, from wrist to elbow. Two pink streaks appeared. When they began to fade, she did it again. Altogether she did it four times, and then four more times on the other arm.*

*Both arms were screaming at her now, along with her thighs, and the places where her eyebrows had been. She was getting impatient with her body.*

*There was the jackknife left, and the screwdriver, and the pliers. Betty couldn't think what to do with the screwdriver or the pliers that wouldn't incapacitate her. She didn't want to be incapacitated. She threw them into the garbage.*

*She took the jackknife and her pills downstairs and filled a glass with water. She looked at the bottle of pills and then at the glass, calculating. She filled a second glass with water and took both glasses and the pills into the living room and set them on the card table. Then she sat down on the sofa and waited.*

*And eventually Heather came home.*

*Betty stood quickly, before Heather even got the door closed. "Boo!" she said.*

*Heather looked at her and screamed.*

Betty ran to the child and threw her arms around her and buried Heather's face in the front of her robe. "How do you like it? It's me, just me, Heather, just me. I'm going to let my eyebrows and my hair grow again and maybe my hair will grow in yellow like yours, maybe then I'll have yellow hair again like when I was young, like you, see? See? Come along now, don't be silly, come along."

She dragged her over to the sofa and sat down, and pulled Heather onto her lap. Heather's face was white and the skin was pulling away from her face, and her lips were pulled back, too. She almost looked as if she were snarling.

Betty lifted her right leg and threw it over the bottom half of Heather's body. She reached for the bottle of pills, which she had uncapped. She told Heather to open her mouth, but the teeth clamped shut. The eyes were twice as big as normal.

The wind started to blow. Betty stopped and cocked her head and listened to his eager rustling around the windows, around the bottoms of the doors, through the open front door. He wanted to get in, for some reason, he was coming in.

Heather screamed again and quickly, deftly, Betty dropped half the pills down her throat. She clutched Heather's chin with her left hand, holding her mouth closed while Heather struggled and kicked and choked. Then she opened the mouth just a little and poured some water down. Heather choked and coughed and swallowed.

More water. Choking, coughing, swallowing.

Betty did this again and again, while Heather kicked and struggled. Through the fingers of her strong hand Betty felt Heather's tears, warm and languid, and the liquid from her nose, warm and sticky.

When she took her hand away, Heather's eyes opened; she struggled, still. It would take some time, Betty knew. But she could wait.

She sat back on the sofa and held Heather in her two arms. Her face stung and her thighs and her arms continued to scream in pain, but stoically she held her daughter and felt herself weeping. She held her and rocked her and wept and waited.

If the jackknife isn't long enough, she thought, there is a long sharp knife in the kitchen; if the jackknife doesn't go all the way, the kitchen knife will.

It was very important that her actual heart be touched.

# 28

*Monday, December 5*

Alberg looked from his office window. There wasn't a
brown Silverado in sight. He wondered if Jack had made the
trip back to Kamloops in a single day, or if he had stopped
someplace Sunday night.

He turned around and leaned against the filing cabinet,
studying his office. He would have done it, he thought. He
would have given up the Job to keep his wife and kids.

And then what? He hadn't the faintest idea. And he
hadn't had the faintest idea then, either. He had never
progressed beyond the idea of quitting to what he might
turn to next.

Isabella rapped on his door. "Can I take an extra half hour
for lunch?" She was wearing a gray and white cardigan,
hand-knitted, she had told him, in a pattern that featured
several Canada geese. Under it, a tangerine-colored skirt and
a yellow sweater.

"Sure," said Alberg.

"Good. Look, I'm going out the back way, okay?"

"Sure," he said again, and she vanished down the hall.

Alberg sat at his desk, put on his reading glasses, and regarded the crowded in basket that he had almost completely emptied less than a week ago. He sat back and tossed the glasses onto the desk. He didn't have the heart for this today.

He was relieved when Sokolowski came along.

"There's a guy out there," said Sid, "wants to know where Isabella's gone to."

"Lunch," said Alberg. "What guy?"

"I don't know, a guy sitting on the bench, reading the paper."

"Not her husband again," said Alberg. "I hope."

"I never met her husband," said the sergeant. "I'll go tell him, anyway." He was back in a couple of minutes. "Yeah, it's him. It's kinda touching, don't you think?" He sat down. "Guy says he's retired, now he can spend more time with his wife." His eyes scanned the notices on Alberg's bulletin board. "Yeah, but—" He looked quizzically at Alberg. "Does that mean he plans to park himself on that bench every day?"

"You've got me," said Alberg.

"Spend the whole damn day there?"

Alberg shrugged.

"We might have ourselves a problem here," said the sergeant worriedly.

"What did you want to see me about?"

"Oh yeah. Right." He held his shoulders back. "I've made my decision. I'm not gonna do it. Not gonna retire early after all."

"Well I'm glad to hear it, Sid," said Alberg. "Surprised, though."

"Yeah." Sokolowski shuffled his feet. "Well it's been a while, now, since she left. More than a year. And she hasn't told me why. And she hasn't said if she's ever coming back. So I figure I gotta hold on to something. My kids are all grown up, and they've always been closer to Elsie, being as how they're girls. And I haven't got her anymore. I don't want the damn house, I'm gonna sell the damn house. So I might as well hang on to the job. Right?"

"Right, Sid. Whatever you say."

Sid slapped his thighs and stood up. "Right. I'm going back to my desk now."

Alberg, watching him go, thought about the sergeant's scrapbooks. Maybe that wasn't such a bad idea. If you could literally close the book on something, on somebody. . . .

For the next hour and a half he dealt grimly with paperwork.

Then he took off his glasses and picked up the phone to call Janey, in Calgary.

He hadn't thought about what day of the week it was, or what time, or whether she was likely to be home; but as the phone rang he asked some god or other to please not let the musician answer.

It rang so many times he thought he was going to get their machine, and then Janey answered, breathless.

"Hi. It's your dad. Why are you laughing?"

"I'm just glad to hear your voice, that's all."

Alberg thought, I stand on such shaky ground with my kids. Especially with this one.

"Janey—" he said.

But then he didn't know how to put it. If he said, What are you doing for Christmas? she'd think he was going to invite them to Sechelt, and he'd have to listen to her searching frantically for a refusal that wouldn't sound insulting. But if he said, Can I spend Christmas with you? that might be even worse. What if she'd already invited Maura and the accountant? and had to say, No, Dad, I'm afraid you can't. . . .

At that moment Isabella opened his office door and sailed in, unannounced, without knocking. Alberg felt his jaw drop.

She stood tall and straight, with her head flung back proudly, and her golden eyes gleamed triumphantly.

"What do you think?" she said to Alberg, ignoring the fact that he was on the phone.

"One moment, Janey," he said. "Isabella has had her hair cut, and I am trying to absorb this."

"Say hi for me," said Janey.

"Hi," said Alberg, dazed. "Isabella. It's beautiful."

It came to her jawline, and from a center part fell gracefully to cup her face.

"Beautiful."

The gray was no longer gray, but streaks of gold amid the brown.

"Thank you," she said. "I am now going to show Richard. It will be a great shock to him. I hope it will shock him back to life."

"Janey," said Alberg. "I'm back."

"Yes, Dad."

"Cassandra's going to Edmonton for Christmas. With her mother. Could I come to you and—uh, Daniel?" Christ. He'd forgotten the musician's name, for a minute.

"Sure. Love to have you. Diana will be here, too."

It was as easy as that.

Alberg stood up and went to his window. The sun was shining again. Parked next to the curb was a big old Chrysler, green, and a bright red Firebird. No brown Silverado. He almost missed the damn thing.

Alberg went back to his desk and picked up the phone to call Eliot Gardener's lawyer. "He's started talking," he said, when he got her on the line. "So now—what can I do to help?"